I0547314

Brinemark-Bienemann Publishing 2012

Copyright 2008, 2012 by Mark Brine

Library of Congress Catalog-In-Publication Data

Brine, Mark

The Book of Odes (Factory Boy)

ISBN 978-0-615-62565-2

Artwork Credits:

Frontcover Artwork by Mark Brine

Backcover Photo of Mark Brine by Sam Holden

Design, lay-out and assembly of final printed edition by Lillian Abernathy
(LACreative, Gallatin, Tennessee).

CONTENTS

THE BOOK OF ODES

(Factory Boy)

- An American Poetic, Musical & Didactic Novel -

by: MARK BRINE c 2008, c 2012

- Based on a True Story -

Dedicated to Therese', my little sister..

And William M. Hobart, my 'in spirit' little brother..

both of whom we so-heart-breakingly

lost in the Spring of Life.

A Tree is Just a Wristwatch

(The 'Rings' Revealed)

A Tree is Just a Wristwatch

that you never need to wind

telling tales, Grandfather clocks

could never hope to find

Registering ancient times

in circulatory script

reminiscing passersby

now vaulted down in crypt

A Tree is like a Wristwatch

you can't strap on your arm

absorbing rays from endless days

and never doing harm

A Tree is like a sundial

casting down a shade

that you can rest beneath it

'til the sunbeams shrink 'n fade

Trees, they speak with wisdom

I'll never hear you say

Dying quiet, in the Fall

reborn on new Spring's day

written: Approx. 1968

(Cambridge, Mass.)

THE FIRST RING

(of this story)

It glared.. Ricocheting and bouncing quickly about the quiet and peaceful alcove room.. Scampering about and pulling his eyes into its flash. Its darting glow, snapping him attentively to it. This, as a result of the early morning's sunlight streaming-in through the undraped, double-windows.. And in the process, into the red ruby stone of his Father's ring.. Momentarily distracting the little boy's focus away from the moving hand it had been studying.. and instead now, out of the near-at-hand panes.. and then further, to the tree-tops and roofs that resided on the bending curve of the below crescent street. His Father's hand, sketching in graceful strokes upon the seemingly-huge art table. This work-bench, slantingly propped-up and constituting pretty-nearly all of the tiny room. His Dad's at-home work place.. A freelance commercial artist, frustratingly laboring over farmed-out Yellow Pages ads.

In a brief glance, Nate scanned back to his Father's pensive stare at the 'in process'. He was a true artist, only now slaving over commercial mundane 'trash'! And for 'pitiful pay', to top it all off! It truly wasn't fair! Even Nate, as a young child, understood this.. And all too well at that!

Then distracting this revelatory and gloomy meditation, the reflective light bounced about the room again, pulling with it the boy's eyes...

In a smearing-together and simultaneous 'flashing blur', the daybreak's reddish sun struggled and momentarily broke-free from behind the thick clouds. And, in the same, through the rising and puffing smoke-line of the factories in the now further-set townscape.. Sparking and jolting Nate back to the cold morning's reality and out of his moment's-before introspect and childhood recall. This memory, bringing in its aftermath, a sudden gasp of desperation and sadness; that (together with his impulsive squint from the burst of light) rekindled only another 'yet-more traumatic' recall from the distant past.. That of an ambulance's red-and-flashing light disappearing into the night, as he watched his Father being taken away.

Having suffered another of his re-occurring nervous breakdowns; earlier that very evening at dinner, he had violently lifted up his end of the table; only to send all of the newly-served meal, dishes and silverware crashing down onto his directly-opposing-him, un-expecting Father (Nate's Grand-dad); and promptly there-after, attacking him in crazed-like fisticuffs. The boy's Mother, at last, coming between them.. and temporarily breaking it up. All of this, while Nate and the other children sat watching in sheer-paraylizing terror.. Until finally, the later-arrival of the authorities.. and the further-discomforting removal of his Father, as earlier stated.

Flinchingly re-surfacing from this memory now, he uncomfortably tangled to shrug it off.. In so, pulling down the brim of his cap; and casting off any lingering and heart-wrenched feelings that he might have had for his Dad, due to the prior and initial recall. Yes, now that he was older, he saw things completely different; and he inwardly reminded himself of that, in these shakened moments. His Father had changed drastically.. Totally giving up his art and any and all of the dreams that went with it. Nate wasn't quite sure why he had; but in his mind, it was unforgivable. Such a waste! That, and the burden he personally carried (As children always tend to blame themselves, whether justifiably or not!..) for being indirectly 'part of the cause' for this 'giving up of one's dream' for the greater good of the family. Or might it even better be said... for whatever 'good' it had actually imparted, as a result!.. This, clearly being beyond debate (in his mind), considering all of the agonies and woes it had brought forth and with it since! But, hey…whatever!…

Either way, he wasn't going to dwell on these things any further.. now or whenever!.. It just brought back too much pain. No, he'd simply 'swallow it' emotionally, and think of something else. So, distractingly he broke into his 'new' inner chant of late, as he forcefully tramped unwillingly-closer to work, along the broken, erratic sidewalk…

'… Come on, Sun.. Lingering..

Warm this day.. 'n make it Spring…

These Winter Blues.. freeze ev'rything..

S', come on, Sun.. 'n make it Spring!.. '

It was simple. Short 'n sweet! Still, he was forever creating little things like that to amuse and comfort himself. He doubted serious, it would ever materialize into a song or anything greater. No, it was just a personal mental heartbeat that had come to him, time to time, throughout this past winter. Sedating him somehow.

In greater reality now, his feet bit hardening-cold, as he trudged even-further and more-awkwardly along the damp, uneven brick pavement. Into the broad-way now. Then, over the railroad tracks and onto the resuming sidewalk. The street (as pot-holed as it was) wouldn't have served any the better.

'Wet-cold' is always a more-penetrating cold than dry! And his ankles tightened and ached in it.. and almost seemed to creak in their forced movement.

Winter storms had subsided, of late. Yet, it was still April and only 'Spring Break' for him. What was normally his part-time job, now became full-time on school holidays and summers. Still, all and all, the seasons were in transition and anything could be expected! And in so, this was the dreariest of morns. Fogged early-hour daybreak.. Or, more accurately, it.. 'fighting' to break! This, for the thick and dusty-like grey and cloudy awning. Not at all spared by the choking-it factory smoke.

His nose ran slightly, giving his face an even-more-tingled chill. Red 'n sore at its lower junction. Sniffling, he tried to hinder its further drip. But, to no avail. At last, abrasively 'sleeve-ing' it!

The factory and freight-yard whistles naggingly blasted in the onset.. Echoing back at him from across the vast airspace and its just-beyond-the-building's river. As likewise, from the opposing (but, hidden, as well..) shoreline's high-rise architecture. This 'valley'-ed-like backdrop, allowing a 'perfectly pocketed place' for reverberation, beyond and through the collage of oncoming brick. He eyed-up the dirty warehouses and smokestacks in glaring disgust.

Routinely passing a little combination corner-store-and-sandwich-shop (that was perched just-beyond Kendall Square's old bus depot); in his continuing jaunt, he side-tracked in closer and peered through its window in search of its further-set, walled clock. 'Eight-thirty'. He was late! Again! Damn! In a sudden jolt, he crossed Main.. making a right on its sidewalk (in so, passing the Houghton Mifflin Building). Then, banging an immediate left onto Carleton, he made down the little side-street, scurrying as best as he could.. Forcing his aching legs on, like a robot! He so hated all of this. Absolutely loathed the mere thought of it all. Yes, another long, boring and agonizing day! He was a musician and a writer.. and that's all he'd ever wanted to be! Even as a very young child, he'd known this.. Never once, having dreamed of, one day, being a Fireman.. a Cop.. or a… Whatever! No, it'd always been the same.. Music! Yes, guitars and music! And, nothing or anything else ever interested him, in the least! But for now, there was just no other choice in the matter.. Born into poverty!.. He HAD to work! But, ah.. one day.. Oh, yes, one day soon.. Things 'd be different! Yeah, totally different! He was sure of that!

Down the narrow, alley-like street, he (at last) reached the Print Shop's entrance on his left. Up the few grey-painted cement steps, he made.. Then, through the doorway to the inner-continuing, slight stairway and its platform. Both of which, leading straight-on-up and into the shop with its greeting-like punch clock. But regrettably in the same, passing the right-hand and see-through, glass door of the front office. Nate tucked low and scatted by.. In this (and the re-erecting of his frame), noticing through the just-beyond-it, higher-placed window, that ole Mrs. Brennan was not at her desk there. She, the 'classic' and stern-faced 'old teacher'- type, who forever had it out for him. Or even better and more descriptively characterized as being, the identical twin of the Wicked Witch in the 'Wizard of Oz'! .. She, the carbon copy.. Only, without the costume! Yes, this.. and a good bit of the 'thinly'-physical likeness and appearance of "Olive Oil" (from Popeye) thrown into the mix.. Though, the former.. truly the more-accurate 'personality' and 'nature' of the beast!

'Whew'-ing in relief of her absence, he swung open the further door and entered the shop.. In so, getting a full whiff of the ink into his nostrils. Quickly removing his outer wear and grabbing his time card, he punched and re-filed it.. Then, in he began, through the furthering rightward gulf. This path, bordered on the left by the backside of the Linotype machine. And in the same, flanked-on-the-right by a short wall, that (at last) gave 'way to a 45 degree right-angled 'off-shoot' crevice with its dead-ending 'hole'. The latter, for raising pigs on its suspended and hooked-chain from the lower-basement's furnace and pot.

Straight on he plowed (tangling his work-apron on, all the while), reaching the upcoming door of the opposite end of the (Reversed both ways-) L-shaped office. Peering-rightward-and-in with his sharp-left-turn, he caught her eye… 'Brennan'! "Dang!" Yes, there she was.. carrying on a conversation with Mr. Hampshire (the boss!), who was presently back-turned. Regardless, her glowering 'head-snap' made Nate's eyes widen in the discovery! So, bolting his own away, he began his retreat in a dart. This, into the even-louder-now press-room. Within seconds, she'd be 'on him'. He just knew it! She just hated him. It was so blatantly obvious!

Into the main cavity he continued in his hurried escape; passing the to-his-left, parallel and lengthy 'lock-up' work bench with its supporting-below, job-case storage bins and furniture racks. Yes, deeper into the on-rush of loud, annoying offset machinery in the workplace rear. They clicking out their insistent rhythms.. Pulsating in herded-like thumpings.. clackings.. and alternating thuds! These steal horses, reigned in constant strain and sweaty slavery! All of this intensifying surge, dislodging a few remaining mental cobwebs.. and making his mind seem less fogged and totally awakened now. Despite the habitual 'loss of sleep' that he forever indulged himself in, this routinely 'did the trick'! Shaking his head and his dark-brown, long uncombed hair in a few quick jolts, he passed the Ludlow and Repro presses on his right. In a sharp-leftward pivot, he entered the camera and stripping room, pretending to be searching-out his immediate supervisor, Roger. For he was often in and out of there, working on or discussing jobs with Glenn and Mike. But this, in truth now, only to try and dodge (and, in so, hide from..) the soon-to-be-transcending 'Brennan'!

The strippers were hunched over their lit tables and the room was dim and mellow.. And in the sudden hush of his entry, seeming so peaceful from the rattling just outside. It was a sort-of intimate spot for its enclosure. Nate had always enjoyed it, having once worked in there for an entire summer.. on the arch table, burning plates. And in the same, making 'devil's pay' for doing a man's job. But he never complained. It was all part of the 'learning process'. And this having been, at the time, a great improvement over the tedious year spent prior in the upstairs' bindery. Yes, now that was true imprisonment! You talk about tedium! And being stuck in one place.. one seat.. hours upon hours upon end!.. Feeding a stitching collator.. Man-o-man, now that is true unmerciful Hell! At least, these days he had worked his way up some. Now he was in the Composition room, doing 'real' printing. Sometimes even running the Linotype machine himself. And the Ludlow. Again though, doing a Pressman's Job for schoolboy pay. But still, the world wasn't always fair.. He'd already learned that! Either way, it was all very impressive to his folks. They had so wanted him to have 'a trade'. And presently, still in his Senior year of High School (and having major-ed-in and studied Printing and Graphic Arts through-out), he was.. well, you could say.. at least working in 'the field'. And seeming to be making great headway too! Still, deeper truth was, he had other plans for his life. No, this wasn't what he wanted! Nor, would ever want! But, for now (and again..), that would all have to wait. Either way, he had to work.. and his nights and weekends always found him studying or working on 'his dream'. So, all and all, he was reasonably content. Though sometimes, doing them both was truly pressing.. Even for someone his age. Still, there was no other way!

Out of breath now, he (as matter-of-factly as he could muster..) gasped out to Glenn and Mike... "Roger in the Darkroom?.."

"No, you imp!.. Y' know damn well he ain't in there!.."

"Well, sumetimes he.." Nate, trying to seem sincere.

"C'mon.. " big Glenn smirking now.. "How often have y' ever seen him in there?.." eyeing towards its black door.

"Well, not too much, but..."

"Nate, you must be on the run from Brennan again.." looking back over his shoulders, out through the doorway and in the direction of the office. "Oh, Lord.. here she comes.. I was right!.. Better hide, Elf!.."

The boy wasn't sure if he was kidding. But figuring not, he nervously eyed the darkroom's door, feeling to dart inside. Yet he knew (if Glenn was serious) he'd have no proper excuse for being in there, when she at last caught up with him.

"NATHANIEL!.." He hadn't been kidding! "I want to speak with you IMMEDIATELY in my office!"

"Yes, ma'am.." He meeked out in embarrassment, as she spun in her spot and began off again, expecting him to follow. Which he did.. to the smirks of Glenn and Mike. Nate raising his fist in mock threat. But they, only smiling wider.

Halfway back through the Composition Room, Roger (who always reminded Nate of a blonde 'Buddy Holly'.. hairdo, rims 'n personality-wise!)

appeared out of the office, shooting in his hurried passing...

"Nate.. when y' through, I need y' t' get on them pigs.. we're almost out!.. Bill worked a double, last night, 'n pretty-nearly cleaned us out! I think there's a few down there, you can send up first.. But then, y' gotta get on t' makin' some more.. Okay?.."

Nodding at him for response, the boy continued in his 'death march' straight into the office. Mr. Hampshire was fortunately-enough trapped in a conversation on his big black desk phone and didn't even notice him pass. Nate breathed freer in that, as he turned the L rightwardly into the further-set area.. Mrs. Brennan's desk being set-up there, by the door and bordering window. She being the accountant, proofreader and self-appointed 'disciplinarian' of the firm. He was only hoping that it would not be the 'issue of tardiness' again. But as expected, it was!

"Nathaniel.. Can you please explain, why.. in the span of one week, you have arrived late three times? What, may I ask, is wrong with you?.."

"Well, Ma'am.. it's m' music.. Nights I perform or practice.. or write.. or study it.. so.."

"Hobby!.. That's a HOBBY, Nathaniel!.. Don't you understand?.."

"Well, Ma'am.. I plan t', one day.."

Before he could finish.. "Foolishness!.. I'll hear no more of it!.. Such childish nonsense!.. I warn you, Nathaniel, if you don't start taking life more seriously and applying yourself to your responsibilities as a future pressman, I will personally see to it that you are relieved from your position"

"But..."

"No 'buts' about it, Nathaniel.. I'll hear no more of your ridiculous daydreams and fantasies!.. You and your shameful HOBBY!.. It's PITIFUL!.. And a boy your age!.."

He held silence. It was no use. If only she knew, in the slightest though, just how hard he'd worked at his music. And his long, late nights at it, while still trying to go to school and keep a job. Not to mention, his homework and house chores!.. No, it was just useless trying to tell people with that kind of mindset. They simply have no clue!

"Well, off with you, young man!.. but, just remember.. you've been warned!"

The pot was already lit. No doubt by Roger, earlier that morning. Still, the basement air was dark and damp. Nate began pouring the molten metal into the pig dies, while he awaited Roger's arrival above at 'the hole'.

When he completed a string of them, he began dumping more old Lino and Ludlow slugs into the bubbling belly. This, very carefully.. using small shovel-fulls at a time, not to create a splash-back on himself. All throughout this and the previous, he had been quite self-absorbed in the silence and solitude.. Lost in dreams of his music and future. His forever past-time! There was also the more-immediate concerns to consider now too. For tonight was 'open hoot' night at the coffeehouse in the Main Square, near the college. Glancing quickly over at the smut-covered 1966 'Funeral Parlor/ Advertisement' Calendar, that someone had nailed into the cement-crevice (between the bricks) of the near-at-hand wall, he re-verified the date. Yes, he'd been right.. it was tonight!.. Yeah, and once again, he had allowed his friend, Willie, to corner him into performing a solo spot at it. Deep down, he knew he longed to do it. But another part of him tingled in the nervousness and anticipation now. He wouldn't have felt so concerned over it, if his band was going to be with him.. There was strength in numbers! But, solo.. well, that was another story! No moral or physical support.. No help.. No nuthin'.. Just him! Gosh, why did he always let Willie get the best of him, like this? Either way, Nate knew he'd never let-up on him, until he agreed to go through with it. So, there was really no way around it, at this point!

Then, like out of nowhere, a sudden glare of sunlight streamed through the smut-darkened cellar window panes. This, bringing back the earlier morning's recall. Yes, of his Father and the alcove. Then, too.. the gut-sickening memory of the dinner events. Replaying all in a quick mental flash, he tried to pull himself free of it, half mumbling a "phhh.." in disgust. Anyone who had all that talent and just threw it away.. and just worked the pitiful, sad jobs he did.. all, just to raise a family.. Well, he'd just have to be crazy! No wonder he was so unhappy with his life, Nate head-shakingly resolved. There was absolutely just NO WAY he'd ever do that! He swore! Never! Not f' nuthin'! No, he saw his Dad in a whole different light now. And there was just no way he'd ever be able to look up to him, as he'd once had. Sure, they'd had great times together.. hunting.. fishing.. bowling.. And yes, he sincerely appreciated all of that. But, 'admiration'?.. Well, that was all history now. No, times had changed. Things had moved on. It didn't mean he didn't love him. Hardly! But, he just truly couldn't understand him at all!.. And he sure wasn't going to make any serious efforts to, anymore, either!

Soon enough after the initial 'pig raising ordeal' with Roger, the morning continued to pass with an onslaught of similar thoughts. And, despite his efforts to ward-off the depressive recalls and thoughts of his Dad.. and these, only further compounded by Brennan's total negativity towards any sort of 'musical' career or aspirations... he, at last, defeatedly took a seat on the edge of a dusty, half-stacked skid of paperstock.. In so, distraughtly cupping his forehead in a sort of retreat and anguish. Inwardly trying to recollect himself emotionally, he envisioned (as he would always do, on his childhood hunting trips with his Father) the image of Hank Williams, walking back-turned and away, down a narrowing and disappearing railroad track. He, in so, engulfed in a foggy mist and rising haze.. inaudibly singing and playing his guitar. Yeah, just like on those drawings of the 'Luke, the Drifter' records! The 'Ramblin' Man'! His boyhood hero! The 'Father' of his Dreams! Yes, that's what he would grow up to be!.. Not all of this!

At last, interrupting his introspect, his supervisor returned and called down through the hole…

"Nate, it's almost Lunch time!.. I'm gonna need y' up here on the stick, this afternoon. So, y' gotta round it up down there.. ok?.."

"Yeah, sure, Roj.. " he responded, regainingly considering how quickly the morn had vanished.

It felt momentarily 'odd' now to be sitting in the sandwich shop for lunch. All last Summer, he'd taken it here with one of the other younger boys, who'd worked in the Bindery. He remembered now how the kid had kept playing this particular '4 Tops' song on the jukebox.. One that Nate couldn't stand! Now, with it only being Spring Break (and he, being only 'temporarily full-time' for the week), it all felt kind of strange! The school cafeteria having become 'the norm', of late. Still, this was better!.. Seeming somehow 'less imprisoning'. Maybe 'cause it was more 'adult-like' too? He really didn't know! But either way, it sure seemed a lot more peaceful. The earlier customers and waiting line had dispersed. And again, with his no longer 'shadow' there to talk his 'ear off' over the Sports World's latest news (Not to mention, to be having that silly song, all the while, blasting in his ear!.. "Sugar Pie Honey Bunch".. 'What the Heck did that mean, anyways?!'), Nate could now more-peacefully jot his notes down and make his forever music plans. No interruptions.

His little beat-up pocket pad and pen surfaced; and with his smut-dirty-smeared face, he sat hunched now.. writing in-between occasional nose-swipes and sandwich snaps.   He found such warmth and enclosure in these pensive moments.. Like a 'team huddle' all his own.. where his mind was at absolute ease.

At last, peering up from it momentarily, he scanned the room and out through the slightly-fogged glass.. In so, faintly seeing a bus visually-consumed by a closer-to-him (and on-his-side-of-the-road) dump truck awkwardly clutching forward and on. Then, back to his retreat. Jotting a few more notes, he re-considered his inner clock. It felt like it was time; and looking back up and at the walled clock, he regrettably verified the hunch. A quick threatening vision of Mrs. Brennan shot through his mind, and he responded promptly.. crumbling his sandwich wrappings and bag together into a heap for the nearby barrel.

On his return to work, he passed the corner bar, where the Printer's took their lunch hours (and likewise, drank at night, after let-out), glancing over at it in his forcing-forward acceleration. Thinking (in the moment) of the times he had been in there, picking up sandwiches for the crew.. and how this one (in particular) reeked heavily-and-terribly of stale beer. Sure, he'd been in a lot of taverns in his life, what with his music and all.. but, somehow this one was just simply rank! Either way, their sandwiches.. (especially, the tuna fish ones).. were always great! In his mental recovery now, a cold wind was tagging him... and he trembled in its alley-like, sudden push. Per usual, he was running up against the clock and shifted into a trot.

Back at the job (despite the buildings heat), he felt an on-going inner chill now. But this, due to the graphite that was staining his hands from the metal type and composing stick.

'.. guess that's why they call it COLD-type!..' he inwardly humored himself in thought (for the more-than-hundredth-of-times that he had with that same line, throughout his reasonably short career!)

Standing and picking through the California Job Case was tedious and grating on the fingers. Not to forget, painful on his legs! And for this, he occasionally tried to re-adjust his position and stance. But it was truly no help. He constantly ached.

Trying to break the monotony, here and there he'd move over to the lock-up table to transfer his completed works onto a waiting galley. But short of this and a few interruptions from Henry (the 'Ichabod Crane'-looking old offset printer, who worked the smaller presses in the adjoining department), the day dragged on without change. Nate always got a kick out of the ridiculous jokes that the old-timer'd come up with. But, (being a bit on the shy side) he found the seedier ones to always get him in a bit of a blush and feeling somewhat uncomfortable. And this, seeming to entertain Henry, all-the-more! And today was no exception. For on at least five occasions, the old Printer had shown up unexpectedly behind Nate's shoulder.. Each time, startling the pensive lad into a rattling jolt!

Henry had that old, beat-up scarecrow look. Thinly face.. always unshaven stubbles.. with a bird-like, hooked nose.. With a few light-colored lengthy hairs, that he combed straight back over his much-more-than-not bald head. They, seeming to be more like 'dividers' than anything else! Overall, he'd have been the perfect candidate and character for the casting of a Dicken's-based movie or play! He could've just played himself!

When Nate first met him and shook his hand, he remembered being quite taken back by the site of Henry's crushed fingers. A few of the tips and ends were totally missing!.. And splattered pieces of fingernails were set (like mosaic chips) into his rough and ink-stained hands. Healed now, yet still quite disfigured and mangled looking! It all, truly sickening for him, in his youthful and naïve discovery. And this, not only for the physical mutilation and the pain it must've caused the old man (getting caught in a press 'n all!); but, as well, for the mere thoughts of (in Nate's case) himself never being able to play the guitar again. Lord, what would he ever do, if that were to happen to him? It could totally and truly ruin his whole life!.. All of his dreams and goals, gone in a split second! What a frightening 'wake up call' it had been.. Making the boy have 'serious second thoughts' on just 'what kind of a meanwhile-career' he'd gotten himself into!

And this was not only the case with Henry, but a number of the other Printers he had met then and since. Rollers have absolutely no mercy! A rag getting caught and pulling you in.. or.. Gosh, there were just a number of other ways it could happen! He would just have to be extra careful and always pay attention!.. For he was in a bit too deep now to just walk away from it all. Not for a while yet, anyways!

By this point though, he had grown a bit more accustomed to seeing Henry's hands and no longer felt odd about it. Still, each time he spoke with him 'the concern' flashed through his mind.

Henry was a real nice fellow.. and Nate always took his (..as well as all of the other Printer's..) ribbing and teasing him with good humor. He remembered (in a moment now), how when he'd first started there in the pressroom, Henry had sent him around looking for some 'polka dot ink'. Nate asking everyone where he might locate it .. Never realizing that, all the while, the pressmen were getting a real chuckle out of his ignorance. An old 'devil's trick'! Yes, Henry was a sly one!.. As were they all!

After the boy had transferred his final settings, he made a quick repro, dropped it off on Brennan's desk for proofreading, and returned to store his work in the galley rack. Glancing out the nearby window, he saw that dusk was falling and got a sudden surge of anticipation. To work off the charge, he quickly washed down the Repro and hit the sand soap in the restroom, near the time clock. Roger was off somewhere in the pressroom now, but that was neither here nor there. It was okay for him to just leave. He'd completed his assignments for the day.

The warmth of the water was comforting on his numbness and he washed longer than usual for it. Drying up with the coarse brown hand towels, he quickly untied his apron, hung it up and poked his head around the Linotype, shooting.. ".. 'night, Bill.." and then, grabbing his hat and coat, he was off.

The darkening chill of the night had moisture in it, and Nate (breathing it in) made an inner wish to himself for no rain. And Lord forbid, no more snow!

Clicking along the deserted side streets' walkway, he became more introspect.. contemplating over whether or not to catch a bus home... Or to just walk, and save his limited funds for that evening.

Reaching the Main Street, he saw his bus waiting at its stop. Tangling with himself, he at last overcame the temptation and decided to 'hoof it'. It was a good haul! But he would take the railroad tracks, believing it to be the shorter of routes (At least, in the 'direct line' sense!). Maybe the more dangerous one, but he wouldn't fret over that now. For he truly needed the little bit of cash that he had.

Entering the dark parlor, Nate continued through the further slight-of-hall into the dim-lit kitchen. His Father (at the table and snubbing-out a cigarette in the ashtray), welcomed him...

"Hi, Nate.. how was work?.."

"Ok, I guess…"

"Feel like takin' a ride over t' the Airport, t' nite?.."

"Nah, Dad.. can't.. got sumethin' I gotta do.." He knew how much his Father enjoyed just walking around it, staring up at the planes that were coming in and taking off. There was an elevated walkway on the terminal roof with big coin-operated binoculars.. And all of Nate's life, it had been a 'ritual' they'd shared. Really, more for his Dad's interest in it (having once been a pilot for a time and still 'longing for the air'. But fate and life had likewise stolen it away. And for that, Nate sometimes found it painful to watch him 'studying the skies'..). Still, it brought his Father joy somehow, he figured. So, he felt a little bit guilty over the refusal and tacked on...

"Sorry.." as he made his way up the stairs. Hearing his Dad's...

"Ok.. Maybe Tomorrow?.."

"Yeah, maybe.." he conceding back, as he touched the top stair. Now (being older) the child-like fascination of it all had long-since totally evaporated. Still, if only to make his Dad happy, he'd give in, every once in awhile. Even though, somehow and again, it just saddened him to watch his Father staring-out at his 'next of' dreams, ascending off 'n away into thin air. Yet and still, he'd do it, here and there.

Leftward and in through his younger siblings' bedroom he made; at last, entering his private and partitioned-off sliver of a room. Closing the door (Otherwise he wouldn't have been able to move about!), he grabbed his acoustic guitar case and threw it up and onto his cot-sized bed. Unbuckling and opening it, he took out the instrument and made a quick check of its tuning.. turning a few.. and re-packing it. Making a speedy and awkward change of clothes, he at last began out, tangling his way through the tiny rooms.

Re-entering the hall and stairway-top, he heard his Mother call from the not-visible back bedroom…

"Nate, is that you?.."

"Yeah, Ma.." frustratedly sensing what was coming.

"You need to eat something before y' go out.."

"I'm not hungry, Ma.."

"It doesn't matter.." knowing he was fibbing, "There's a pot on the stove.. corn chowder.." (one of his favorites!) "..you can warm it up, 'n have a little.."

"Ok, Ma.." giving in.. But checking his watch, as he fumbled further down the stairs. Willie'd be waitin', but there was nuthin' he could do to prevent it.

Other worldly.. The Poet.. The 'Poe' fanatic.. Fragile and thin-framed.. Sensitive to a fault.. These were all Willie. And Nate was totally awed by him…

as, too, of Willie's knowledge and extreme perception of everything 'out there'!
A tightrope walker on an ungodly high string!.. Always bringing to Nate's
mind, the character 'Fodder-wing' from the movie "The Yearling", that he'd
once seen. And, his friend.. even looking like the very boy in the film.. only, a
bit older! Yes.. The boy who could fly!.. and would, whenever he was ready!

In the town-square (near the University), there was a lack of routine
traffic, vehicle and human alike. This, possibly due to the deepening cold front
that had crept into the evening hours. But on second thought, the weather rarely
effected it, any other time.. So it was probably and more-likely 'Spring Break'
for the college (coinciding with the Public Schools', this year) that made for the
greater absence of beings. A lot of folks, out-of-town, he figured.

The two-some hurried along passed the old graveyard and through the
start of the center, yappin' a mile'a minute. Nate's guitar-case occasionally
banging his knee-side.. making him, momentarily, lose footing each time. On
one occasion of this, he aggravatedly snapped…

"My Dad.. he wanted me t' go with 'im t' the stinkin' airport again
t'nite.. Man, like I really wanna be doin' that!"

"Well, your Dad.. he wanted t' be a pilot.. right?… " Willie, defending..
" I mean, he prob'ly really enjoys it, Nate.."

"Yeah, 'n so?.. He wanted to be an Artist!.. 'least, once, anyways!…
Quit that too!.. So, tell me, how can y' look up to someone like that? .. " shaking
his head in disgust..

".. 'Sides, Hank Williams.. Bob Dylan.. They're the real heroes in my
book!… Heck, they…"

Willie, cutting him short, slightly angered now…

"Nate-o.. you shouldn't be talkin' like that, man!.. 'bout your Dad 'n
all!.. you could lose him in a minute!.. 'Sides, he's a really good guy!.. You
oughta be grateful that.."

Nate, cutting back in…

"Willie.. you're always sidin' with him, man!.. Why?.. I mean, you don't even know the half of it, so… "

Firm-like and refusing to be moved…

"Hey, Nate.. I don't need t'!… 'Sides, you got it all wrong.. 'n totally backwards, when it comes to REAL heroes, man!.. Yeah, those guys are all Stars!.. 'n they're great!.. But, it's everyday folks that truly make a difference, in this world, man!... And, your Dad.. Well, he's a real good Father!.. I do know that, for sure!.. So, you oughta…"

Nate, giving it up, raising his hand in 'stop'…

"Ok, Willie Boy.. Got it!... Whatever!... Ok?..."

In this, he began walking briskly ahead.. with his friend 'in tow' and barely keeping up.   But, at last and nearing the coffeehouse, Willie (un-encumbered by an instrument) darted ahead.. and took the lead.

Down the stone stairs of the basement-set coffeehouse they scurried, Nate now feeling a sudden mixed sensation of joy and dread pumping through his veins. In through the doorway, he fought to ignore it.. following Willie to the register (where the names were being collected for the 'open hoot').. His friend excitedly shooting out his name so quickly, that the 'sign-up fellow' thought it to be the speaker's own. And in so, he turning to Nate with.. "You, too?"

"No.. Nate.. That's me!.." trying to clear up the confusion.

"Oh, I thought.. Well, ah.. Oh, yeah.. I see.. you're.." looking at Willie and stopping. Then turning back to him.. " Well, at least one thing's f' sure.. You sure got ONE eager fan!.." . Nate awkwardly smiled, then pushed Willie forward and on, to try and conceal any further signs of embarrassment.

Into the crowded club they made; in so, noting a few open seats at the opposing-and-far end of the stage. Working their way around and through the masses (and after a fair struggle in it), they plopped themselves down. Studying about the smoke-filled, dim-lit and bustling room in their settling, Willie whispered loudly..

"Whatcha got planned f' tonight, Nate-o?.. Gonna do that one 'bout your Grandma?"

"I dunno, might… " He, feeling a bit antsy.

"Yeah, do it!.. That one's a sure winner!.. I really like it!.. Hey, what about that new one.. y' know, 'bout the factory 'n all?.."

"I dunno, Willie.. that's really kinda 'too-new' .. I mean.. y' know, I ain't really memorized it yet!.. 'least, not good enough t' chance it here!"

"C' mon, man.. do it!.. it's a cool one!.. You'll remember it!.."

"And just, how d' YOU know that!.." Nate facetiously shooting back (for he was truly starting to un-nerve him now!).. and, in the same, staring steadfastly into his narrow and more-sunken face.

Willie detecting his humor, returned…

"You DO know it!.. You're just.. too.. CHICKEN t' try it!"

"No, I ain't!.."

"Yeah, y' are!.."

"Damn, you, Willie.. You're a real pain in the butt sometimes!.." and he, turning away, like to ignore him.

Saved by the approaching waitress, he swung-up, in the same, to order a coffee (despite his already-on-edge nerves!). With Willie's "No, Thanks..", Nate (figuring him to be broke again) shot out (as she left).. "make it two!.." and then, smirked a smile at his grateful friend. "Now leave me alone", he offered with a cynical, kidding-like look.. and turned away to mentally try to collect himself. Willie (knowing the routine) allowed him his solitude, studying about the crowd himself now to wait-out the festivities.

There's a strange paradox that exists in 'apprentice entertainers' of a nerve-racking dread that overwhelms the mind, while waiting to be called upon to perform. And in the very same, a horrendous sense of forthcoming disappointment, if not! The latter of these two, being now 'eliminated in a flash' with the introduction of Nate to a very- sparse scattering of 'polite, welcoming him, golf-course-like' applause. And, in this, leaving only the first! Yes, wobbling forward now and lifting his guitar 'sideways' (as to not bang any of the about-him heads), he worked his way onto the stage.

The songs were nice enough.. but, the performance itself was somewhat weak. Or better yet, shakey! But, all was executed properly-enough, despite... and after all, that was the purpose of attempting these feats, to begin with.. Yes, to learn!.. So, nothing was in vain. Though, much was spent in pain!

Between the long day at work and the exhausting pressure of the evenings' events, Nate just couldn't make the long jaunt home without a stop-off in the outer-square's park. And his partner complied willingly.. all the while, 'carrying-on empathetically' throughout-it-all about his "superb performance". Yeah, Willie was stretching it 'beyond belief' for moral support.. But, hey.. Nate knew better! Still, any disagreements would've been pointless.. And only further fueled Willie's attack. So, he just gave in, and sat on the chilly bench, letting him rattle on.

In the quiet and peacefulness of the surrounding winter's-like night and its late hour, Willie, at last, worded himself out. And, after a long cold silence, his mood swung.. deeply saddening, as it often would. And he began talking about his Mother. After having lost her at a crucial stage in his development, he now seemed 'still and overly' obsessed with her death. And, as well, yet trapped in the overwhelming heartbreak of it all. Nate (having fortunately-enough not suffered the same) couldn't fully understand... Still he always listened very caringly.. And somehow 'vicariously' felt his deep pain.. for the loss of his own and so-dearly-beloved Grandmother (only a few years prior) still ached!

At last..

"See that star up there, Nate?.. I betcha that's where my Mom is, right now.."

Nate instead of 'following suit', (as inconspicuously as possible) peeked over at his friend's arched-and-staring-upward face.. Studying it, peripherally and sporadically, there-after. There were tears starting and increasingly gathering, as he suspected.. so, he softly responded...

"Yeah.. probably.." Then went silent, to allow for Willie's release.

"Damn, do I miss her, Nate!.. Y' know, I'm gonna..." Stopping to momentarily try to control himself. But it didn't work, and he further blurted out in his pain.. "Y' know, I'm gonna go t' her soon.. I mean it, man!.."

Nate, turning and focussing in towards him now...

"Willie.. Listen.. I don't think y' Mom'd want that.. I mean, you got a whole life t'.."

But, he.. cutting him short.. and, in the same, directing his reddened-eyes sharply at him now...

"I don't care, Nate!.. I mean it with all 'f my heart!.. ".. Then, hopping up to his feet and walking away into the near darkness.. To hear no more of it.. Trembling and groaning to himself, in his anguished furthering. It was painful just to watch, and Nate felt the start of his own tears for it.

Under the eerie-looking, moon-bathed and bare tree-line, he stood.. Alone, for the moment, in the shadows and his wrenching agony. Nate continued to watch him.. and tried desperately to think of something to say to console him. But, nothing would come. He was just a boy himself. Yet, in his limited-ness, he knew there must be something worth-while he could grasp. Something that would make things right again. But, what?

Allowing Willie his privacy for a time (..but, with the chill of the night seeming to increase), he at last raised himself and lifted his guitar-case from beside the bench. He moved on towards his friend's still-turned back and lowered head, putting his arm around his shoulders and giving him a pal-like squeeze.. Noting, in his quick observation of Willie's face, that a 'resolve' had already been taking hold. He was grateful in that... For 'timed wrong', he might've received a totally different response. He further offered a reassuring smile, that was received by the still-red, yet-trying-to-respond-to-it-accordingly face of his friend. Life can be so painful. Never ever let it be said, that 'youth is free of its fair share of suffering'!

Just as they came to the Common's end, Willie (to try to lighten up things a bit) said...

"Y' know, Nate-o.. Maybe if I was t' someday get married t' your sister Katie, like I always told y' I'm gonna!.. well, maybe I could..."

"What?.. 'n have you f' my Brother-in-law!.. No way, man!.." Nate, facetiously.. "Get out'a here!.." jostling Willie's shoulder with his free hand, then pointing.. "You just stay away from m' little sister, y' hear? .."

"But, I really love her, Nate!.. Really!.."

"I don't care.. you stay clear!.. Hear me?.."

Both laughing and carryin'-on, they disappeared further-off and away into the night.

And, in a distant recall, the Poet wrote...

Love Appears a Knight in Armour

Poets fall in love so easy

always seeking arms

fire-placed, romantic moments

whiled away to Brahms

Seizing sentimental spirits

persuasively lassoed

pursuing clothed security

as if, a shivering nude

Love appears a Knight in Armour

gallant to degree

clutching ropes from falling depths

of insecurity

"Look it 'er go, Nate!.." his Dad turning to him, as the far-off ascending airplane climbed into the dark horizon. It was a sight to see! But after years and years of watching countless others in their 'take-off', by now this had totally lost its charm. At least, for him. But, his Dad still found excitement in it. So, Nate (to appease him) moved in to the iron guard-rail that enclosed the tower-watch, putting his arms up on it for support. He peered out, trying to seem enthusiastic. But, obviously not convincingly-enough…

"What'a y' say we go get us a cup 'a joe?" His Dad always called it that.

"Sure.." Nate nodding with a slightly forced smile.

Turning and beginning off the platform, they reached the thin stairwell and started down. Through the long aisle-like, deserted corridors they walked on, not saying much. But, Nate thinking a lot. Mostly of his Dad's tragic loss in not becoming the pilot he had always longed to be. That and his abandoned art work (his other dream) seemed totally illogical! Or, better yet.. unfathomable! And it deeply saddened him. And, in the same, that ol' guilt feeling returned. It was an inner-sickening feeling, when momentarily considering the painful episodes his family had had to deal with, throughout the years. Yes, the depression and sickness that had followed, as a result! And at last (for all of the anxiety it caused him now), Nate had to dodge and shun it away for his inability to understand and deal with it on any fair ground. No, all he knew was, when he grew up.. nuthin'.. no, absolutely nuthin'.. would ever come between him and his dreams! There was just too much at stake! For all parties concerned!

His father had his first nervous breakdown, early on.. and for it, he'd become ineligible to ever attain a pilot's license there-after (As Nate understood it). A heartless decision (the boy felt) on some government officials part, considering how many people have had to deal with such issues in their lives. Regardless, this had (in the process) squelched any remaining hopes that his Father might have had, for a future in the cockpit. Still, his undying love for it, found him (for his likewise 'artistic talent'..) constantly devising wing-structural concepts and aeronautical body designs, that he would sketch-out and send to the builders.. Hoping and praying they would see his creative talents in the field and bring him 'on board'. For, at least, then.. he'd be close to it all! But, being the sincere and trusting 'good-guy' he was.. (believing in the 'better person' in everyone) he had never patented any of it. This, probably and as well, for his very limited funds. Either way, many of his 'ideas' were just flat-out thieved. So much for the 'truer nature of man'!

After what seemed like endless miles of scenic-travel posters, closed offices and construction re-routing plywood-and-planked-like corridors, they at last reached the main terminal. Entering the huge and brilliantly-lit lobby, they saw the coffee shop still open at the far-end.

Reaching it, they found it serene and quiet, with only one other customer seated in the much-dimmer-now extension. And he, a pilot in full uniform... in-between flights, it appeared.

"Want coffee, Nate?.."

"Yeah, Dad.. that'll be fine.." finding a seat near the glass partition to peer out at the vast cavity, while his Father ordered. With his return and the drinks...

"Here y' go, Son.." sitting opposite.. "Well, that sure was fun, huh?"

"Yeah.." Though, not with any true spirit.

"Well, I guess you're gettin' older now.. 'n maybe you're just.. Well.."

Nate knew what he was trying to say and to thwart it, he offered...

"No.. it was ok!.. Really, Dad.. Y' know, I just got a lot on m' mind.. 'n.. "

"Music, I bet!.. Huh?.."

"Yeah, well.. some.."

"Maybe some sweet young lady, huh?.."

"No, not really.." turning a bit embarrassedly out the window to stare away.

"Well, y' know, Son.. it's pretty natural t'…"

Still refusing to break his further focus, Nate didn't respond.. Just acted as if it all was going unheard.

Nate slammed the locker door shut.. spun the combination lock.. and grabbing his books up from the floor, took off for home-room. Arriving late (per usual!), he entered as sneakingly as possible. But it didn't work. Mr. Kilder had eyes in the back of his head.. and without even a slight head pivot, he interrupted his daily 'blackboard' announcements with…

"Nate… I'll see you for Detention tonight…" smartingly adding.. "Again!.."

Then (with still no physical turnings) he resumed in his addressing the class and his ongoing 'chalk-screeching' scribbles. Nate dropped his shoulders in it.. and, at last, made for his seat.

With the sound of the First Period Bell, he began into the hall with the others. Halfway up the third floor's flight, it all began again… Coming from behind him…

"Hey, Elf.. when y' gonna get a haircut?.. If it gets any longer, you're gonna have t' start wearin' a dress!.. Not only that, queer.. but, this is an all-boys school.. They'll be kicking your little pansy ass out of here, 'fore long! "

He tried to ignore it. Ray Bolger was the quintessential 'dumb jock'.. A total greaser! And his accomplice-in-crime, Brad Russell was a carbon copy, chiming-in his two-cents with…

"Man, let's put lighter fluid in it, Ray.. 'n give him an instant haircut!"

Nate just kept on climbing, feeling his heart-poundings increase.. Still silent to the taunts.

In through the fourth floor's hallway doors, they moved.. he trying to (as inconspicuously as possible) pick up speed. But it didn't work, for the hecklers (like dogs sensing his fear) darted faster, grabbing him by the back of his head and hair, and pulled him down into a painful surrender. Then, lifting him up by his shirt's front, they spun him.. in the process, pushing his back up against the cement corridor wall. In the sudden stop and jolt (..Causing his head to bang for the natural, retreating-reflex), they began (right up close, and in-his-face) …

"Listen, you little queer.. y' better have your hair nice 'n short by tomorra.. or we're gonna cut it ourselves!.. You heard Brad.. 'n that's how!.. Hear me, boy?.." Ray staring violently into the reddening-deeper face of Nate. But he wouldn't respond. So, Brad reiterated.. "You hear, Elf?…" Near tears, but holding desperately, he, at last, gulped out.. "Yeah, I hear y'…" with a pale, but dry-look of defiance.

Class bell rang and he was saved. Letting him go in an abrasive fashion, they laughingly began off, not to be late. Nate was truly stunned.. for in the past few years, this taunting had all been verbal. Things were escalating and he really didn't know what to do! Fighting meant immediate expulsion. He sighed deep, trying to regain a sense of composure before entering class. Boy, did he hate them guys!

Nothing more happened throughout the day.. and detention kept him beyond normal dismissal. And this, conveniently-enough.. for the after-school fight that might've occurred. But this, too, not without cost! For Mr. Kilder was in rare form now, giving him the longest of his disciplinary sermons…

"Nate.. Do you want to know what your problem is? .. You lack 'motivation'!"

Yeah, if he only knew how hard Nate was working at his music and writing! If he only knew how much of a 'balancing act' it was, what with all else in his life! If he only knew about the late night's performing at music jobs..

then, having to get up bright-'n-early for school! And, when not, instead for work! Yes, at the Print Shop. Then, on top of it all, the long tedious hours of practice, reading-about and studying what he loved.. and planned to be. If he only knew 'the truth'! 'Motivation'? .. Yeah, Right! But, the boy knew all too well from past experience, it wasn't even worth trying to explain.

Mr. Kilder became so emphatic in his pounding and preaching, this time.. he actually concluded it by sitting down, with his head in his hands (upon his desk), seeming to be in tears. Nate was quite sure that he was crying.. Only, knowing his past history of being a Marine 'n all, made it seem unlikely.. impossible.. or maybe even, just a mirage that he was seeing. Not really happening! But it was. Still and in so, he was never truly self-convinced-enough to be completely sure. But, the whole event.. Well, it was just.. really.. so STRANGE!

Being, finally, excused, Nate walked through the school's main courtyard and passed the Library. Then, out further and onto the main street he made, to catch the bus for work. What a weird day this had all been!

Brennan was off.. and it set the mood for a quiet and remaining day. Despite the ever-continual rumble of machinery in the backset-end of the building, there was a peace and pensiveness in the front shops' air; and Nate greatly welcomed it. Still, though.. throughout all his work, his thoughts kept gravitating back to the earlier and upsetting events at school. Scraping the final handful of slugs from the Lino, he placed it along with the previous-others that were on the new galley and took a line gauge reading. Thereafter, making a repro, he checked for nicks.. removed them.. and ran a second. Then, leaving it on Brennan's desk for later proofreading, he proceeded to wash down the press. And (per his earlier instructions..) he, at last, fed the Ludlow (beforehand) for its next assignment.

After his immediate business, his thinking returned. What was he going to do about all'a that? He wished he could just beat the living Hell out'a both of them. But he knew full well it'd be an unlikely stretch. Why'd he have to be so small 'n thin? I mean, maybe if he got lucky and was really mad enough, he might bring down one! But, two? Pretty far-reachin'!

It was still too cold to swim. But several of Nate and Willie's friends had taken a late night drive out to Stiles Pond. A 'spin in the sticks', as they called it. Just for nuthin' better to do! Summer was in the air, but so too was Winter's dying nip. Buzz (a mulatto boy with a high-strung nature and a wacky-quick wit) was the oldest, having the license and car. He and Zack (Nate's drummer and lifelong friend), at this point, had taken off for the village market up in Boxford. They'd be returning soon.

Sitting by the thicket on the pond's edge now, Nate and Willie shivered a bit in the darkness. Several creature-calls echoed from across the chilly sky in the dark distance, leaving only deathly silence in their aftermath. The latter, broken on occasions by the slight rippling waves hitting the shoreline. Nate hadn't said anything to his other friends in regards to his school problems, for fear of ridicule. But with Willie, things were always different.. and seeing the quiet and perfect opportunity arise now, he took it…

"Man.. School.. I got these real jerks on m' tail!.. They really hate me!.. say they're gonna burn off m' hair with lighter fluid, if I don't get it cut!.. Y' know, them real greaser types?.. Dumb jocks.. I just can't stand 'em!.. Man, they just won't leave me alone!"

There was a silence. Willie (sitting in front of him and closer to the shoreline) didn't respond. Just kept looking forward and out. Nate wondered if he should've just kept it to himself. Finally, in a whispered-like under-voice (never turning back to look at him throughout)..

"They're jealous.. Just jealous, Nate."

Another silence.

"Why d' y' say that?.. Jealous of what?.." Truly confused.

"Your music and art 'n all.. Y' know, they wish they could be like you.. play the guitar 'n .. " pausing slightly.. " Well, y' know.. 'n be cool!.. You're everything they ain't!"

"Y' really think?.."

"Sure!.."

"Well, still.. what 'm I 'sposed t' do, Willie?.. I ain't inta fightin'.. I hate it!.. 'Sides, this late in the year, that'd be all I need t' do.. Yeah, go 'n get myself expelled.. 'n…"

"No, don't.. Y' don't need t' do that!.. Just ignore 'em!"

"IGNORE 'EM?.."

"Yeah, that's what I do!.. Doncha think I deal with that same crap?.. People hate artists, man!.. Deep down, they really do!.. Look 'it Poe.. Everybody hated him!.."

"Really?.. I thought he was pretty famous!.."

"Was!.. Still, the people that knew him up close, they detested him!.. The people that read him.. Sure, they loved him 'n all.. But, his contemporaries.. Heck, they loathed him!.. says so, in the books!.. 'n believe me, I've read 'em all, when it comes t' him!"

"Yeah, Willie.. I sure know y' have!"

The answer wasn't exactly what Nate had been looking for. Still, there was a feeling of resolve (at least, on Willie's part!) in the silence that followed. So, he gave it up.

Willie.. at last, turning back now....

"Hey, Nate-o.. Sumeday y' think y' could write a song about Poe?.. I ain't never heard one!.. What'a y' think?.."

"Sure, man... Sumeday!"

"Why not now?.."

"I ain't got a pen on me!" Nate, being silly. Willie, cracking a branch beneath himself, as he gave a quick sarcastic-like smirk .. and then, in the same, quickly turned back out and away.

A darker and stiller silence transcended in the aftermath. Only chilling, sporadic ripples heard in it. Cold stars and a full moon looking down. Slight occasional wind, bringing an occasional human sigh. Then...

"Hear that, Nate?.. Listen!.." Willie arching up, nervous-like.

There was nothing more in the stillness he could hear...

"What?.. " in a gasping whisper.

"Angels!.. Hear 'em?.. comin'.. comin' from.." stopping and looking about "from.. over there!.. " pointing forward and up above the opposing shoreline.

"Angels?.."

"Really, Nate, I ain't kiddin'.. listen, they're singin'!.."

"Don't tell me.. a song about Poe.. right?.." Nate thinking that hilarious.. but, Willie turning dead-serious and angered...

"I ain't kiddin', Nate!... just listen.." Then swinging back.. and waiting a few seconds.. "Hear 'em?.."

Nate believing now, but still not hearing a thing.

Willie hopped up, shaken-like, as if mesmerized and totally a-feared by it. Nate following suit, but more out of respect and guilt (for his moment's before joke). But there was nothing! Absolutely nothing he could hear! Though he was convinced now that his friend could hear something.. For there was nothing 'staged' about his un-nerved reaction and awkward stance. Nate was totally 'lost for words'.. and just stood waiting, not knowing what to do next. Feeling a strange rise of deeper fear mounting inside, he peered about himself, then out further to try and focus on the external. The water ripples sounded harder and colder now.

At last, Willie relaxed somewhat and slowly reseated himself, though still with his back to him.. Running his trembling-some hands through his hair-sides.. Not explaining or elaborating, in the least. It was obvious that he was still somewhat upset and lost in the deeper thoughts of it, so Nate just sat down as well and held tongue.

The sound of Buzz's car pulling in on the parking lot's gravel was a true relief. Nate spun momentarily to witness the headlights, without system, searching and bouncing off the behind-them shrubbery. Turning forward again in excitement..

"Willie.. They're back!.. Ready?.."

Without another word, they both began up the slight grade.

Hunting Trips

We used to go on Hunting Trips

We'd walk the railroad tracks

rifles head-locked through our arms

plaid shirts on our backs

Every Autumn Saturday

fingers crossed, good luck

maybe we'd return that night

with pheasants or a duck

Tramping fields of dying grass

in Sat'day's drizzily dawn

shotgun shells of different colors

scattered 'bout the pond

When navy skies spoke for themselves

and dusk warned all of night

we'd hurry home to beans 'n brown bread

to climax it just right

Dusk had nearly passed. Since morn, his Dad and he had 'seeming-endlessly' tramped through dying foliage and drying shrubs. This, without a single shot being fired. His Dad most times, steps ahead, with his shotgun arm-locked and braced, walking in thoughts of his own. Nate (toting his own rifle) tagging behind and rarely speaking. But they, together! This 'quiet' the norm, except when crossing the brush-infested and dangerous swamp lands. And then, they.. engaged in nervous banter and conversation over the quicksand-like mud ponds and the rebounding snaps of wire-strong branches. There was always the 'half time' relief of the gravel-graded train tracks though, that ran dead-center swamp; allowing for a well-needed break from the strenuous travel. Yes, and it was always then, that Nate would imagine seeing 'ole Hank Williams rambling along them' with his guitar and singing "Ramblin' Man" (or some other of his 'wandering songs'), as they made their slippery way across. Then, after a brief sit-down-'n-'break', they'd be right back into the marsh and thicket again.. Tangling through thorn bushes and twisted pussy willows.

But now (the day spent and dusk near-completed), they were making their one 'last round' of the pond. His Dad, still ahead. Then, Nate heard them! The ducks quacking in the deeper-darkening horizon. They were coming in their direction! His Dad lowered himself ahead to a final half-kneel. The boy stopping cold in the anticipating silence. Boom! Boom! Boom! It echoed across the cold night. Three shots. Two ducks dropping! One, into the un-see-able distance. Another, directly into the pond ahead. It splashing frantically. His Dad turning and calling him forward, as the swimming duck neared the shore.

It, at last, aground and wobbling-about erratically…

"Here, Son.. y' need to finish him.. Quick, it's suffering!.." pulling Nate into the caress of his shotgun. He, nervous and confused. His Dad helping him hold it up in his arms. Boom! The awful kick-back of the gun. The spray of pellets. Then, silence. Ear ringing silence!

Boom!.. Again! 'Again?', Nate squinting his nose and eyes in disbelief.. and discomforted perplexity! He knowing fully well that there was never another shot fired then. Shaking his inner wits, he outwardly focused now and saw a puttering-on bus, jockeying its clumsy and fume-spitting way further down the avenue in the direction of his High School. It had been a back-fire! He'd just been so lost in the recall, he'd totally forgotten where he was. But with the sight of the school's entranceway, in the distance now, it brought back all the dreaded reality.. And the 'lighter fluid'-threat quickly re-echoed in his mind's ear. Damn, there was just no way he was going to deal with that today! Absolutely no way! And with all of the other tensions in his life now (compounding his inner turmoil), he instead made a quick about-face and hoped no one that he knew had seen him. Beginning back in the direction of the Square, he felt the odd sensation of nervous tension that grips one's lower torso in times like these. But he would ignore it. It would pass. He knew that from numerous similar and past experiences.

There was a peaceful silence that settled itself upon the reservoir.. Mingled with the earlier morning's dew. Its still-vapor, now further ascending itself like perfume up and into the day break. He still felt a bit nervous for what he was doing. But miles away from the school-grounds and general-area now, it seemed a bit safer. There was a special place he would always enjoy sitting, on the sloping side of a particular hill that overlooked the water. This is where he sat now. Alone. The reservoir was always deserted this time of day and week. Rarely would a person appear. And Nate especially liked that idea.. Yes, everyone else.. working or trapped in their worlds.. But, he.. free! Or at least, temporarily free!.. Thinking his thoughts of music and the like… And his 'one day' dreams. Yes, of when he would be grown up and able to leave this place. The school! The factory! Yes, the life he longed to leave behind.. And never again return to!

By 11 am, having ached to play his guitar (and knowing he'd be expected late day at the print shop), he returned home. Not to try and hide things from his parents, he simply gave in and appeared. Walking into the kitchen…

"Nate.. what are you doing home so early?.."

"I didn't go, Ma..   Sorry, I just couldn't t'day .."   The sincere and distressed look on his face, brought no argument. Upstairs to his room, he went.. with not another word of it said.

With all that Nate's Mom had to do with raising eight children.. regardless and in spite of all.. when her oldest and musical son performed at his 'whatever' local events, it was she that 'taxi'-ed the crew around. Maneuvering the ol' Olds' 98, filled with the band members and their equipment, she'd drop them off and pick them up every time. Re-organizing her schedule and unending tasks to accommodate and support his music and love for it. A true Mom!

Pulling up and double parking outside the school auditorium, Nate (passenger side) slivered out first. This, to assist Zack with the removal of his bass drum from his crunched-and-supporting- it lap in the backseat. All and everyone else, soon climbing free from the 'four-door' and 'sidewalk-side' opening.

Tonight it would be a "Battle of the Bands" and everyone was secretly on edge. All desperately hoping they came out 'winners' for once. And not that they weren't good, might I say.. but, only because they were 'different'.. doing the music their own way. And for that in itself, unlikely to come in first over any of the typical 'copy'-style bands that sounded like everyone else (that the audiences were already familiar with.. and loved and accepted!). So, it was a stretch that they would prevail. Still, they always tried.

Likewise, there was always the contributing factor of their old, beat-up and second-hand equipment. The more 'well-to-do kids' always showing up with the newest and top-rate amps and so forth. The best in the line! The best in clothes and matching suits too! The best in everything, except talent!.. At least, in the truly creative and artistic sense! But then again, what did the judges and these audiences of 'media-brain-washed' kids know about 'Art' to begin with? The 'superficial' always perpetuate the 'superficial'!

So, there was really no true contest here, except the always 'high' going-into-it hopes, that maybe.. just once.. the music and originality would count. Oh, the blessed innocence (or is it 'ignorance'?) of youth! Either way, it was an opportunity to play their music and possibly promote themselves, in the process.

Stephen was a good solid bassist.. Of Chinese descent, but a pure bred American boy, all 'round! Nate had known him long before the formation of the band. As in the same, Tim (the lead singer) and Ben (the other guitarist). They had all grown-up together in the same neighborhood. All too had been in 'Scouts' (Which is where they met Zack, the drummer).. and well, they'd just literally 'cut their musical teeth' in this unit! From the songs and playing, right down to the 'system of unloading the equipment', this was all fine-tuned clockwork! And soon, the Olds was emptied and 'riding higher on the road'!.

"Ma, is 10 ok?.."

"Yes, Nate.. but, be ready.. y' hear?.. " as she, in leaving, opened the driver's side door.

"Yes, ma' am.. we will!"

"And behave yourselves too!.."

"We will!.." He answering for the crew. This final comment of hers, in reference to their last school auditorium performance, where Tim (the forever ladies man!) had riled up several jealous boys. Their girlfriends taking a big 'liking' to the singer's on-stage dancing and theatrics; and for that, a 'near gang fight' had almost occurred outside after 'let out'! Fortunately, no one ended up fighting, in the least, though. But this, only for the old, infamous 'mike stand' trick. Yes, the.. 'putting them up over your shoulders, with their cast-iron bases blatantly exposed'-threat!... Hey, that can deter even the most heated of customers! This and the 'just in time' arrival of several Squad cars worked wonders! Thank God, all 'battling' was prematurely squelched! Still, it was quite a scare.. And, one that Nate's Mom sure didn't want to have to re-live again. Nor anyone in the band, might I say! But such is the life for High School bands without security and so on.. There's always the chance!

Backstage, Nate (with his nicknamed "Queen Jane", red-sunburst, Hofner f-holed guitar strapped and hanging from him) was trying desperately to get his cord untangled, when Tim approached. The latter asking..

"What'a y' think we should do t'nite.. Some Stones' stuff.. or... I dunno, what'a y' think?.."

"I'd like t' do 'There'll be no teardrops tonight' myself.." Nate, lifting his head from the un-raveling.

"Are you serious?.." over-hearing Ben shot back in grimacing disbelief.

"Yeah, I am.. Why not?.. We do a pretty good version 'a that!.."

"You gotta be crazy, man!.. I mean, doin' an odd ball, old Hillbilly song like that, at a thing like this?.."

"Hey, Ben.. What's the difference.. . Heck, even if we do sumethin' current, it ain't gonna matter none!.. So, why not just enjoy ourselves!.."

"But I don't ENJOY that one!.."

"Well, me 'n Tim do.. Right?.." looking at the singer now. And, he...

"Yeah.. Well.. Let's!.. Why not!.. 'n.. How about some Pickett too?.. 'n maybe 'Stand by me'! .. What'a y' say?"

"Yeah, ok with me!.." Nate agreeing.

Ben.. further 'teed-off' now.. turned and moved away.. Knowing fully well, it was useless to argue. They ran the group. Despite the fact that he, too, was one its founders.. and had once shared in the decision making and so on. But now, things were all different.. Ever since Nate and Tim had taken to co-writing together for the last several years, and had become 'better friends', everything had changed! His once-voice and power had diminished completely. And being more of a rhythm guitarist than anything else, most of the time (not singing or doing more than an occasional lead guitar part), he'd almost become expendable. And he knew that. No, it wasn't fair at all.. But, it was life.. and he had somewhat resolved himself to it. Though, there were still 'those moments'!

And so, the cover tunes had been picked. As well as two of the songwriter's selections. One, having Nate's lyrics.. "Old Mrs. Brennan" (a 'biting' little number about Mrs. You-Know-Who!).. and the other, "She's My Little Girl", a Tim lyric.

Actually, it was a pretty exciting and precise performance, all 'n all! The band seeming to really cook and enjoy themselves. Still, it was 'musically' different. The 'Beatle' bands with their racked Marshall's (.. as expected,) getting the greater applause.. Despite their stale approaches to the truly, well-crafted material. Almost insulting it, in Nate's opinion! But, again, it had worked for them. And, in the same, it had all been for-seen.. So, no great surprise!

Yes, they lost again. And 'packing up' was meditative and silent. The only joy being the sudden, quick moment that they hit the balmy cool night air. It, and the auburn-stained sky, stealing their breaths.. And, somehow helping to calm and swing their moods in a flash. All, short of Ben's.. who (.. in a sharp, under-the-breath-type voice.. As if talking to himself, but loud enough for all to hear..) exhaled, with a snarl…

"Damn, man.. I just knew it!.. we gotta start doin' some current stuff.. I ain't takin' much more 'a this!.. 'n I mean it!"

No one responded. It went as if totally unheard.

The Duel

We stood as one.. like back to back

The sweat rolled off my chin

The smell of death.. it reeked the air

For either me or him

I was confused.. maybe I'd lose

For one destined a fall

Was I prepared.. to let myself

Stand naked to it all?

Among the other thoughts.. that came..

Distracting to my mind

Tempting sweet desertion

What route was I to find?

I turned to run.. to realize..

That it would be in vain

And so, in agony, I stood

Until myself regained

Nate stood in front of the third grade class, breathing into the ear of his teacher's adult and grown-up son. The latter (having dropped by the school to see his mother briefly) was now stooped down and listening to the intimidated, young boy.. totally oblivious (at first) for all or any reasons why. But, this.. strictly at the beckoning of his mother, standing stoically aside them at her desk...

"Well.. What do you hear?…"

Nate continued to breath heavier at her motioning command; as she was a dreadful figure and a staunch disciplinarian, to begin with.. and the last thing he wanted to do, was 'set her off'! She, with her heavyset and huge stature..(not to forget, her renowned 'short fuse'!) had the 'most well-behaved' class in all of the school! It was common knowledge! So, despite the embarrassing situation he was now in (having the entire class sitting and staring at him, impatiently waiting!.. And for, Lord knows, what reason?.. he, himself, completely unsure!), he would simply comply. What's a young child to do, otherwise?

"Well, come on now.. What do you hear?.." She persisted on to her son.

He (obviously more compassionate than his mother.. and now, at last, realizing the reason) was pretending not to be hearing anything (in the boy's breathing).. and just kept lifting his hands like ..' I dunno?'... Not wanting to actually verbalize it, for the 'high-intensity' and un-nerving scene that it all was causing.. And even greater, for the lad's sake!..

Finally, frustrated for his delaying…

"The WHISTLE!.. Hear it?.. The WHISTLING!.. He has ASTHMA too!.." She, thinking this all just so grand!.. And like it would 'somehow' alleviate his (her son's) suffering and plight with it!.. or whatever?.. Only the Good Lord could've known her intentions!

"Oh, yeah.." He, trying to make light of the ordeal.. Though, truly saddened for the traumatic embarrassment it had all caused the unknowing and unaware boy. It showed in the way he padded his shoulders and moved in now, obstructing the class's view of him. But, regardless, the harm had been done.. and Nate's return to his back-of-the-row seating was truly painful, in its aftermath!

That had been on a Friday morning. Nate remembered it all, very clearly now.. despite the many years that had passed! Traumas are hard to forget! Regardless, for some strange reason, it had just re-surfaced 'out of nowhere' (in spite of his present condition and the at-hand moment)! For, now.. he was sitting in the high school nurse's office, waiting his turn to be seen.. and feeling the furthering flush of a climbing fever, hanging and hazing over him. And, he.. a good bit 'delirious' for it! This.. causing him to drift mentally in-and-out of focus.. and, in so, into the resuming memories of it again…

The Sunday night immediately following that 'embarrassing' occurrence, young Nate and his Father had gone over to his Grandparent's apartment. All weekend, the abasing 'whistling' episode had preyed on his mind, and he'd been quite withdrawn for it. Still, he held it in, refusing to discuss it with his parents or anyone else. The thought of going back to school, Monday, and having to face them all, though.. was deeply troubling and sickening him. But, he also knew it inevitable!

Entering his Grandparent's parlor, he saw his Uncle seated in the corner, in front of his record player, listening intently to a Hank Williams record. Moving in closer to him now (for his mutual appreciation), Nate noted it to be a 45 rpm; hearing better in this... "We're getting closer to the grave, each day..". It sounded so good! .. But, his Grandfather (sitting in the opposite corner) didn't appreciate it as much, mumbling out.. "I'm sick as a dog.. 'n I gotta be hearin' somethin' as depressing as that!.." to Nate's Dad, who had entered just behind him. The boy (and his uncle) continued to listen, despite.. and just let the adults have their say. It was such a moving and great piece! And the first time he'd ever heard this one! .. And, Hank.. Well, he was just.. 'T.H.E. Man' in Nate's eyes!

"That guy was nothin', but a drunk!.. That 'n a dope addict, like all of them others!.. N' wonder all he ever sang about was Death!.." Nate caught that out of the corner of his ear.. His Grandpa continuing in his verbal disdain for it, to his Father. But, the boy had heard the same-and-similar before from his Mom.. and knew it just to be a 'ranting'.. But, in the same, a sincere and pure-hearted 'ranting' though.. with only a didactic intent!.. Not particularly malicious or maligning. And, yes, it was true.. ole Hank DID die like that! Hey, we're ALL sinners! Still, there was a real good part in Hank, that wasn't easy to see! A deeper thing! His very soul! And, Nate (be assured!) 'knew' that soul!.. Yes, he 'knew' his very spirit!.. 'n better than any words could ever express or describe, either! This, 'n that Hank had been.. 'a man with a real sincere and truer-faith-than-most in God'.. Plus, someone with an obvious and genuine concern, that his audience 'learn and gain' something from what he wrote and sang about!.. And, it showed through 'crystal clear' in the words of his songs. Not to mention, the very deep-hearted conviction he applied when singing them!.. Lord, it was just.. so.. so.. obvious!.. He wondered, in the moment, why his elders couldn't see, understand or share the same. Either way, it was what Nate himself hoped to do, one day.. Yes, with his own music and writings!.. to hopefully 'move' and lead folks to what is really and truly 'more important' in life!.. and what sincerely counts the most!

When the recording was through, his Father beckoned him over…

"Son, c' mere.. 'n hop-up on y' Granddad's knee.." The boy (feeling like he was getting a bit 'too big' for that now) looked quickly down and away. But, with his Dad's.. "C' mon, now.. don't be like that.. ", he complied.. figuring his Father was just trying to (through him) comfort his own Dad in his sickness. It did seem to brighten-up his spirits, in the outcome. So, Nate was glad that he had done it.. For his Grandpa had always been so loving and close to him, throughout the years. His beloved Grandma, too!

The next morning, he woke up feeling weak and ill. He wasn't sure if it had been from sitting on his 'sickly' Grandpa's knee?.. or just the simple 'sickening dread' of 'having to face his schoolmates' for that previous Friday morning's incident.. But, either way, he tried to convince his Mom that he should stay home. But, having been absent a whole week , only two week's prior (with his asthma), she thought he couldn't afford missing now. So, off he went..

That morning in class, they were reading from their Health Books.. One by one, standing by their seats to read aloud a paragraph or two. It was the study of the inner ear. The discussion of it (plus, the ill-at-ease tension of being called-on to read-it-aloud) mounted and increasingly preyed on him, as his turn neared. That, and the likewise-compounding-it fever (and the 'physical weakness' that it was causing him!) were beginning to boil! So, when finally his turn came around, he awkwardly complied.. standing up and starting in.. But, before he could conclude his section of the text, it all overcame him.. and he passed out in the aisle. This (in the reviving and final conclusion) only further embarrassing him and complicating his 'societal' and 'world' view.. Or even better said, absolutely 'traumatize-ing' it! And, that, being the very piece of dirt in the oyster! Yes, the one that makes the pearl! He.. withdrawing deeper and deeper, further away from the world there-after!.. And, into his guitar playing and music.. and his writing! Surrounding and building his guard! For.. no one could touch him there! Yes, that was 'his world'!.. A world where 'cruelty', 'hypocrisy' and all of the other 'evils of mankind' were only attacked, condemned and chastised in the lyrics that exposed them!.. Yes, but, short of that.. they, being.. totally 'non-existent' entities!

"GET SOME WATER!... SOMEONE.. GET A GLASS OF WATER FOR HIM!.. Y' HEAR ME?... SOME WATER!" .. he heard his teacher calling-out, loudly.. in the coming-back-to-reality of the moment..

Nate (in the very same.. and his likewise 're-surfacing from the memory') looked up at the nurse, now approaching.

"And what's wrong with you?.." Arrogantly.

"I got a bit 'f a fever, I think.." he responded; wondering, in this, what he might've done wrong. .

"Maybe it's because of all of that HAIR on your head!.. Your brain can't get any AIR!.." she shot back. Nate, making a dis-believing squint, like as if to say.. 'What?.. How can you joke now?' But, she wasn't! .. Just as serious as pneumonia!

"Come over here.." she frustrated-and-aggravatedly resumed; pivoting away and pointingly directing him to take a seat on a sofa, that was in the further-set room. This, directly adjacent to and right beside her desk. Marching to the latter, she collected a thermometer and returned to literally 'jam it' into his mouth. Nate felt to get up and leave (for her attitude).. But, as sick as he felt, he knew it would only cause him greater regret in the end. So, he held tight.. drifting in-and-out of conscience-ness, here and there, through-out.

In the waiting, his mind quickly returned to the third-grade episode.. Remembering how he'd likewise had a recurring 'fainting spell' in the seventh.. But, this one.. due to the still-lingering fear and displacement caused by the subject matter (the inner ear!).. Yes, the 'association' and its lingering complexity! Ah, but, finally and at last, he had won-over and 'broke the hex' in his High School years (and the further studies of it).. Refusing to be moved by the phobia!.. And he was momentarily proud of himself now for his victory. This, only to be rudely awakened from it, by the violent tug of the glass-instrument out-of his mouth.. And for this, momentarily wondering if he'd lost any teeth, in the process.. and tongue checking them, in a quick-'n-dry swish. At last, in his blurred re-focussing, seeing the nurse's reading of it..

"One hundred and three .. Hmmm.. " She, truly regretting now that he'd been telling the truth. Despite, she tried on.. "Well, I'm going to call your Mother.. and see what she wants me to do!.. " resuming in threat-tone with.. "That and while I'm at it, see what I can do about you getting that hair of yours cut!.. " All of this, like as if, conceding.. but, in the same, ultimately and triumphantly going to 'win-over' and 'get something out of it' herself! Whatever!.. Nate was too ill now to care.

"Well, now.. what's your phone number?.." She seating herself at her desk. Nate looking over at her and giving it. Fading mentally, back-and-forth, in her dialing and the wait.

"Hello?.." She, proceeding to inform his Mom of the situation. Where-upon the latter told her, that she would be down to pick him up at the front door within the hour.

Still not satisfied with herself, she then pryingly injected.. "Can I ask you a question, Ma'am?.. Your son's hair?.. Do you think it's very healthy for him to be wearing it so long?.. I mean, the germs that… "

In this, Nate wearily raising his head and noting her sudden, interrupted stop. That, and the 'totally shocked'-look and bewilderment that covered her face, as well!.. This, as his Mom (appropriately enough!) proceeded to 'tell her off'! .. And, in the same (..to put it mildly!..).. to 'mind her own damn business'! Yes, and though Nate himself couldn't hear the same, it was all so 'blatantly obvious' by the nurse's returned apologies that followed (confirming just exactly 'what WAS being said' on the phone line)!

When she, at last, softly clicked down the receiver and somewhat recomposed herself…

"Your Mother wants you to meet her downstairs at the main entrance soon. Why don't you rest here a bit.. and I'll let you know when to begin down.. Ok?.." Then, turning away and inward for her 'still obvious' embarrassment.

Nate lowered himself into a curled-and-lying position now, thinkin'.. 'There is a God!.. See, I told y' !'.. like as if, facetiously trying to convince himself.

The 'lighter fluid threat' never ignited. Nate had returned to school without even another word said of it. Still and regardless, he had continued in his wait thereafter. But now, with only this 'one more day of classes' upon him, he was feeling somewhat easier. There was the glimmer of light at the end of the tunnel! Maybe it had been forgotten? He had no idea of why or how it had been overlooked, but he surely wasn't about to ask. Still, it preyed on his mind all day.. And, the hours passed very slowly.

Short of his buying two Eskimo bars (to celebrate the school year's end!), lunchtime in the cafeteria was pretty routine and typical.

And when, at last, the final bell rang.. and he was (in a flash) two blocks away with no 'tormentors' in sight, then (..and only then!) did he take a deep breath of relief. Yes, he'd made it! Graduation would be in about a week. But, short of that, it was over. Yes, finally over! Thank God! Sure, there'd be the fulltime hours at the factory to deal with now.. But still, summer was here.. And the sounds, smells and sights of it were everywhere about him. He felt so free and elated!

After flattening the handset job with the planer block, he tightened it with the quoin key and carried the lock-up over to the Hand-fed Platen press. The early morning sun was streamlining down through the southeast-set windows.. and (like a prism..) settling its rays directly upon him, as he tried to secure the chase into its bed. The mid-July heat of it, making him momentarily pause in his efforts, to fore-arm and smudge the sides of his dripping-profusely-now brow. This, grey-ishly 'face-painting' him for his soiled ink-and-graphite-stained hands. And after all, not really solving the problem, in the least! For no sooner was he back into the task, when streams of salty sweat over-ran the dams of his eyebrows and instantaneously blinded him in a stinging frustration. It was in times like these that he cursed Ol' Guttenberg! Still and despite the bitter blur, he at last secured it all into place.

Having previously inked the hand-feeder with black.. and evenly distributing it for the run, he now (in his recovering-sight and slightly-better focus) did a print on the bed's manila wrapping to set his gauge pins. Razor-ing and clipping them in, he cleaned off the original with a naphtha-rag and took a proof.. Checking it for proper centering with his line gauge. It was perfect! Dang, was he gettin' good! Still, it would have to be okayed by Roger. But, looking up and about for him now, he found the pressroom empty. Where was everybody? Suddenly hearing through the propped-opened window their voices outside in the bordering parking lot, it hit him.. It was break-time! The coffee truck was in. He hadn't even noticed the driver's honk! Rushing out without his normal hand-washing, he made for the canteen's side.

At last, he secured his 'regular'... A rectangular-shaped blueberry muffin and a coffee-milk. It was simply 'too hot out' for regular coffee now! In paying, he motioned Roger's attention away from the other pressmen (gathered in a semi-circle and talking).. and told him he was ready for him to check his proof.

"Ok, Nate.. be in, in a minute".. then, turning back and away, he resumed in his on-going conversation.

In this, the boy wandered off, finding himself a seat on the nearby curb to savor his breakfast. Looking about the little side-street, he breathed-in the Summer. The initial novelty of it had worn off, by now.. But still, it was quite 'impressive' in these few moments of fleeting freedom.

An old milk truck rattled and passed by them, heading up towards Main Street.. And it brought back the very sounds and recall of hearing them in his early childhood. Yes, like a sudden jolt back in time, that he was transported to, in but a flickering moment. And, then he remembered, in the recovering second's after .. how, each morning, his Mother would leave the empty bottles out for their 'pick-up' and the soon-'exchange and new delivery'. There weren't many of these trucks still on the road, these days. But here 'n there, he'd still catch sight of one. They, looking so much more worn and tattered now though. Rickety in their awkward movements! The glass bottles jingling away inside, in their metal crates!

At last, creaking himself afoot, he began back in along with everyone else. Their break being intentionally-timed to end with the start of the Bindery's. But, seeing that they always dragged it out a bit later, Nate turned now and saw (in this) the old women entering the rear loading dock area.. Clamoring and yapping their ways, down the slight of metal stairs. Per usual, they.. cursing, swearing and carryin'-on like a bunch of drunken sailors! And he remembered, in that moment, how he used to have to listen to 'the like', all day long. Not to forget, all of their catty 'gossiping'! Sure, they seemed friendly-enough, when they first met you.. Even, sort of, 'awed' by you!.. But, this.. all and only to get information that they could use against you later! Yeah.. 'familiarity' SURE DOES 'breed contempt'! .. a lot 'f truth in that! And, in the same, he recalled, as well, now (as he moved further away), how he'd always hear them whining and screaming about, how 'the man-in-their-life' didn't treat them 'like a lady'! And he, all the while, thinking to himself (even back then!), how.. 'if they'd only ACT like ONE, then maybe they WOULD HAVE'! But, never expressing it aloud though. No ways!.. For being 'the quiet one' (as they teasingly called him) and a bit on the shy side, they baited him enough as was! To have said something like that, would've only made the hatred and torture worse! Still, it was true! Either way.. hey, fact was.. they just truly sickened him! And moving even faster now, he began inside before they'd even 'near'- arrive.

Getting his approval from Roger, he spent the rest of the morn in pensive and silent work. The big metal wheel.. spinnin' and clockin'-it away. Daydreaming. Ah.. but, very cautiously!.. For, one false move and all of his dreams would 'literally' be crushed in an instant!

He loved the mood of quiet mornings like this though. Dreamy and peaceful. And he recalled in it, how when he was a boy (and he'd be home sick from grammar school, lying on the sofa) there was a certain calm and introspective joy he'd felt then, that he truly loved. He remembered, too, how he'd so enjoyed the Captain Kangaroo Show with its rural, farm-like settings.. And the 'always casual-and-slow talk and conversations' of the characters. Not the loud, screaming crowds of youngsters like on the Howdy Doody Show. That was unbearable! Very early on as a toddler, that show had actually frightened him, what with all of its boisterous nonsense. No, he enjoyed quiet and peaceful things. And now, alone in the shades-drawn-down pressroom (despite the further-set rumblings of the offsets), it was still pretty tranquil and serene, all 'n all.

Linger Softly.. Oh, Dear Morning

Linger Softly.. Oh, Dear Morning

With your dew across the Earth

Linger Softly.. do not grow up yet

You're tender now in birth

- 57 -

Linger through the meadow's trees

And green, in misty blur

Scent the forest scenery

And for hours, please endure

Share with me your fragrance

Through this A. M.'s tender bliss

Linger Softly.. Oh, Dear Morning

When, in time, I reminisce

After lunch, Nate returned to have Roger tell him that he'd be making a delivery of letter-heads to a Doctor's office cross-town. He, being overjoyed at the news.. As he so-loved these occasional 'outs'. Yes, a chance to escape 'on the clock' for a while! Boy, was this day really shaping up into a beauty! Hurriedly, he washed down the Hand-fed and hit the bathroom sink for clean-up. Spinning the spigot, he quickly rinsed off the sand soap and grabbed a few brown paper towels for drying.

Into Mr. Hampshire's desk, he went to collect the goods. After receiving the directions and bus-fare from his boss, he began through the office and out, passing Mrs. Brennan at her desk. She, mumbling (to his happy 'Hi') something about his sloppy hair and appearance. But, he.. too elated now to listen or even care. Through the door and down the cement stairs, he exhaled.. "Thank y' , Lord!", as he hurried off and away.

Main Street was rumbling now with traffic (Vehicle and Human alike) just everywhere! Nate made across and through it all for the terminal, but the bus wasn't there yet. Still, he didn't mind waiting now, unlike evenings when he'd be heading home. No, there was absolutely no rush!

Placing the two boxes aground, he peered back at Main, noticing two checkered cab drivers yelling at each other. Arguing over a space, he concluded. One was a Mediterranean descendant, judging by his appearance and hand-movements.. and the other, a white-haired, but big fella with a solid German look. Both were pretty upset, and Nate thought them to be acting quite silly. I mean, being that 'grown-up' and allowing themselves to be getting 'that worked up' over a parking place. Both of them must've had much 'great problems in their lives' that they were venting. Still, as young as he was, he noted the ridiculousness of it all. Yes, the childishness of mankind!

Then, to distract him, sped-passed a mint-lookin', Studebaker Silver Hawk (His favorite of cars, all-time!).. right in front of the arguers.. whizzing by gracefully.. And Nate (in this).. dartingly focussing-in on it, as it continued in its leftward direction. Soon enough though, it was blotted-out by the terminal's far-end brick-wall and the building-resolve. 'Dang, y' don't see many of them anymore, now do y'?.. And, that pristine too! Yeah, someone sure must'a kept-up on that ol' boy!.. And, or.. just never used it, all that much!.. Man-o-man, what an absolute gem!'

Pulling up close at hand, the bus awoke him from his meditation, and he stooped for his goods and boarded. After downing his fare in the change machine, he took a seat in the rear, near an already-opened window.. Placing the delivery on the outside seat to prevent another's sitting. But, there was really no need.. The bus was pretty-nearly empty. Still, he hoped it would deter any passengers that might be picked up along the way.

As they started off from the center and went several blocks away, he heard a siren coming head-on and fast.. And peering out the window, he followed the quick entry and passing of a police patrol car, speeding back in the direction they'd just come from. He wondered in this, if the two 'fussing' men had gotten into a serious tangle. But it was too late now to see or be concerned over it.. So, turning forward again, he started to mentally sort through what he had planned to discuss with Tim (the lead singer in his band), that night. They were to meet at another of the numerous coffeehouses in the college square, that always played Mose Allison records for background music. The owner must've been a fan.. and, in the process, had made the two boys into the same. Real bohemian-lookin' café! A lot'a mood! There was never any 'live' music there, but it was just a great place to go and talk.. and sometimes bring their girlfriends. But, tonight they would be having a meeting about the band. His relationship with Tim, of late, had been faltering. The tension had been mounting.. and Nate had, at last, devised a scheme to try and save the seeming-possible 'future'-break-up of the group. His solution being, to record a 45 rpm. Yes, there was going to be 'big business' plans made tonight!.. And Nate was anxious.. For.. how would they get the money, when they couldn't even afford the proper instruments and equipment that they needed, and were already going without? It didn't matter, they'd do it somehow! He just knew it. However long it took! Yes, this was 'big-time important'!

Pausing from his thoughts now, he studied ahead, down the many rows of seats, to the front of the bus and the driver's back. It was so sedate.. Only a few passengers (all deeply lost in their own thoughts), with rarely one being picked up or dropped off. This day seemed almost 'odd' for the eerie-quietness of it. It was almost like the heat had over-powered all-and-everything into a total submission. But then, there had been the 'craziness' of the two men, far behind them now. No, he just seemed to be, personally and luckily-enough, running into a lot of it today. And he only hoped it would last!

Finally reaching his stop, he un-boarded and began his foot journey into a small village-like center and its main-through-fare. Passing some second-hand stores, a five-&-dime and then a café-looking eatery, he continued along into what-was the start of a residential area with home offices. Picket fences and lawns.. and, at last, no sidewalk. A half block further, he saw the white hanging sign for the Doctor's Office.. and, in so, proceeded up the driveway and onto the graveled-walk that led to the front porch.

Knocking, then trying the handle, he found it to be open. And as he continued in, onto the hallways' red carpet, he noted the receptionist in the further-set doorway ahead, out of her seat now and coming to open it.

"Sorry.. I didn't know it was unlocked.."

She, graceful and friendly-like, motioning him in. And when he was close enough..

"Yes?.."

"I have a delivery.. 'f letterheads."

"Oh, yes.. Thank you!.." and it was done. All, but for his return to the shop.

The rental boats were strewn and chained along the dark and sparsely-lit Stiles' shoreline. Each, having their fair share of missing paint-chips. The crescent moon only slightly illuminated the bare bodies of the four boys running along the pond's beaching edge, goofing and laughing as they entered the water, splashing each other.. But, trying not to be too loud or disruptive. It was late. Still, there were people's homes lit-up in the viewable distance and beyond, that circled the pond.. and no one wanted to get caught.

Once in the chilly-feeling, thick-and-heavy water, the noise hushed and the night sounds returned. This, short of the close-hand gasps of exertion and the whisper-level conversation of the swimmers. Nate dog-paddled his way in closer to Willie and Zack..

"Y' don't think there's any snakes in here, d' y' ?.." Nate, through jittering teeth.

"I.. I dunno?.. Y' think?.." Willie, serious and stammering out.. and, in so, glancing worriedly down at the water.

Zack paddled in even closer, gasping..

"Prob'ly are.. but, I'd be more concerned 'bout snappers!.. 'specially now!"

Nate adding.. "Yeah, them snappin' turtles can literally chop y' finger off.. let alone your.." looking down quick in his dog paddle .. " Well, y' know.."

There was a pause.

Then…

"Man, you guys.. y' always messin' with me!" Willie catching their game and raising one of his arms to splash them away. Then pivoting himself, he swam a bit further out. But, stopping in short order (for the realization that no one had followed him), he dog-paddled about, staring off and away at the deep.. like as if, contemplating something.

Soon, Nate and Zack overtook him and made their way much-further-out and beyond. Buzz (who had immediately went out ridiculously-far and well-beyond any logical or safe distance) was now returning, and met the two halfway. Just as they reached each other, a shooting star flared across the sky. Paddling in now…

"Did y' see that?.." Buzz, gasped.

"Yeah, man.. Cool!.." Zack, exerting closer.

"with the sky this dark, it really stuck out.. huh!.." Nate added with heavy breathing.

"Hey, I wudn't talkin' 'bout that.. I mean, that shark fin out there!.." Buzz, further gasping and looking as serious as he could muster.

"C' mon, man.. this is fresh water!.." Somehow, both still getting a sudden chill for it. Darkness is funny like that! Not to mention, cold water!

"Hey, man.. there's all kinds 'f crazy stuff like that, that goes on in this world!.. Y' don't have t' believe me.. Why d' y' think I was hurryin' back..

Hey, I'm out'a here.. Stay, if y' want!" Buzz, plowing off.

A silence remained between Nate and Zack, as they watched him swim away. Neither wanted to admit their mounting, inner fear. Besides, it didn't make any sense.. Who was he trying to fool!

A large fish jumped and splashed further out, towards center pond.

"Damn, man, I'm out'a here too!.." Zack, digging in and Nate following in the same fashion, close behind. And this, until both and all were ashore.

Sitting on the land-capsized boats, they all stared back out at the pond and shivered themselves dry for a good spell. Eventually conversation broke out, at a bit louder volume for their slight distances. Nate began it…

"Hey, man.. someday I'm hittin' the road out'a here!.. Yes, sir.. prob'ly thumb my way down South!.. Y' know, hit the Turnpike west 'n head right on down!.. I mean it, man.. Me, I'm gonna see the world!.. Ever since I was a little kid, I always dreamed of bein' just like ole Hank Williams.. Y' know, like them pictures of 'Luke, the Drifter' on them records 'n all.. just wanderin' around, playin' his guit'r.. 'n singin' for people, all the time.. Yeah, man.. I'm gonna be a Hillbilly singer!"

Willie seemed totally taken back and disturbingly-confused by the thought of all this. He.. (unlike the others, who seemed to be 'totally oblivious' as to what had been said, either way) gawked over at him and responded…

"Hillbilly Singer?.. Man, Nate-o.. you're crazy!.. Them southerners.. they ain't never gonna accept some Yankee doin' that!.. Singin' Hillbilly stuff 'n all!.. Ain't never gonna happen!..

Yeah, you talk about 'clan-ism'.. Man, you'll just NEVER penetrate that!.. ,

"Well.. " Nate, trying to salvage his dream.. " What about Hank Snow then?.. Heck, he was from Canada.. 'n that's even further north than here!.. 'n he made pretty good for himself in Country music!.. Right?"

"Sure.. but, it's like y' said.. he was from 'Canada'!.. They didn't fight Canada, did they!. Hey, man.. I know.. 'n you're gonna find out, too!.."

"Well.. whatever.." Nate, still defending.. "I just think if you do sumethin' from your heart.. Y' know, sincere 'n all, then.. people will appreciate it!.. 'n see the truth.. 'n that's what really matters most in music anyways!.. 'Sides, there's knuckleheads everywhere in the world, man.. Y' know, mean 'n prejudice .. Yeah, just plain stupid people!.. F' that matter, we got tons 'f 'em here too!.. Still, all 'n all, most folks are reasonably level-headed.. 'least, I think!.. So…"

"Yeah, well.. I'll admit.. Y' right on one thing.. We sure do got a far-more-than-fair share of idiots here!.. " Willie conceding.. " Still, I just hope you're right on that, Nate-o.. Y' know, 'bout bein' able t' rise above all'a that nonsense.. Hey, I really do!.. 'least, f' your sake, anyways.. " A brief pause to let it 'air out' some. Then, he resumed..

"Either way.. 'travelin' 'round like that.. 'n leavin' here'.. I mean.. You serious, man?…."

"Yeah, Really!.. This place stinks!.. The Factory 'n all!.. Man, I gotta get out'a here, one way 'r another.. or I'm just.. gonna lose m' mind!…

Yeah, I'm gonna be a travelin' musician.. That's my life!.. " Like as if nothing negative had been said, regarding any of it.. " I sure ain't gonna be no printer!.. or nuthin' else, f' that matter!.. No ways!.."

There was brief silence.

Then, Willie wittingly conceded… "Hillbilly singer, huh?.. Well, in a way, that IS kinda like a Folksinger.. Ain't it!.." implying that regardless-and-despite, he was going to win out in the end , either way 'n after all.

Nate (seeing how he'd verbally 'painted himself into a corner' now) begrudgingly acknowledged…

"Yeah.. Well.. I guess.. I mean, yeah.. I guess y' could say that.." then, turning away.. until, surrendering.. "Hey, whatever…" and going silent to think on it some. I mean, as much as he didn't want to admit it, it did pretty-much make complete sense!

Looking up at the few sparkling stars flickering in the above jet-black sky, they each (in their own introspect) momentarily meditated on their futures.. Until Nate interrupted it with..

" ..'n you, Willie.." turning back to him and their conversation.. "What 'a you gonna be?.. Y' know, when you get out 'n on y' own 'n all?.. What's the plan, man?.."

There was a pause. Then..

"I ain't got one.. " he, uncomfortably, surrendered.

"What'a y' mean, y' ain't got one?.. Everybody's got some kind 'f a dream.. or sumethin'-'r-other, they're lookin' forward to!.. It's just, well… y' know.. the thing y' do nowadays" meaning 'at this stage in one's life'.. "So, c' mon, man.. what's the deal?"

Willie withdrew for another few minutes.. All the while, looking like-as-if he was becoming increasingly, and more-deeply, perplexed at having to supply an answer.. And, the further it dragged on, the more frustrated and physically-distressed he began to appear.

Nate, at last, noting this (after the lengthening silence), dropped it all with...

"Hey, man.. It's really gettin' chilly!.." directing this at everyone else there. Hopping up in so, he began locating his clothes. Feeling a bit guilty for having pressed Willie (Despite the fact that the latter had seemed to be doing so, to he himself, only moments prior!), he resumed the change-of-subject with.. "Where's my clothes?.. Man-o-man, I'm freezin'!..".

Zack, in this, jumping up and adding his 'always-comical' two-cents, with… "Yeah, Nate-o, me, too!.." and then with a fake-'n-quivering, womanly high tone..

".. I'm shrinkin'!.. I'm shrinkin'!..", vocally mimicking the Wicked Witch in 'The Wizard of Oz'.. But, this.. suggesting something totally different. All.. getting a chuckle out of that!

In the car, there was a sense of warmth for the enclosure, and Nate leaned forward from the back to rest his arms upon the front seat's felt padding. Buzz had switched on the radio and was reaching for the station dial, when he shot…

"No, don't!.. Don't change it!.. I like that song!.."

"Yeah, me, too!.. " Willie raising his hand, like to stop him from the front seat's passenger side.

The song went.. 'In the event of something happening to me.. There is something I would like you all to see..'

"Who is that?.." shot Nate.. "It ain't the Beatles, right?.."

"No, you knucklehead.. It's the Bee Gee's.. They're new!.. Now, shhhh, man!.. I wanna hear it!.." Willie responded in a quelling motion.

They all listened intently, as Buzz slowly pulled out. Willie hunched in, raising the volume level for the grumbling gravel below. The station was a bit distant and it only made it sound more static-filled. Still, all and all, it was audible enough.. and everyone sat hushed and listening throughout. When it was over...

"Man, that's my favorite song!.. " Willie declared, as he spun back around.

"Yeah, it's cool!.. But, what's that instrument in there?.. Y' know, that low sounding string thing?.." Nate asked.

"It's a cello, stupid!.. You're the musician.. Y' didn't know that?.."

"Well, no.. I didn't.. But, hey, what's the big deal.. I ain't no CLASSICAL musician, y' know!.."

Willie goofingly reached over like to start a pushing-and-shoving match.. and Nate (happy and relieved that he had, for the earlier 'silence'!) responded accordingly in fun. Everything was okay now!

"Hey, guys.. cool it!.. I'm trying t' DRIVE, f' cryin' out loud!.." Buzz reaching over to physically subdue Willie, for he being the closest.. "These damn country roads are BAD ENOUGH .. without you two makin' it worse!"

Nate thought sure that everyone would be sleeping, when he arrived home. But walking in through the darkened parlor, he noted the kitchen light to still be on. Entering, he found his Mom still up and sitting head-in-hand at the kitchen table.

Seating himself opposite of her, he noted the red-and-white, checkered table-cloth to be crunched-up unevenly beyond her forcing-it-so elbows. He could tell she'd been crying and it immediately darkened his spirits.

"Y' ok, Ma?.." He whispered.. knowing, all the while, that it must be something truly bad.. For he knew she rarely ever cried.. Or, even ever showed this kind of 'despairing-like' emotion. No, he'd always seen her as being the "Katherine Hepburn"-type (Even, looking like her, with her dark wavey-hair and very definite features!) .. and, in the same, having a strong 'country girl'-like 'will and presence' about her. Yes, she was the 'rock' of the family. The one he could count on. The one he related to deeper.. and had always pictured 'himself' to be the greater-'like'. So, this all was very disturbing.. and too 'out-of-the-norm' for him, seeing her like this .. and he began feeling over-anxious for it.. And, increasingly unsteady, as he awaited her reply.

"Your Father's sick again.. Your Grandfather took him over the V.A., earlier. I don't know how we're gonna make it.. Things 're bad enough as they are!.. I don't know how much more of this I can take.."

A cold silence overcame him with a surging tinge of fear. This, for the sudden desperation of the at-hand situation.. And then, even greater, for the furthering thoughts and disturbing recalls of the violence that he had witnessed, in the past.. Yes, that often seemed to accompanied these episodes! A distressing guilt hit him too now; feeling that he should've been there.. to have tried to protect her. This, compounding everything else that was crashing down on him! He took a deep breath to try and recover.. But his stomach only further sickened.

Then, in a heart-wrenching flashback, he inwardly re-pictured the traumatic events that had led up to and during the last of these episodes, roughly a year prior. Only, on that occasion.. when he had, in fact, been there to experience and witness it himself.. And, having stayed home throughout the entire day, for that very and sole purpose.. Yes, of 'being there' to try to protect her, should the worst occur.

That memory came rushing back now, and he tremblingly recalled his Father angrily pacing about the house.. ranting and raving to himself.. and tote-ing a Cross through-out it all. A fair-sized, wooden one.. with a heavy, mahogany-sheen-ed look. . He could see it now, so vividly.

With his Mother in the kitchen, at one point.. and he and his Father in the parlor.. all of a sudden, Nate saw him take-off in a near-run .. Then, before he could even fully- unseat himself, he heard the wallop of the Cross hitting his Mother's head. And, her immediate shriek of pain!.. The boy.. jumping up during all of this.. and dashing in to find his Mother trying to seat herself at the kitchen table, with blood profusely coming from the top of her scalp. Grabbing a dish towel, in an instant, he rushed to her, momentarily comforting her, and telling her to hold it there and apply pressure until he returned. Then, in the angry-maze of it all, he took off in heated-pursuit of his Father, who had continued on upstairs, and into their back bedroom.. The boy, little expecting that when he taggingly entered (as well), he would have the Cross lifted-and-fixingly-aimed at him.

Just inside the doorway, he froze solid.

"You want it too?.."

Nate couldn't even verbalize a response. He was so paralyzed! Their eyes were locked.. and it seemed to go on forever! Nate was in absolute terror.. But, trying desperately now not to show it!

At last, his Father somehow came to his senses, in all of this.. and realized what he was doing.. and, in the same, broke down into tears. The boy (having no relief or words to offer), simply turned and darted out.. returning to assist his Mother.

Snapping out of all of this now, Nate came back to the moment at-hand.. And, further shaking his wits, he refocussed in on her, and blurted out…

"He didn't hurt y', Ma… Did he?.." starting to show a slight rise of anger now. "If he did, I swear I'm.." The typical 'boy's way' of dealing with 'the overwhelming'… When, truth be told, he already knew that he was hardly 'any match' for his Father!

"No, Nate… no, he didn't.. " She cutting in.. and to further address and thwart his temper… " Besides, y' know he doesn't know what he's doin', when he gets like that.. He's a totally different person!.. He never even remembers any of it… " Then, recoiling inwardly and shaking her head.. "I'm just…so.. so tired of all'a this.. How, in God's name, am I going to… " rocking back and forth a bit in her chair for emotional relief.

"I'll help, Ma.. Don't worry.." knowing fully well, he didn't make a hardly-decent salary to begin with.. "I'm makin' more now, with school done 'n all."

"Nate, don't be concernin' y' self with it.. You just go up t' bed now.. ok?.."

Despite, he remained. Until…

"Please?… " looking up sadly, but firmly.

Knowing she needed to be alone (and not wanting to upset her any more than she already was), he conceded… "Ok, Ma…" and slipped off. But the heavy depression and worry stayed with him, long after he pulled the covers up over himself.

Laying upright and staring at the dim street-light glow (that shone through the slightly-cracked blinds of his window and into his tiny room), he thought on it all for a seemingly-long time.. Hearing, on occasions throughout, the disruptive sleeping sounds of his seven brothers and sisters just beyond him and the thinly wall; all bunk-bedded and huddled-together in the next room.

Being the oldest, he felt that he should be able to do something greater to spare them from the fore-coming hard times. Oh, what an awful feeling this was! He felt so overwhelmed by it all, and literally trembled in a physical pain beneath the further-entrapping-him sheets. All of the fun of the earlier evening at Stiles was now dispelled and gone.. And, had been crushed, in an instant! And, replaced with this!..

What would he do? What could he do? He had absolutely no idea!

The lazy days.. of Summer Love

With the smell of flowers.. 'n flickerin' stars above

The night of balm.. when, arm in arm

We'd stroll in the sparkling moon-glow charm

Lana lived right near 'the hill'.. Which was a name that folks had given to that section of town, for its 'earthly elevation'; as well as for its 'loftier-living inhabitants'. Numerous mansions domed its 'upper-crested' mounds. Nate would always do his 'shoveling' up there, come winter for its better paying rates. But Lana's family was hardly rich and only resided on the bottom edge of it. Still, getting to her house meant passing through it often enough.. and in so, Nate would always point out a particular chicory-stained mansion with a matching barn, that he planned to buy, one day.. On the upper corner of Lancaster Street and Washington Ave. Yes, one day, when he grew up and 'made it big' in the music business. And this, not so much 'cause he really wanted it. But rather, more in that he could then say.. "I used to shovel this walk, when I was a poor kid!". Yes, that kind of 'accomplishment' thing!

Ascending in its direction now, with her by his side, 'winter' seemed so inconceivable and distant. Almost unreal and unimaginable! For it was such a pleasant and quiet summer night. Even the concerns of his family situation seemed lost in the balmy peacefulness of the moment.

Lana had been Nate's steady girlfriend since his first year of High School.. and, by now, they'd come to know each other quite well. Within that time, he'd become more-and-more of a Folk Music Fan, due to his trips to the coffeehouses in the square.. And, in so, was totally lost in Bob Dylan and his writings and music now. Having purchased all of the singer's LP's, he had since pretty-nearly dissected and memorized the entire catalog. And, presently one of the melodies rang in his head, as they continued up towards 'his' mansion and along the uneven brick sidewalk that edged it. It was the song, "To Ramona".. which Nate especially liked.. as that was his Mother's middle name.. and he always had fondly related to it, for that.. Not to forget, it's plaintive and beautiful melody!

Having topped Agassiz Street (only moment's prior) in their continuing climb to Lana's house, she (at this point, having 'talked herself out' .. and in the echoes of it all, having finally noticed Nate's disconnect and introspect..) focussed-in-on and contemplated his displacement. Preferring to see it as the 'beauty of the evening' distracting him (and Lord forbid, not her gibberish-ness to fault!), she took a deep breath of it in and exhaled...

"Nate, what are you so deep in thought about?.."

"Ah, nuthin'.. just thinkin'.. y' know, 'bout a song.."

"Oh, I was hopin' it wasn't anything I said.."

"No.. no... just a song.. that's all.." then, taking silent, hoping that that would do. As, truth was, he had absolutely no-earthly-concept of what she'd been saying for, at least, a good several blocks now.

At last, making the further ascent.. and then, its continuing-descent down and across Upland Road (..and beyond 'the hill'), they finally seated themselves on Lana's front porch. There-upon, she broke the since-silence with...

"Nate.. How's Willie?.. Have you seen him lately?.."

"Yeah.. he's okay.. I seen him a few nights back.. 'went swimmin' out at Stiles.. Me, Zack, Buzz 'n him.. Why?.."

"I dunno.. Last time I saw him, he just seemed so depressed and.. well.. lost, for a lack of better words.."

"Yeah, sometimes he gets like that.. but, he seemed pretty up then.. 'course, we always have us a time out there!.. " Nate pausing a second.. "Y' know, he's got his eyes on Katie.. Maybe she's still refusin' to go out with him!.."

"You silly.. you know, right well, he loves her!.. It's so obvious!.. He just needs a little push!.. Either way.. You're always giving him a hard time about that!.. Why?.."

"She's my Sis!.. What 'a y' expect?.."

"Well, Katie told me he writes some real pretty poetry.. You ever read any?.."

"Don't need t'.. He's forever recitin' it t' me 'n everyone else!.. and, or.. carryin' on about Edgar Alan Poe!.. Yeah, him or some other demented, dead poet!.." still being facetious and difficult.

"Well, tell me.. I'd really like to hear one!" Lana, earnestly prying.

"I dunno!.. I can't RECITE one!.. What'a y' think, I MEMORIZE 'em!.."

"Well, what are they like?.. I mean.."

He becoming a bit frustrated now…

"I dunno, Lana!.. Dang!.. " She putting on a sulk. "Ok.. ok!.. he's got one.. called 'Man-child'.. it's about some motherless boy.. an Indian brave.. who walks into a lake and drowns himself. Y' know, like he's so unhappy 'bout losing her 'n all, that he commits suicide over it."

"Gosh, that's eerie!.. You don't think he's.."

"Nah!.. not Willie!.. He's just expressin' it out 'f himself!.. I know, I'm a writer!.. Just.. y' know.. unloadin' all the built-up pain 'n hurt of it!.."

"I dunno, Nate.. I wouldn't be so.."

Cutting her off.. "Nah.. no ways!.. " shaking his head.. "You girls.. You're always over-reactin' t' stuff like that!.."

Manchild

I watched the Manchild descending..

A motherless, Indian Brave…

Hopeless of all mending..

T'wards the lake.. and to his grave

Trance-like to the ripplin' edge..

Defeated, through the glade…

Out across the shoreline.. as

His hand released his blade

Then, into deep surrender..

I watched him further go…

'til the water's surface settled still.. upon

his womb, beneath, below

Having passed Zack's bottle of Coke to him.. and now popping off the lid of his own Moxie, Nate threw the opener and the two caps into his tackle box. Thereafter, taking a quick, savoring swig. Then, putting it down, he reeled in and checked his line.

It was early Saturday morn and the mystic waters were dawned with a haze. Nuthin' was bitin'! This had been a ritual for Zack and he, every summer. But, of late, Willie had been tagging along too.. And per usual, he'd taken moody and introspective, wandering off on one of his 'solitude walks' (as Zack called them). His fishing equipment lay dormant on the nearby hillside shoreline now.

"Hey, Zack.. how'd it go, this year.. Y' know, with the Printin' 'n all?.. What were y' studyin'?" Nate curiously turning in his direction and trying to make conversation.. for they both had been majoring in it.. Only, his friend (being a few years younger) had been a Sophomore, prior. And, he.. living in a town away, had been taking it at a different High School, as well.

"We were just startin' t' do some actual work on the Platen.. " he responded, half-heartedly.. taking another swipe from his Coke.

"Yeah, we got one at work.. 'n I use it a lot" Nate, slightly arching his shoulders in his head-swing-and-return.. "They're kind 'f neat!.." .. but, noting in this, a total dis-interest in discussing anything 'school related' now. And, so a silence settled in.

Then.. "Hey.. What'a y' figures eatin' Willie?.." Zack offered sideways, thereafter returning to his scanning view.. though, still looking concerned and innerly-perplexed over it.

"I dunno?.. His Mom, I guess.." Nate, half-sighing with understanding, then turning forward and away.

"Really?.. Again!.. I mean, y' always say that, Nate-o.. And, y' know, every one loves their Mom 'n all.. but, I mean… " pausing to try to collect his words and not sound insensitive..   "Well, don't y' just think that…"

Nate knew what he was trying to say..   "We still got ours, Zack.. " Then, turning towards him and taking a deep breath, he sort of lowered his glance... "I mean, we really don't know what it's like.." Then, focussing back up and out, away at the waves.. " Y' know, just since my Dad's been sick 'n gone 'n all.. Well, it sure makes things hard!.. I mean.. I think I can understand a little bit"

"Yeah, I guess y' right, Nate-o.. 'n really, I hope I never DO know what Willie's going through, t' tell th' truth! " He, going silent and into his own thoughts now. Then, at last, to change the subject and break the hush… "Boy, they dang sure ain't hungry t'day!..."

"I dunno, Zack.. Maybe Willie's feedin' 'em from the other side.."

They both getting a chuckle out of that.. and Zack adding…

"He prob'ly is!.. That little sneak!.."

They both giving each other a smile; and like clockwork, reaching for their sodas.

After a pause, Zack turns… "I'm gonna kill him, when he gets back!" This, catching Nate totally off-guard and causing him to choke and burst-out his half-way-down soda.   Zack, in seeing it, breaking into an uncontrollable laughter, as well.. And for a good five minutes, the two of them rolled about their places in a side-splitting agony.

The graphite run-off from the cold-type was sweaty and mud-like in his hands. It was a sweltering late August day outside, and Nate glanced out at it through the dingy, clouded-like windows.. Then back down at the California Job case he was imprisoned over.

There was a lot of commotion and yelling going on in the back of the larger room. Two of the offset pressmen were fussing over something, cursing at each other.. and Nate only hoped they wouldn't start swinging. Glancing back over his shoulders, he verified that they weren't. At least, not yet!

Back out the window he escaped, yearning to be swimming. It was just a perfect day for it!

Bill (having tired of being forced to listen to the backroom argument) got up out of his Linotype seat, walked around to the coat rack near the time clock.. At last, returning with his little Toshiba transistor radio. Having collected it from his jacket, he now frustratingly snapped it down on the lock-up table beside him, and turned it up loud- enough to over-ride the fuss. Ironically it blasted out "I can't get no Satisfaction" by the Rolling Stones, and Nate thought it very fitting. Then, in the same, Bill re-sat himself down to enjoy the 'outlawed' (on the job!) music. It was likewise (without him saying a word) his 'little way' of letting 'the office' know that something was wrong.. and they best show themselves, before all Hell broke loose!

Nate knew (..As much as he was enjoying it now!) that, it all wouldn't last long though.. What, with Mr. Hampshire (and worse, Mrs. Brennan!) on aboard! Yes, soon the ax would fall! Meanwhile, he'd hang on every note and try to savor the sounds and moment. Not only that, but it was Bill's problem.. and nothing that he himself was guilty of!.. So, why be concerned?

Still and regardless (and as surely as should've been expected!), when Ole Brennan DID sweep in on her broom, first thing out of her mouth was...

"NATHANIEL!.." executed in such a sharp and ear-piercing fashion, it made the addressee jump and cringingly coil in an instant! The Linotype Machine blowing up, would have been less of a scare! Nate gasped in the aftermath, as Brennan stood (hands on her hips) waiting.

Bill cut in, defiantly (for he had absolutely 'no fear of the evil one'!)...

"It's my radio!.. I put it on!.. I'm sick t' death of havin' to listen to them argue back there!.. You have a problem with it, you go tell Mr. Hampshire! Otherwise, why don't you just go back there y'self, 'n tell them to shut up!.. OK?"

Brennan (put in her place now and dealing with another adult) held her tongue. Even in her continuing head-bowed, eye-stare of Nate, she just simply festered and fumed, trying to re-collect herself. At last, she pivoted in a sharp-like spin and shot inside the office.

Nate wondered if she'd gone to get Mr. Hampshire.

Bill.. in looking over at him…

"What a damned ole witch she is!.. huh?.."

The boy nodding a yes.

"She sure hates you, kid!.. That's as obvious as the witch pimple on her crooked nose.. Ain't it?.."

Nate (still wordless) smirked another yes, and quickly eyed a glance back at the office door.

"Yeah, I know.. he'll be out soon.. But, I don't give a flyin' crap!.." turning back to his keyboard and re-starting. The boy, likewise, returning to his work.. listening to the music, while it lasted.

But no one appeared. Brennan had surely squealed. But, Nate figured Mr. Hampshire must not have wanted to deal with it, and simply let it go. It was truly a mystery, but one that he was happy went unsolved. For the rest of the day became more bearable and pleasant with the music. He wondered why bosses didn't allow it.. For it seemed that it put the workers more at ease; and in so, they seemed to get more done. Better productivity! So, why was it always banned? What was the harm in it?

Still, he knew all too well, that once the heat of the moment cooled… Or, better yet, by tomorrow morning, all would go back to 'normal', as they say.

And you know what?.. he was right!

"Y' know, when I was like **8** or **9**.. I dunno, maybe **10**?.. I used t' eat in here everyday!" Nate told Lana, as they sat in Tommy's Lunch.. "Yeah, I used t' ride around.. Y' know, on m' bike.. 'n deliver The Chronicle in the Square here.. My route came right up t' this side street.." he quickly motioned to his left, up towards the back door that they'd entered from.. Then, resuming.. " ..'n yeah, I just always LOVED their hamburgers!.. Ain't they the tops?.." facially pointing down at hers, as they sat together on the counter's stools. Then, glancing back up at her.. "Well, what 'a y' think?.."

"Yes, they're really good.. " She agreeing, but obviously having difficulty 'sharing the nostalgia'. But, then.. noting the disappointment in his face.. "Yes, they're delicious, Nate!… Thank you!" This, making him seem, at least, somewhat contented. Then (to change the subject).. "Do y' think it's gonna rain?.."

"I dunno, Lana.. Sure looks like it " he, trying to focus further and rightwardly, out the front windows now, to take a reading. But, from their position, it was just too hard to see.. "..'least, it sure looked like it, before we come in!.."

A thought-filled pause.

"Y' wanna stay here.. or, in the Square somewhere's, 'n wait it out?" implying he didn't have the bus-fare to dodge it, if it did come down.

She, reading his thoughts… "No, that's alright… we can just walk back, if y' want.. I don't really mind getting wet.."

"Ok " .. as he swallowed his last bite.. "Well, whenever you're ready.."

Holding hands, they, at last, crossed Langdon Street.. coming upon the old apartment building where his Grandparent's had lived, years past. It had been a first floor flat, cornering and facing the main street.. and as they passed it now, Nate slowed to a stop in its bordering driveway. Glancing back up and into the sparely-lit parlor (for its shades were opened), he thoughtfully stared in. Remembering. Being a quickly-darkening-day all about them, it's inner light was on.. But (being a low wattage bulb), it afforded, but, a very dim and scant view.

"I wish y' could 'a met my Grandma, Lana... " he speaking, but meditatively focussed beyond.. "She was a real sweet lady.."

Just then, thunder sounded in the above sky.. but, nothing fell, so he resumed..

"She died right in there.." meaning the living room. His voice remaining soft..

".. sitting in a chair.. on a Sunday mornin'.. I'll never forget it... We were all just comin' back from church, 'n before I could get in the door, they..." he stopped, for the overwhelming sadness it was causing him.. and to catch himself from crying in front of her.

Lana squeezed his hand and just listened for his resume. The sky was erupting more now, but the rain was yet to come. It would be soon, though.

"Y' know.. my Granddad.. he has a sister that's a Nun.. up in Halifax. Well, my Grandma had a dream, several nights before she died.. and she wrote it all down in a letter to her, and then mailed it. She said in it, that she'd dreamed she'd woke up and went into the parlor.. and Jesus was standing there in front of a Christmas tree.. and motioning her to come closer 'n all.. and then, she just woke up. But, y' know, before my Granddad's sister got that letter, my Grandma 'd died! .. Weird, huh?.. And, y' know.. that was in October!.. Ain't that strange?.." Nate looking at Lana.. "It must 'a been like one 'f them premonitions, I guess... Huh?"

"Yes, Nate.. I've heard about people having those kind of things.. I guess God wants the people that He especially loves to not be so shocked, when they die.. or whatever?"

"Gee, Lana.. that's a good way t' look at it!.. I never thought of it like that, before!.." he seeming relieved and happier now, for that reasoning. "Well, we best get on, huh?..", as the sky began pounding worse.

Not, but a block away, it came down.. in buckets.. drenching them within minutes! This, making for a total mood swing.. as they began frantically searching for a covering. But, nothing was available or near-at-hand. So, laughing and carryin'-on for the chilling-ness and craziness of it all, they just gave-up looking.. and instead, tried to enjoy it. And, once they'd made up their minds to do that.. and just relax and 'go with it', everything seemed to be fine! And, ultimately.. fun! And Lana was so 'obviously grateful' now to see Nate's change-in-temperament, she actually became giddy. And, he.. too!.. Because of her! It was hilarious!.. At least, they sure thought so!

And even later, when numerous 'escapes' did appear along the way, they were just too wrapped-up in 'enjoying it' to go in them.. No, they kept on walking and clowning around.. just like in that old movie, "Singing in the Rain"!.. Heading towards her house.

YET ANOTHER FALLS

When Summer Falls, Winter Springs

When Summer Falls..

Winter Springs

Bringin' with it..

Snow 'n things

like Christmas Trees

'n ching-a-lings

Santa bells

red ribbon strings

Then, Winter Falls..

to Summer's Spring

warmth returns

so comforting

the beaches boom

the seagulls sing

days are long

vacationing

'til Halloween.. 'n..

the Goblins sing.. again..

When Summer Falls...

Winter Springs

Autumn brought with it the return of the college students. And this, for one, meant the reformation of the Wild Cat Jug-band! Near 'the avenue' (where all of Nate's friends hung out) was a large Victorian house, that the college owned and rented to a few of its students. And in this particular abode (as there were others scattered about the town), several members of this band roomed.. and had, now, returned for their school year.

Nate and his fellow band-mates looked up to these musicians and had learned so much from them, throughout the past few years. They had all the really cool records, too.. Obscure ones and the like, that he and his friends would sit and listen to for hours upon end. Muddy Waters' "Folksinger" LP was a top player, as well as other black Blues artists. And then, there were all of those Jug-band records!.. and the Hillbilly stuff!.. They just had an endless collection between them; and were always more-than-willing to welcome in the 'townies' to share of their wealth. Nate and the boys especially loved sitting around their rehearsals, as well.. Listening to them do 'the classics'!.. "Stealin' ", "Walk Right In".. you name it, they knew and did 'em all! And, top-rate, too! And it truly awed the boys for their vast knowledge and precise musicianship.

Mike was the washtub string bassist and Nate's particular hero. And this, for the way he looked and carried himself. The boy just thought him 'the coolest of all'.. But, it was more of a chemistry thing than the instrument he played, that attracted him. Yes, Mike.. sort of looking like he could've been an older brother to him! .. And, the latter (being the oldest in his family) had never really had one to look up to. So, it was almost to be expected.

Now, Zack (on the other hand) was totally mesmerized by Jim, who played harmonica (the boy's second instrument)… and (on many occasions) he would teach him parts and give him other harp tips and so on. So, Nate and Zack were their most frequent visitors. Willie, too.. But, he.. more for the company of his pals. Stephen, likewise, would show up often enough, as well. And on this particular night, all four were there, sitting on the couch in the main room, listening to them rehearse, center-floor. Some of the Wildcats' girlfriends.. college girls.. were lounging about on the surrounding chairs, as well.. and the band was in rare form. Truly cookin'! Stephen excitedly turned to Nate on his immediate right…

"Hey, Nat.. y' know what I'd really like t' do?.. Remember how we filmed the band in the basement, last year?.. with my Dad's camera?… Well, I wanna do that with these guys!… What'a y' think?.."

"Yeah, why not!.. 's long as they don't mind.. Yeah, that's a great idea!"

It was one of those kind of high-spirited moments when people say things, and you never really know whether or not it would ever happen. But, knowing Stephen (and his love for photography, film and so on), he assumed it probably would! Willie (sitting directly opposite side of Nate, having moved forward and in now) offered…

"Yeah, man.. Y' should!.. 'n save it for prosperity.. just like that other one y' did with Tim, Nate-o, you 'n Zack 'n all! That was really cool!.. Where is that film anyways?.. You got it, Nate?" turning further inward.

"No, my Dad's got it.. filed away.." Stephen assured.

"Y' gotta make sure 'n save it.. and do one 'f these guys too!.." Willie adding.

As the two continued and carried on with their conversation over his lap, Nate re-focused beyond to the players and their music.. and gradually (while still listening), around and about at the dim-lit smoke-filled room and its seeming-so-cool décor. The Victorian-looking fireplace with the artsy paintings on its shelve. Then, up to the high ceilings with its several flags and college streamers hanging down. And at last, back down to the desks and book shelves surrounding, with the numerous and stacked text books and study tools lying about and on them. And all their piles of records too! This was a different and new world he was seeing. And a totally alien lifestyle, that he so admired. Downright Bohemia! It all looking-like and reminding him somewhat of the "Bringing It All Back Home" front-cover on Dylan's album!.. But, only.. this was in 'real life'!.. Not just some photograph!

His Parents and Grand-alike called these people "Beatniks" and disliked them somewhat. And, not so much just for their 'general weird-ness'.. But, more for the fact that the college itself was, flat-out, eating up all of the city's real estate.. And, as you'd say.. 'taking over everything' in a big-time way! But, Nate found great appeal in them and their students now. As a younger boy (for this general-town-folks' disdain of them and anything even-near-related to 'the college'!), he and his pals would throw rocks at the Institution's private police.. And, sometimes, similarly 'disrupt' and 'prank' their student's 'backyard parties' and the like.. Each time, frantically running off, hoping they'd escape from their 'well-deserved' wrath, in the end! But, yes, now.. things had changed.. Totally!.. And, he saw it all in 'his own' way. For.. having worked for the college (as a kitchen boy and so forth, a few summer's prior), he'd come to find them to be quite friendly and warm people. And, very different than what he had been led to believe! "Don't criticize what you can't understand".. Bob Dylan had said something like that.. and Nate knew it to be 'a greater truth of life' now!.. And, it rang in his ears, in this very moment, despite all of the otherwise-about-him music and noise. But then, he also knew, as well... Had his parents had been sitting there right beside him now, and listening.. they would've surely agreed. It was simply an 'unfamiliarity'-type thing. Something not experienced. Too removed. And, in the same breath.. that, in itself.. being the 'perfect environment' for the breeding of 'clan-ism' and 'prejudice'! Or, better.. Where it takes root! Yes, where 'gossip and hearsay' become 'the rule' and 'simple fact'! But, then.. in his parents' defense, he knew all-too-well, they were not 'prejudice people'.. Hardly! Simply, mis-informed by their peers!

Either way, Nate loved it so! And in the coffeehouses, he had experienced that same 'mystical excitement'.. Wonderful new and different music was taking shape now (Among other things!).. and these dark and intimate rooms made his young mind and dreamy thoughts whirl in an 'almost ecstasy' over it! Yes, these were "The Times!.." And yeah, ol' Bob was dead-right.. they sure were "a' changin' "!

Getting a bit anxious now from all that he was thinking (not to mention the sudden entry of a negative thought that had been plaguing him of-late), Nate began up and off the couch.. "..'scuse me, guys.." and wedged his way through the talking-over-him Stephen and Willie.

Afoot, he began through the people that were strewn about, continuing off and into the kitchen. Two students were standing and talking to each other, beside the table.. and Nate entering, pressed pass them on his way to the connecting 'john'.

Re-appearing from it, he found Willie waiting outside, concerned-like…

"We weren't interruptin' y' listenin', were we, Nate?.."

"Nah, I just had t' go.." nodding back over his shoulder.

"Oh, seemed like you was pretty deep in some serious thought 'r sumethin'.. Was hopin' you weren't upset with us?.."

"Nah, not at all, man.. Really!.. " But (Nate seeing a golden opportunity to make an 'opinion inquiry' here), he further offered.. "Y' know, I've been thinkin', though.. about the band some… Maybe you can tell me what y' think on it?.."

"What 'a y' mean?.." Willie hooked.

Nate, in near whisper now… "Well, I been thinkin' like how we've all grown apart .. Y' know, Tim 'n me, especially!…'n well, short of Zack, I don't really see 'em others all that much anymore!.. Just at rehearsals. I'm just thinkin' like I'd like to go into sumethin' else.. Y' know, like some other band 'r sumethin'.."

"Well, I always told y' , you should just go on y' own, Nate-o .. Y' know, folksingin'!.. 'cause, f' one thing, the lyrics are deeper.. 'n more poetic 'n all!.. Y' know, just like the stuff you write.. 'n…

But, hey.. if you're still not sure 'f that, maybe y' could form a new band, where you could do a lot more 'f the singin' 'n all!.. "

"I hear y', Willie.. But it's more involved than just that. I mean, we finally got the record done 'n all.. 'n heck, y' know, we even got signed to make some more records with the company.. at THEIR expense!… and here we are, ready to fall apart!.. I mean, that was m' whole purpose in pushing the recording thing, in the first place.. I thought it would bring us all back together again… But, it seems t' have only made things worse!"

"Yeah, well.. still Nate-o.. sumetimes y' gotta do what y' gotta do in life.. n' matter what comes of it!.. Y' know, y' gotta think of y'self.. 'n.."

"Yeah, I know, Willie.. but we've been together f' so long now.. it's hard to imagine things any other way!.. Geez, man.. we literally learned t'gether!.."

"Sure, but if you ain't happy with it n' more, why bother?.. It's sort 'a… well, y' know.. defeatin'.. Right?"

Just then, Stephen entered the kitchen. Nate 'shhh-ing' Willie quick-like.

Stephen (not noticing it, but sensing a private conversation going on between them) only moved in close enough to offer…

"Hey, Nat.. I gotta head on out… We rehearsin' Saturday?…"

"Yeah, can y' make it?.."

"Sure.. see y' there! .." turning to leave. Then, stopping and re-swinging back.. "Oh, before I forget.. Is it ok if I get Johnny.. Y' know, that organ player we all saw play, last week.. t' come out 'n sit-in with us then? "

"Yeah, I guess.. I mean, if y' want.." Nate, trying to show enthusiasm, though not at all keen on the idea. But, Stephen had talked Tim into the possible-and-ultimate inclusion of Johnny.. and Nate (knowing this) had simply conceded to keep the peace. Truth be known, he viewed him as a spoiled, little rich kid.. from 'the other side of the tracks', as they say .. And, not to mention.. on a musical level, a totally un-necessary addition to an already-full-enough band. But, with the 'already-tension' in the group mounting of late, he just figured he'd agree on 'an audition' (Knowing already which way he'd vote!).

"Ok, thanks, Nat.. I'll call him.."

"Yeah, alright.. y' do that.." Nate forcing a smile.

"Well, see y' !.. You, too, Willie.. catch y's later.."

When gone…

"There's my other problem, Willie.. That Johnny guy!.. I mean, that's the last thing we need.. Another player!.. "

"Well, man.. Y' know how Stephen loves that Animals' sound!.." Willie offering.

"Yeah, I know… Hey, they're a good group!.. But, it's not the kind of sound I want t' have for us!.. " Nate trying to be understanding. Regardless.. "I mean, if they keep pushin' this thing, it's gonna be the final straw f' me!… I mean, I hate to say it, but it's really true!.."

Willie nodding.   Then.. "Well, y' wanna head back in?.. "

"Yeah, I guess…"   and they doing so.

Zack was still sofa-ed and totally absorbed in the Jug-band's music. When they re-sat themselves beside him, he seemed startled and completely unaware of their moment's-before absence.

Autumn Time

Autumn Time

Weather's fine

Summer's grueling

Heat's behind

Death consenting

leaves descending

golds 'n orange

scarlet endings

Painted, splattered

Spotted, tattered

His easel flung

In blessing, flattered

Naked limbs

Of no more trim

In morning mist

Defined, but dim

Corn stalk fields

In harvest yield

In reverence now.. it's

Stance seems kneeled

Bounty blessed

Farm, barn-house rests

In silent, stilled…

Thanksgiving-ness.

Thanksgiving was cold. Very wintery weather had set in. And after the annual family gathering, Nate made for the avenue hang-out. Feeling more stuffed than the bird he'd just helped to consume, he forced on. Momentarily relishing the thoughts of having kept Johnny 'at bay' to date, he crossed the main-way in his regulation P-coat, catching site of Willie wearing the identical same. And, he standing in the approaching store-front's entry and crevice, along with a few other stragglers. Next door to them (and to Nate's left..) Brigham's Ice Cream Parlor was dim-lit and closed.. But, the right-sided Chicken Delight was open and bright.. with a few moving-images smeared beyond its thickly-hazed glass. Snuggling himself into the strapped-up collar, Nate moved in closer now and shot out…

"Hey, Willie.. 's gotten cold, huh!.."

"Y' ain't kiddin', Nate-o.. ' think winter's here!.."

"Damn, Willie… 's too early f' me!"

"Me, too!.."

Their other friends seemed to be in a conversation of their own.. And, for that, neither were missed as they started away…

"Nate.. I gotta talk with you about sumethin'.. " meaning privately.. And, the addressed sensing that, began to follow him around the corner, pass the 'blurry-ed' take-out/eatery and away-on-their-own. Then, continuing and further-entering the mouth of Martin Street, he resumed…

"Nate-o.. y' know I'm y' friend, so.. well, I just gotta let you know this.. or I just wouldn't feel right… Y' know, it's hard to tell y', but…"

"Well, what's the deal, Willie?.. Just lay it on me!.." following curiously into the darker-set road.

"Well.." as the engulfing nearly-bare-now trees covered their escape.. "It's Lana… I heard word that she's been two-timin' y' some....'n…"

Nate, stopping dead in his tracks and cutting him short… "Y' sure?.."

"Look it, man.. I wouldn't be sayin' this, if you weren't my pal of pals. Y' know that.. Right?.."

"Yeah, man.. but, how 'd y' know?.. I mean.."

"Well, Nate-o.. like I said, I heard it.. but then, the other night, I seen it f' myself.. Yeah, she was getting in Larry's car.. 'n.. "

"Larry?.. " an older guy who hung around with the avenue crowd. A real lady's man with a car to back-up his advances.

"Man, Willie.. Y' really sure?.."

"Yeah, Nate.. I'm sure.."

"Well, thanks.. " dropping his head, inner-perplexed. "Thanks f' tellin' me.."

Willie remaining sympathetically silent.

"Yeah, thanks.." repeated and spoken unthinkingly, for Nate was still introspectively lost. Willie continued in his silence a bit longer, that he might have time to take it in. At last.. "C' mon, man.. Let's walk…'k?..", putting his right hand on his friend's left shoulder, and gripping it firmly-forward to begin.

"Yeah.." Nate glancing dumbfoundedly back up at him, as they started off.. "Yeah.. Ok.."

Following 'robot'-like, Willie led him even-further now, down the sidewalk and beneath the streetlight-reflecting trees.

"Oh, yeah!.." Willie remembering something.. " Hey.. I been meanin' t' tell y'.. That story y' wrote.. " hoping it would distract his grief... "Y' know, the one that y' gave me last week t' check out?…"

He becoming curious now, despite his inner turmoil.. and, in so, looking over at him, as they trudged together over the warped-'n-awkward, brick walkway and deeper into the night. "Yeah?.."

"Well, I finally got a chance t' read it, t' day… It's cool, man!.. Neat story!.. " Then.. "Y' know, your writing style.. Well, ' reminds me a lot 'f Hawthorne's!.. "

"Hawthorne?.." Nate, truly confused.

"Yeah!.. you've heard 'f him… Right?… "

"..'f course.." Nate being truly and curiously pulled in.. " But, how'da y' fig'red?.. I mean, I never read any 'f his stuff.. Just only what I HAD TO!.. Y' know, in school 'n all!.. 'n as little as possible, t' tell the truth!.. Heck, I can't even remember a bit of it now!..

.. 'sides, wasn't he one 'f that 'Concord' crowd?.. Y' know, them college professors 'n elitist snobs?.. Man, Willie.. I ain't got nuthin' in COMMON with that bunch!.. Y' know that!.. How can y' even suggest it?.." Then, like away and to himself.. " Man, what a night this is becomin'!!"

"Nate-o.. Man, you don't understand!.. " Willie responding sincere-like… "Hawthorne.. he wasn't no high-class guy!.. Heck, he was just a street kid from Salem!.. Yeah, just a reg'lar townie!… Nah, he was just like us, man .. Y' got it all wrong!…

..'n yeah, well.. ok!.. sure, he got involved with all'a them people later.. y' know, when his work got accepted 'n all.. but, even then, he never really related to them!.. Thought 'a them just the same way you do!.. No, Nate.. you just THINK y' know him!..

Either way, whatever y' thinkin'.. he was a real GREAT WRITER!.. 'n what I was sayin' was only meant t' be a compliment!.. Yeah, I really liked y' story!.. 'n I think y' should continue in it!.. Y' know, write some more of 'em 'n all!..

.. 'n Hawthorne.. well, he's just the closest I could come up with, in describin' y' writing style 'n approach!.. That's all.."

A pause. Then..

"Yeah, I know, Willie.." Nate conceding.. " ..Yeah, I.. I know that!.." feeling guilty now for his over-reaction.. "I'm just really kind 'a BUMMED t'nite, man.. Sorry!.."

" .. 's ok, Nate-o.. I understand.. No big deal.. "

All day next, at work, Lana's 'infidelity' preyed on his mind. Even the thought of it being Friday and the weekend at hand, made for little relief or comfort. 'How could she?' he fumed, as he poured gasoline onto the clean-up rag for the Lino slugs that he'd just repro-ed. Should he confront her? I mean, they weren't married. Still, that didn't matter! They were supposed to be going steady. It was a matter of trust! And she'd failed him! Should he just forgive and forget? I mean, maybe nothing much had happened on the occasions she'd been with him? Should he confront Larry? Well, for one, he really didn't want to end up in a fist-fight over it. I mean, what would that do.. or prove, either way? She was the one that had made the commitment!.. Not him! Maybe he should just forget it? Nah, that sure wasn't gonna work.. I mean, it was all that he could think about now!

What is it about life, that when you're down and troubled, someone's just gotta come along and kick you right in the face?....

"NATHANIEL!.. "   Brennan stood near the office's doorway now, hands on her hips, giving him the most defiant of looks ever.

"Yes?.." Nate raising his head and responding, though not moving any closer. Hardly in the mood for this!   She.. still silent and glaring.

"Well?.." the boy added, as politely as possible.

"Nathaniel.. When are you going to get that hair cut?.."   Studying his disgust-filled stare-back.. "You look like.. like.. Joe, the 'street sweep' from that Dicken's 'Bleak House' Book! .. Yes, like some little beggar!.... It's absolutely SHAMEFUL!.."

Forming his face and lips to spit-out the worse of rebuttals (for this was truly IT for him, what with all else that was going on in his life now!); out-of-nowhere now, in chimed Bill (just in the nick of time too!), who happened to be entering the composition area from the back pressroom, behind Nate...

"Mrs. Brennan.. Would you PLEASE stop PICKING ON this boy?… He does his job finely enough!.. What's the damn difference WHAT his HAIR looks like?.. Why is that SO IMPORTANT to you?.."

"Nathaniel represents our company!.. When he goes out to make deliveries, he is speaking for us!.. "   She, in a hissy fit now.. and totally flabbergasted for his defending him.

"Fact is, Mrs. Brennan.. You have had it out for this kid, ever since the day he started here!.. You simply don't like him!.. Never did!.. And probably never will!.. So, why can't you just leave him alone?.."

The greater truth really cut deep.. and in a jolting-sharp twist, she began back inside of the office, spitting out vehemently, as she left…

"I will discuss this with Mr. Hampshire, sir!… Be assured!.. "   and then, warningly.. "and BOTH of YOU can answer for yourselves!.."

"Fine, we will.." Bill responding flippantly as he made his way further into the Linotype's crevice.

When she'd left and a silence fell in…

"Thanks, Bill.. But, y' really didn't have t'.."

"Yeah, Nate.. I did!.. People like that just really aggravate me!.. If it wasn't your hair, it'd be sumethin' else!.. Anything else!.. People like that just live to pee people off!.. Y' know what I mean?.. "

"Yeah.." Nate nodding.. "still, y' didn't have t'.."

"Forget it, kid.. I wanted t'.. "

"Well, thanks.." soft enough that he wasn't sure Bill had heard it. Then, recoiling into his work, the thoughts of Lana returned to only bring back and further deepen his grief.

Tim had asked Nate to get Howlin' Wolf's autograph for him.. as he couldn't make it to the Coffeehouse in the Square, the night of his performance there. Nate was a big fan of him too; though not quite as emphatically as Tim..

And as strained as things were becoming between them, these days, Nate didn't want to fail in his mission (As un-nerved as it was making him now!).

Willie, Stephen and he sat on the opposing side of the smoke-filled room, during what-was the intermission. The Wolf was directly across.. sitting (likewise) on the bordering-and-propped-up-against-the-walls, ice-cream-parlor-style booths.. talking with the immediate people surrounding him. Willie anxiously reminded...

"Nate-o.. if y' gonna git it, now's th' time, man!..."

"Yeah, I know... but..."

"No but's about it, Nat.." Stephen interrupted, though looking quite uncomfortable himself.

"Yeah, Nate-o.. He's right!.. No but's about it!.. C'mon!.." Willie getting up to go.

"Alright, alright!!.. " Nate unwillingly following. Stephen staying to secure their seats.

When there...

"Ah.. ah.. Mr. Wolf... m.. my name's Nathan.. " he muttered out.. " I.. I ..I.." Willie nudging him, and he turning briefly in a grimace towards his attacker.. Then quickly back.. " I.. I was wunderin' if I might get your autograph for a..."

Before he could finish and put forth the paper and pen, the Wolf reached up and comforting-and-supportively grabbed it all with both of his huge black hands. Then, in the same, he cupped the boy's unstable hand in a firm grip, and said.. ".. 'f course, young man.. I'd be mighty proud t'.. " ..being just so friendly and appreciative of the boy's admiration.. Then, "Lemme see here.." re-adjusting the writing tools (In the moment, Nate being glad now that he hadn't finished his sentence, regarding Tim!), moving out and towards him, the

Wolf began writing.. Looking up on a few occasions.. "Now, I's gonna write my address here, 'n I want y' t' write t' me… ok?.. Promise?"

"Yes, sir.. I.. I will!.." he, totally taken back by the old man's kindness. That, and his genuine goodness! Such a sincere, polite and warm man! A Star, for sure!.. But not a trace of egotism or big-headed-ness about him! Totally humble! This was a complete epiphany for Nate.. Yes, an on-the-spot 'lesson' of how an artist should treat his audience! He'd never met a 'Star' like this before! But, he swore to himself, right then and there, that this would be the way he would treat 'his audience', one day! .. Yes, when he was a grown-up 'Star'!

In the haze of it all, Willie pulled him away; for Nate was still standing there in awe, when the Wolf ended. Thanking him for his friend (Then, Nate doing so himself), they made their awkward way back across and through the crowded room.

Re-seated now, he turned to Willie.. "That's how I wanna be.. just like that!.." Stephen pulling in closer now to hear, as he continued.. " Yeah, that's a REAL Star!.." His two listeners not gathering the deeper meaning of what he was saying though. But, it didn't matter, all 'n all.. He was really just talking to himself.

When the rivers are frozen..

And the glade leaves dead brown…

With snow, intermingled..

Upon the hard ground

And the cold winds, so bitter..

Blow in and blow out…

And chimney's are puffin'..

Like a pipe smoker's mouth

I'll call on my mem'ries..

Of Summer, now gone…

'n pray they will keep me..

internally warm.

It was really starting to get bitter cold now. Nate stood alone in the elevated train depot, pacing in wait. Hand-pressing his ears on occasions.. But, lightly!.. for they felt brittle from the biting wind.. and, like as-if, they would break-off, if he forced too hard!

The train seemed to be taking forever! Looking about to distract himself, he considered how this huge, hanger-like-building looked very similar to the train depot in the beginning of the Beatles movie, "Hard Days Night". Only this, a lot dirtier.. And much more abandoned, silent and stark in comparison!

This thought, carrying him back to another memory from his own times, that had coincided with the movie's release. Yes, when he had been in a downtown store's 'bargain basement', one mid-week morning (Hooking school.. a bit nervous and planning on, as-soon-as-possible, being 'more hidden' in a nearby theater!); When out of nowhere, a massive herd of women transcended down upon and into the shopping bins that he was pensively rummaging through (for a cheap pair of Beatle boots). This 'stampede'.. entering without end.. filling the entire basement floor in seconds!.. All and everyone of them.. screaming, pushing and shoving-one-another un-mercifully in their frantic rush for 'deals'! Yes, in the terror and moment of it, he had assumed the "sale hour–bell" had just 'rung' and a 'corral gate' opened from somewhere's above! It was truly hilarious; though hard to find humor in, when it was happening! For thinly-little Nate had all he could do, but to save himself from being absolutely crushed, at the time! Now, in retrospect, he could laugh about it. But, at the time ..it had all been just.. too unbelievable and scary! He considered for a minute now, what the Beatles must've felt like.. What, with all those girls chasing them around 'n all! Yes, the actual horror of it! He'd never thought of it that way before. Surfacing from the recall now, he shook his head (for it) and re-focussed on the cold, hard steel and cement enclosure all about him. Noting a huge gust of entering-and-passing, freezing wind.. working its way through and out the tunneled-like other side. He pulled back into the slight billboard-ed coving. Being that the entire depot was building-top level, these attacks were pretty-much 'totally un-thwarted'.. And very painfully sharp and penetrating, in the same!

Just to be moving again, he (clothing-ly) nestled himself inward; and walked to the nearby opening and overlook.. Just below and beyond the station's 'Sullivan Square' sign. His body literally ached. Staring out at the deep-and-darkening night, he surveyed the vast and far-off city's massive skyline. This, and the running-out-into-it , bridged-and-raised train track from his stance.. It, curving and winding far beyond.. just above the closer and more-defined rooftops. They, with hard-crusted, snow caps. Considering in the moment, how this same bleak view (Short of a few very-distant and horizon-lined skyscrapers now) would have been identical to what his Father (and even, his Grand-father!) might've seen, years past. The thought momentarily depressed him.. bringing-in-its-aftermath, a very desperate feeling!.. An overwhelming and 'fear-filled' one, that took his steam-hazing breath away! Blurry-eyed and despairingly he fought the mounting-and-sudden 'adrenalin surge' internal, hoping that he could re-gather and distract himself enough.. And, in the same, remember and (instead) focus on his own 'greater' plans. No, he wouldn't be here forever! He must remember that! This was all just.. temporary! That's all! Just…just.. for a time!

Pulling back and feeling through his pockets to try and further divert himself from the lingering negativity and panic-like anxiety (.. and, in the same, to make sure he hadn't lost the enveloped check that he'd received from the customer, that he'd just delivered the letterheads to..), he noted in this re-swing the coming of his train. Thank God! ..Oh, yes.. thank you, God!.. He could escape! Still, he just hated getting home so late though! But, then, daylight's savings time always made everything seem worse.. It just took so long for folks to adjust to it! Either way, here and there, he'd always been sent on errands like this. And, after all, it did get him 'out of the shop' for awhile.. So he couldn't really complain. There was 'good' in it! .. Yeah, he might as well try'n relish it!… 'Sides, tomorrow was Christmas Eve.. There was a lot to look forward to!

'Ree' was the baby. The eighth in a long line of five girls and three boys. The blonde, stocky-built toddler. And she, preceded by Anna, the thinly, black-haired one with the 'Mick Jagger' lips (as Nate would tease!). Then, continuing in reverse order, came John, the equally dark-haired 'quiet' brother. Peter, before him, was the bold one… blonde and ' proof and product' of the slight-'sliver' of Swedish blood in their family tree. Tess was next .. and the over-sensitive, little rebel of the female side. As a baby, she would cry so hard and heavy (when she didn't get her way!), that she would ultimately lose her breath.. pass out.. and the fire department would have to be called to revive her. This all, causing an ever-traumatic scene, each time! A child with a heatedly strong will! From the very start! And Nate's 'pet' for it. She, too, being clearly attached to her older brother.

'Niney' was next. The loving, caring sister with a heart too big for her own good. Naïve and trusting. So much so, that Nate could easily trick and tease her with his 'big brother' pranks. She was gullible to no end. Easy prey.. and he just couldn't resist it!

Now, Katie (the oldest girl).. well, she was a whole different story! Pretty (as were they all!).. but, sharp and less tolerant. Being that she was born in a closer time frame with Nate.. having the identical dark-brown hair and complexion (The others, gapped a few years behind them), she looked-to-be almost his facial-twin. But, in the same.. having been his playmate, when they were toddlers… Well, all that could be said of that was.. there had sure been some serious scrapes and tangles between them!.. And, now.. being older (.. And, when they would still occur, on occasions..) Nate would simply choose to dodge or ignore them. In other words, they loved each other; but much more cautiously-and-distantly than the little ones; that they were both more partial to, by nature. So, it was with great reserve that he would ever 'even consider' discussing any of Willie's 'pleas for favor' with her. No, all of his friend's coaxing would do no good.. but, Nate just simply couldn't find the right words (Nor, the heart!) to tell him that!

Presently, Niney ripped her way through the huge box's Christmas wrapping, finding inside another slightly-smaller, gift-wrapped square.

Confused, she looked up at its giver.. But, Nate just sat smiling at her (and then, around at everyone else, when she wasn't looking..), as she excitedly removed it and began ripping through the next and new one. Tess and Ree moved in closer now, distracted from their own 'openings'; despite all of the Christmas morning madness about them. What was it? It was such a huge gift!

At last, Niney concluded this procedure.. Only to find another, slightly-smaller package. And, yes.. it, gift-wrapped, as well! Now, even Peter and John's peripheral overcame them and they curiously moved in, as well. The morning's excitement died-down and the entire family soon followed suit.

But, with this un-veiling, came yet-another smaller gift. Wrapped too... Though, now.. they were starting to slowly decrease in size.

Finally, after numerous others, an earring-sized gift-box appeared. Niney was getting flustered and intense now. What could it be? Tearing it open and popping the lid, she peered in. Her face dropped. It was a piece of bubble-gum. Bubble-gum? Yes, BUBBLE-GUM! She resurfaced, confused-like.. looking up at her giver.

Nate smiled and asked..

" Can I split it with y' ?..."

She raised her fist, threateningly... Then, began up with..

"Nate!... I'm gonna kill you!" Everyone was laughing. She tanglingly continued her ascent, as he un-seatingly took off.

After the festivities, Christmas day always dragged out. Each child, ultimately finding a corner for their games and toys. And, Nate.. off to his 'seniority' suite.. where he lay listening now to his new transistor radio.. and, in so, mumbling along.. "pa.. rup.. pa.. pum, pum". He'd already-and-pretty-nearly worn out the two new LP's he'd received.   So, stuffed from dinner, he'd retired with his Toshiba.. and was laying there now, nearing 'nap mode' quickly.

He'd considered walking down to the main street 'hang-out' (as bored as he had been towards the late day!) to see if anyone else had appeared.. But, the extreme cold and occasional snow flurries had thwarted it. At least, until now! Yes, the inner angst was truly getting to him. So, hopping up, he began through a few 'mock' calisthenics to try and shake off the mounting dozy-ness. It seemed to work some.. He'd do it. Yes.. even if no one was down there, he just needed to get out!

The cold was biting, at times.. but, he trekked along despite.. until he, at last, reached 'the avenue'. Everything was closed.. There, and along the way.. only seeing (in all his travels) one coffee shop with a few stragglers beyond its glowing-lit, glassy haze. The bitter was getting to him now.. So, with no one about the usual 'hang out', he hurriedly crossed the snow-brushed street, and made for the far-corner's laundry mat. Usually it was open (regardless of holidays).. and he prayed now that it still would be. Reaching the glass-and-metal-trimmed door, he found it was. Thank God! Sliding in across the linoleum, he began walking about the deserted storefront, blowing warmth onto his numbed hands. And, as well.. stomping his feet lightly, to try to rid the outer-slush.. and, likewise, awake the blood cells in them.

After five or so minutes, the slight warmth of the room began taking some physical effect.. Though the mental haze (caused by the extreme cold) was still spinning his head. He sat down on one of the fiber-glass chairs now, to take a much-needed breather. In so, introspectively remembering a long, long passed event he'd experienced near that very site. Yes, three or four doors down, at the once-coffee-shop that was located there.

It was during his early Grammar School years, when they (his class) would walk (every Tuesday morning) up to the local church for religious education. It was a good mile or two hike; and in the process, they would always pass by this very spot and the eatery, traveling to and fro. He recalled one particular winter morning, how.. on the return back to school.. he had been so cold, he just simply couldn't go on.. So, in blinding tears and excruciating pain, he had left the line and gone into the coffee shop. This, in total disregard of the rules and penalties for doing so.. But, it was just that desperate a situation! He remembered now a nice young woman (that had worked there, at the time), who had taken such compassion on him.. At last, leading him to the counter and getting him a warming cup of hot chocolate. He recalled how truly grateful he was. And still was, to this very day!   It's funny how little things 'of kindness' like that are never forgotten.. And how they forever live in your heart!   He wished he knew who she was, that he might thank her .. Despite, all of the years now passed and gone!   For it had just meant so much to him!   He felt a tear now in his thawing eyes and brushed it, that no one would see it.. This, on impulse; not remembering his location and solitude.

Surfacing now, he gazed about.. Noting in so, that the soft and pumped-in radio station (above him) was airing a Muddy Water's selection. He loved Muddy! Wow! Focussing sharper, he recognized it to be "Goodbye Newport" from the 'Live at Newport' LP.   How strange to be hearing that on the radio now!   Then remembering, it was the Sunday "hootenanny show' broadcast! What with the Holiday 'n all, he'd totally forgotten that it'd be on the air, that night! Cool!   He stood up to hear it better. At last, moving to the window; listening and scanning the abandoned, winter night. What a lonely and odd feeling it was to be here, on such a night! Almost eerie!

The walk home was faster and brisker. He, taking the back-roads and more-direct route.. and in so, passing along the same streets that led up towards the earlier-noted church (and its education classes).   In this, another recall from a different Christmas Day came. Yes, of him being in the car with his Father, enroute to a Service. He remembered how (at the time) he'd told his Dad, that he had been disappointed with his gifts that morning.. And how, even though he'd asked for a real army helmet; now that he had one, there really wasn't much he could do with it, that day. In this, he remembered his Father telling him..

"Son, sometimes the things we ask for in life.. even if we get 'em, that doesn't mean they'll make us happy!.. Y' know, just 'cause we WANTED them!..

And then there's times when we just don't get what we want at all!… That's just the way life is!..

But, hey.. As long as we get what we NEED… that's what's important!.. RIGHT?" looking down at him, in this.

It didn't make a lick of sense. And why would it to a boy! Even now, Nate saw nothing in it worth a hoot!   He shook his head, and walked on..

At last, passing by Walden park.. and then, beyond it, through a huge construction site that bordered and led-into Sherman St., he noted it all to look like the artwork on his new Manfred Mann LP.. You know, where they'd taken their publicity shot for it 'n all.. This, making him anxious to get home and listen to it again. Lord, was it so windy and bitingly colder here, for the huge opening and space!.. Truly forceful and piercing! First thing he'd do when he'd get in was.. put it on the turntable, crawl up in the dark, snuggle in warm, and go to sleep with it playing!

> The naked lakes of Winter-time
>
> With breeze across them blows
>
> The coming snows.. 'n temps below
>
> Yes, soon they'll all be froze

It brings me back.. in youth, to days

Of skating, other games

We played in mittens, scarves 'n hats..

Until the evening came

Whereupon we'd stiffly wobble home

To warm up by the heat

'n thaw-out, happy, talkin'..

our hands and numbly feet.

THE SECOND RING

The electric trolley's still ran in this section of the city. Nate, at last, unloaded himself from it, at his closest stop.. the one, bordering the huge V. A. Hospital. Having immediately made for the right-sided-and-nearest sidewalk (as not to chance crossing the street's full width in a single effort), he stood now looking up at its massive concrete-and-glass exterior. This, while the trolley resumed its further journey; screeching off like some enormous fingernails slowly scraping across a gigantic blackboard.. Ear-piercing and brain-drilling!.. Only making his already-discomfort and nervousness worse! Yes, he truly wanted to visit his Dad, but still.. it was all making him feel quite uneasy. Either way, he'd come a long way and was going in!.. Hell or high water!

So, crossing the avenue with its centering tracks, he proceeded uphill and beyond the front parking lot.. and, at last, through the awning-covered entrance. Approaching the receptionist, he inquired about his Father's location. She, giving him the ward number and some brief directions. Taking the elevator up a good amount of flights, he finally un-boarded.

Entering the hallway, he immediately noted the extremely-rundown nature of the ward. That, and the pitiful stench! But, despite and through-it, he continued.. at last, coming to the nurse's station at the corridor's end. Explaining that he was there to see his Dad, she pointed out a combination Recreation-and-Lounge room entrance near-at-hand, where he could wait. Following her instructions, he went in, taking a seat on a shabby-looking sofa. It, being propped-up in front of a huge window pane, that overlooked the further-city's skyline.

As the wait continued, he felt more-and-more uncomfortable. And, in a moment, he wished he'd never came.. Sicker now, for the mere sight of the 'sub-standards', all about him. This was supposed to be a 'health' facility! That, and not to forget, his own personal concerns weighing on him. Yes, it was all becoming pretty 'intense' now!   But, again.. he was going to go through with it, no matter what! Yes, regardless of 'whatever', he would hang in!

Growing more antsy and on-edge (for the lengthening wait), he, at last, unseated himself to scan through the magazines and other reading materials supplied on a nearby metal rack. They were all so 'out-dated'!   It was truly shameful! Regardless, he took a National Geographic back to his seat. Anything for a diversion!

Flipping through the pages, he was, at last, interrupted by the entrance of his Father. Placing it aside, he hopped to his feet, greeting and hugging him. The latter, feeling awkward, at first.. but he was glad that he had, in its conclusion.

Re-seating, his Dad did so, as well.. in a chair propped right beside him...

"Thanks, Nate.. Y' know, f' comin' 'n all!.. It's really good t' see y'!.." He, looking brightened for it, but still pale and depleted. Heavily unshaven and worn too! The boy, trying to ignore this..

"Yeah, sure, Dad!.. Good t' see you too!.."

A slight pause.

"How's your Mom?.. 'n the kids?.."

"Fine.. Yeah, fine!.. I mean, we sure do miss y' .. 'n well.. y' know, it's been kind'a ha-...   Well.."   Nate stopping, as not to bring up any of the 'roughing-it' negatives now, that might (in turn) make his Father feel bad.. Or more-accurately, 'worse' than he surely and already felt about it.   But, it didn't matter..

"Yeah, I know, Son.."   his Dad realizing how hard it must've been for them, without him being there to support them and so on.

A longer silence fell.

Nate wanted to say something.. Just anything!.. to fill the void.. but, couldn't think of a single thing now! He'd come all this way, and never really planned any 'conversation'! And, his Father had seemed so 'depressed and effected' by what he had already said.. that he was just.. well.. totally lost for anything 'family-related' to take a chance on now. Inwardly, he tangled with himself.. at last, blurting out…

"Hey, Dad.. D' y' ever hear of Hawthorne?.. Y' know, Nathaniel Hawthorne?.."

His Father looked at him confused-like…

" Well, yeah.. y' mean the author?.."

"Yeah, him!.."

"Well, sure, Son.. wasn't he like a famous writer.. from.. Salem?.."

"Yeah, that's him!.." Nate unsure of why he'd even brought it up, in the first place. But, being that he had.. Where to now? Forcing out.. "Well, Willie.. he says I write a lot like him!.. Y' know, my stories.." pausing to think. Then.. "Y' know, he says my style is similar to his!.. Did y' ever read any 'f his stuff?" Was he sinking or swimming?.. He really couldn't tell!

"Well, no.. not that I can remember.. Ah, I dunno.. maybe, though..?" His Dad pausing to think.. Then.. "But, if y' ask me, I think you write more like your Granddad!.. Yeah, you get all 'a that honestly!.. Y' know, from him!.. He wrote books, too!.. 'least, one that I know of, anyways!.."

This was purely, and nothing short of, 'revelatory'!.. And it sincerely caught him totally off-guard!.. For Nate had never heard a single word of his Grandfather being a writer!.. Let alone, completing an entire book! No, in all of his years of growing up, he'd never heard anyone speak of it, in the least.. Even, his own Granddad! Nothing! Was this..

".. for real?.. That really true, Dad?.. " Nate, stunned-looking.

"Yeah!.. 'f course!.. " his Father surprised.. "Y' mean, you never knew that?.."

"No.. really.. I never did!.. "

"Well, 'guess y' do now!.. Huh?..

Either way, 'n yeah.. I think your style's a lot like his!.. " his Dad, reiterated.

Nate was beyond confused. I mean..

"When 'd y' ever read any of mine?.. Like, how'd y' .."

"Your Mom!.. " his Father cutting in.. " She showed me one.. when I was still home!.. Awhile back… Y' know, when you were out 'n all.."

"Really?.. " whispered-like, thinking how he'd never really figured they'd have had that much interest in what he was writing.. Nor, even 'the time', what with all the other kids t' deal with 'n all! Re-focussing.. "Well, what was it about?.. Y' know, Grandpa's book?.."

"Well.. I read it a long time ago, Son.. I mean, it's been years!.. I dunno?.. " His Dad truly caught off-guard and getting confused now.. yet, trying to focus.. ".. seems like I remember it as being a murder mystery or whatever?.. No, maybe it was a romance novel?.. I.. I can't recall!.. Either way, I do remember it all took place on a Tropical Island!.. Yeah, that I'm sure of!.. in the South Seas somewhere!.. But, again, it's all just been.. too many years!.." looking truly uncomfortable and fatigued by it all now. That, and like as-if, starting to withdraw.. for some sort of 'distant memory' it might have brought back to him. That, or something otherwise!.. But, whatever.. it, being clearly upsetting and unpleasant!. . Regardless..

Nate couldn't let up there.. Excited and unthinkingly, he persisted…

"Well, d' you still have a copy of it, Dad?.. or does Grandpa?.. or anyone else?.. I mean.. I'd just really like to read it! "

"No… No, I..   I, I..   I.. don't.."   His Dad, dropping his head and withdrawing deeper.   And, looking very-internally-frustrated now..   In this, 'spacing' even further!

'Possibly from my pressuring him?', Nate, at last, noted and concluded. He surely hadn't meant to! Either way, he immediately felt guilty..   For, only seconds before, 'the visit' had all been so pleasant and so positive!   Quickly, he offered…

"Dad..   It's no big deal..   Don't worry about it!..   Ok?..   I was just.." stopping, as he could see that his Father was beyond hearing him.

"No, I..   I, I .. I really can't…   can't.."   He, rising to his feet in this. Then, in the same, starting to pace about..   In so, running his fingers through the top and sides of his hair, like trying to comfort himself.   There was a total disconnect.   He was mentally miles and miles away now!

"Dad..   I'm goin' t' get the nurse.. ok?..   "   Nate (upset and sensing the urgency)   hopped up and started off..   "I'll be right back…Alright?.. Everything's gonna be ok, Dad..   Yeah..   I'll be right back!"

As the empty trolley screeched and scraped along, jarring back 'n forth from stop to stop in its awkward return, Nate sat hunched and huddled-over in the last of seats.. sick to his stomach.. wrapping and coiling himself into his old High School jacket and scarf.. and crying uncontrollably.

All through-out the Winter, Buzz had been talking about getting an apartment and rooming together with Nate (Now that he was out of school). But when, all of a sudden, he announced that he had secured one with a deposit, the latter was stunned. He had sincerely thought it all talk. But, now upon him, he had to make a decision...

"Well, yeah.. I guess.. I mean...Yeah, I sure want t'.. It's just that.. Well, y' know, with my Dad sick 'n away 'n all.. Well, maybe I should talk with m' Mom, 'n see if she thinks it's ok.. Y' know, she prob'ly won't mind, so much.. But, still.. I prob'ly should."

"Sure, man, I understand.. " Buzz.. but, further tempting .. " What'a y' say we go see it though?.. I got the key!.." dangling it, in the process.

"Yeah, well.. " looking down at it.. "Yeah, sure.. Why not."

Soon enough, Buzz was leading the way up a dark stairwell and the spiral hallway of an impoverished, old and huge apartment house. It, being located in the far northern section of town.. on the main road, directly across from the railroad tracks and the Cedar Street Junction. A housing so large, that a bar was located below it on the avenue, along with a few other flanking-it and empty-now store-fronts.

Reaching the second floor, Buzz put the key in, as Nate glanced about and at the other opposing-it doorway on the same level. His friend (Noting this in his head turn) pointed out.. "That one's available too.. They're pretty much identical, so I just went with this ..." opening to, at last, enter in.

It was a reasonably large, dusty and dingy-looking flat. Furnished. With three poorly-lit, but good-sized main rooms in a row directly ahead of them (The third, not viewable yet from their stance though). Nate noting these (the immediate two) right away, as they stepped into its leftward-leading hall. To their entering-and-immediate right was yet another tiny, alcove-size room, that was boxed and directly-adjacent to the straight-ahead parlor.

Walking their way down the long connector, Buzz pointed out a tiny bathroom on the left. Then, further in the rear, they entered what-was a fourth room in-the-line, a kitchen with an extending leftward-and-beyond-it, small pantry. Walking through and across it in rightward motion, Nate, at last, glanced out its opposing windows to look below…

"Car Lot down there, huh.."

"Yeah.." Buzz matter-of-factly.. "Well, what'a y' think?" now that the enticement had been completed.

"Yeah.. Well.. Yeah, I like it!.. and I'm sure it'll be ok."

It was a done deal.

The work days were even-more drawn-out now. Boring and tedious, beyond belief. His time was being wasted! The things he could be doing otherwise to further his Art. But, not unless he made an escape.. To somewhere that he could perform 'on going-ly', for a living 'n all. And really, he was unsure of exactly where he'd go.. and how all of that was done, to begin with! But one thing for sure.. he knew he wanted to, at least, attempt it! He had to!.. Or he might be trapped forever in this 'hell-hole' of wasted time! He stood at the Ludlow now, staring out into space.. thinking deeper.. as his molds were being set.. Contemplating all of this.

Then, peering over at Roger at the stone (lost in his own tasks and thoughts), Nate considered his life. It would always be like this! Yes, the same thing, until retirement. He wondered if his Supervisor (like he) had ever had any greater dreams.. Or was 'this' his dream? To simply be a Printer? He figured so, as Roger had never expressed otherwise. Well, that was ok, he thought.. If that was truly all he wanted!

Pondering on this now, he was at last pulled out of his introspect, with…

"Y' ready to head on over there?.." Roger, awakening him abruptly.

"Oh, yeah.. I didn't realize it was s' late!.." Nate, a bit embarrassed, in that Roj might've known what he was thinking about .. "Yeah, I'll be done in a minute".

Roger had been working nights at another pressroom in the downtown's north end district. A Printing Shop with a very odd and serious stench of burnt. Nate wondered if it was from fire damage or simply from the aged Linos and Ludlows. Whatever?.. it was a powerful smell!.. and it was the very first thing that he noted upon his initial entry, that first Friday night that Roj brought him on-board for some moonlighting. But, Nate needed the extra cash now for his rent 'n all, and had finally conceded to helping him out.. Just as long as he'd give him a lift home afterwards. That, being the only stipulation.

So, at last, climbing the creaky, old stairs to the third floor of this narrow-and-angled-on-a-hill building, Roger got him started on cleaning nixs from some Lino proofs. Then, leaving him alone, he proceeded to go downstairs to attend to his own tasks.. In so, the boy returning to himself and his earlier meditations. This, for several hours.

Roger, at last, calling up the stairwell and pulling him out of his introspect..

"Nate.. Y' at a place where y' can stop?.. We need t' round it up.. It's gettin' kinda late!.."

When all was accomplished, he settled into Roger's passenger-side and sunk back, huddle-like, into a half-doze. At last, reaching his apartment, Roj nudged him awake and thanking-ly dropped him off.

Entering the cool air and the blurred lights of the surrounding night, Nate waved him 'goodbye' and stood on the sidewalk affront of his new home. There was something really 'nice' in the freedom of just being 'out on his own' now.. Something profoundly and inwardly moving.. and, in so, he paused for a moment to relish the thoughts of it, before heading upstairs. He was absolutely exhausted from the extra long day.. Still, breathing-in the almost-magical 'presence' about him, he experienced something he'd never before felt.. A sudden moment of 'youthful discovery' beyond words.. The odd epiphany of 'coming of age'.. where the 'long-awaited childhood of yearning for it' is left behind. Yes, the dawning of manhood! It (and he) had finally 'arrived'! .. and it was strangely overwhelming!

At last, climbing the stairwell (in the lingering thoughts of this) and turning the key, he pushed open the apartment door; only to find that a small party was in-process. Buzz calling out from the parlor...

"Nate.. C'mon in, man.. Have a beer..."

Totally and physically beat, he was in no mood for this. But, holding it all in, he proceeded to the doorway of the living room, making his stance there. This, to show his unwillingness to join in.. and, to (in the same and likewise) peripherally eye-rightward into his little alcove room and verify that no one was 'trespassing' or getting 'into his stuff'.

In his return and scan of the parlor, he saw Willie .. along with a few other faces he'd seen before, but didn't 'namingly' re-collect, right off. Then, it came to him that they were members from another local band in the area. Yes, they.. a bit younger than he and his group.. and in so, admirers. Getting up from their seats, they came through the handful of other 'unknowns' present, offering their hands for a shake...

"Hi, Nate.. Y' remember me, right?.. I'm Wally!... and you've met Kev before.. " turning to his partner. "He plays bass with us!..."

"Yeah.. I remember.." Though, vaguely!.. "How y's been?.." shaking their hands.

"Nate.. next weekend we're playing in Southie.." Kev began.. "..'n Wally can't make it.. He's going out'a town with his folks.. Would you be willin' t' fill-in f' him?.. Y' know, on lead?.. So's we can still do the job?.."

"Ah, what night?.."

"Friday.. " Kev responding.

"Yeah, I guess.. But, what time y's gotta be there?.."

"It's 9 til closing.. It's a bar.. " Then, Kev trying to entice.. "..with Go-Go-Girls 'n all!.."

"Yeah, but what time y's leavin'?.." concerned, but unimpressed.

" I dunno.. Guess we could pick you up here at 7.. Is that ok?"

Willie had, by now, moved in to listen and greet Nate… "Yeah.. ok.." focussing back to Kev to answer… and he responding…

"Great, man.. Thanks!.. We'll look forward to it"

"Yeah, sure.. See y's then.." As Buzz called out (again), distracting him…

"Nate.. 'least, take a sip, man!.. C' mon?.." and Kev and Wally dispersing now, contended.

"Nah.. Not now.. 'k?.. Really!.. But, thanks, anyways!.."

Willie, having waited patiently.. "Hey, Nate-o.. How y' been, brother?.."

"Ok.. yeah, ok.. " Nate diverted, but now re-focusing in on him .. "But I'm really kinda beat.." looking away momentarily in disgust of the commotion.. Then, back.. "I gotta hit the sack"

Willie trying to hold his attention (seeming a bit uneasy and anxious in it)…

"Nate.. D' y' mind if I crash here tonight?.. I had an argument with.."

Before he could complete his sentence… "Sure, man… Y' know that.." Nate, still a bit dis-oriented, but trying to comply.

"Thanks, man.. " real sincere, and breaking his friend's further distraction…

"Sure, Willie boy.. Y' know y' always welcome here" and the addressed sadly smiling in this... "Now, I gotta get some sleep…ok?" Willie nodding in a perk. And Nate retreating quietly into his little half-room by the front door.

Behind the makeshift-curtained-doorway, he undressed and flopped on his cot-like bed. But, the noise persisted.. and he, at last, got up to put on his favorite LP, "Folksinger" to sedate him and hopefully drown-out the background commotion. To the closer sounds of "My Home is in the Delta", he re-settled in and, at last, drifted off.

Morning, he got up creakingly, and began out through the rubble. It was a total war zone. There were discarded beer cans and snack-wrappers scattered everywhere; and working his bare-feet slowly (as not to step on a 'pop top' and cut himself), he passed the parlor (seeing Willie still zonked-out on the couch).. And then further and passed it, to Buzz's next-in-line bedroom (its owner, snoring away within). Then, at last and just beyond, he retreated quietly into the bathroom.. Relieved in knowing Willie to be the only flopper from the night before.

When dressed, he proceeded out of the flat, clicking the door softly as not to awaken anyone. In a further quiet down-climb, he began out onto the avenue. It was nearly ten A.M., but felt like much earlier for the general silence and emptiness of traffic. Taking an immediate right, he began down the main street towards a little 'greasy spoon-like' restaurant, several blocks away.

Ordering his 'regular' (of late) "eggs over medium", he awaited its arrival; sipping on his coffee and staring out the cracked, but-taped-together window. To the tempting-and-overwhelming smell and crackle-popping sounds of bacon cooking behind him, he thought now about the band… and how their attendance at Saturday rehearsals, of late, had been sporadic. Each member (the disgruntled ones, anyways!) seeming to miss one much more frequently now.. Though, a different player each time. He wondered who it'd be today. Yes, things were falling apart awful. And worst of all, the 45 RPM they'd recorded had just finally been released.. and with all that seemed to be 'going in their direction', they (to the contrary) were quickly 'heading in the exact opposite'! Nate decided he'd hit the phone booth across the street after eating, to call them and get a sort-of 'reading'. So, checking through his pocket-change now, he verified that he had enough dimes on him to make the calls.

Despite living away now, his parent's basement was still the band's rehearsal space. His Mom and Dad were the only complying parents (of the band's) willing to put up with the 'weekly' noise. What, with eight kids, I guess they were used to it! And, noon found him there, this time with Ben not appearing. But, Nate wasn't so concerned over him, as being only a rhythm guitarist, he was expendable. That and his becoming worse-and-worse attitude and temperament .. Not to mention, his 'personal problems' and seeming-to-increase 'disorientation', it was probably for the best that he be absent and dealing with whatever necessary.

But, either way and all 'n all, the practice went reasonably well enough. Still, the tension was obviously mounting.. And all the 'dodging of it' wasn't seeming to be helping, in the least. Yes, things were unquestionably coming to a head. But, Nate was at a total loss for how to solve it.

That evening, when he returned to the apartment, he sat in his room discussing it with Willie.

"Well, Nate-o.. it's like I been tellin' y', all along, man.. y' need t' start folksingin'.."

"Nah, Willie.. y' know how I feel about that!.. "

"Well, then.. what about joining in with those guys that asked y' t' play with them next week?"

"Nah, man.. that ain't gonna work neither.. that's just a one-time fill-in thing!… 'sides, I'm not into what they're doin', all s' much!.."

"Well, how's about you formin' sumethin' new.. Y' know, your own band?.. Where you do all the singin'.. 'n …"

"Willie.. we've been through all'a this before.."

"Ok, Ok, man.. but, y' gotta do SUMETHIN'!.."

" I know.. I just don't have any solid ideas yet.." Then, to change the subject.. "Hey.. let's take a walk… Alright?" Nate hopping to his feet to push the point.

"A walk?.. Where?.. I mean, sure!.. if y' want!.. but, where y' wanna go?.." Willie, puzzled.

"I dunno.. just anywhere.."

"Ok...."

So, into the beginning-to-darken night they went. Crossing the avenue straight away, Nate began leftward.. leading-the-way towards Cedar, the angled-off side-street that ran in the direction of his parent's house. Down pass the cornering-it cleaners and along the very-familiar (to him) side-street, they made; silent now for the beginning exertion.

After a number of blocks, they reached the intersection with its huge church on the opposing end of the tiny square. Across the way they made for it, walking slower now and talking, as they followed along the churchyard's flanking side street and bordering-it chain-linked fence…

"Man, this is a really neat lookin' church!.. Huh, Nate?..."

"Yeah, I guess.. if y' say.." he wondering what the great attraction for it being. But, then.. Willie was notorious for such abstract observations and comments! Nuthin' new!

As they walked a little further along and down the sidewalk .. "I got a strange feelin' about this place, Nate!.." looking up and around the huge structure and its solemnly-sedate surroundings. Then..

"Wow, 'n that chapel on the side there!.. Man-o-man.. do I get a REALLY FREAKY VIBE from that!!.... Yow!!.."

"Yeah, 'n what's new 'bout that?.. you're always gettin' 'freaky vibes' from EVERYTHING!"

"No, really, Nate.. Laugh me off, if y' want.. But, sumethin' gonna happen here, that..."

"Willie.. Stop!.." And he doing so in reality to accentuate it.. " Please!.. You're always tryin' t' spook me 'bout stuff!.."

"No, man.. I really mean it, Nate-o!.. Sumethin' big 's gonna... "

"Whatever, Willie.. Whatever!.." cutting him short.. turning away and beginning back towards the apartment, that he might not continue in it.. For, in an odd way, it was making him internally uncomfortable. Why?.. he really didn't know!.. Just was!

"Nate?.. " But, the addressed continuing on and refusing to turn or answer.

"Nate-o?.." He, still ignoring him and walking ..

"Ok, then!.. OK!" Willie conceding to drop it and follow.

Late that night, Nate passed through the hallway and 'again'-party (that Buzz was hosting in the parlor) to find Willie in a completely mesmerized trance; seated in a 'meditating monk'-type fashion in the back bedroom. All alone and totally unaware of his watching him.. He staring dead-ahead into a stereo, that was playing "Within You, Without You" from the 'Sgt. Peppers' LP.

Stopped now, Nate waited for him to notice his presence, but Willie was completely lost. Yes, totally enthralled in his 'other world'! Somehow he felt such an empathetic (or was it 'sympathetic'?.. he really wasn't sure!) concern for this 'fodderwing' friend of his! A certain, mysterious compassion for him. And he thought on this as he watched now, in the moment. Just what was it about Willie that seemed so 'painstakingly' compelling?.. His desperate need and fragility? What was it that worried Nate so deeply about him? He really didn't know! Yes, there was his poetic nature and undying belief in Nate.. but, even greater and still, there was something that he sensed about him, that overwhelmed and outweighed all of that. But, what? And in those very fleeting moments, he snapped a mental picture that he was sure (even then) would last a lifetime. He just knew it! It was beyond words or explanation! And.. sort of scary, in a way! But it burned an image so deep in his subconscious, he somehow knew he'd never forget it. Life itself is just 'so weird' like that sometimes! Why do such little, seeming-insignificant 'snapshots' stay, while other things of much greater importance fleetingly pass so easily into nothingness?

At last turning away, he walked on thinking 'What a strange day this has been'!

"What 'n the hell, you listenin' to, man?.." shot Buzz, as he stood now, leaning up against the bedroom's door frame, gawking and peering in.. "That's Hillbilly music.. right?"

"Yeah.. it's Hank Williams.. " returned Nate, looking up from the seating on his bed, where he sat strumming along with it.. In the same, facially motioning to its LP jacket lying on the record box, just below his roommate. The latter.. stoopingly reached in, picked up the empty sleeve, and read..

"..'Lost Highway and other Folk Ballads'.. What the... " pausing, with a look of total disbelief and innate disdain. Thereafter, dropping the cover flippantly back to its place.. "Is this that guy you 'n Willie were talkin' about, out at Stiles, last-"

Cutting him off.. "Yeah!.. Hey, I like him!.. Have f' a long time!.." Nate, trying to defend his taste.

"Really?.. That's weird, man!.." Buzz smirked-out.. Then, condescendingly " I thought you were hipper than that!.. I mean.."

"Y' mean 'what'.. like Hank ain't cool?.. " Nate, slightly aggravated.

"Well, I dunno?.. " becoming a bit unsure of himself now.. "Well, who do YOU know that listens to this kinda crap, up here? " (meaning, 'in the north').. ".. name me one person!"

"Me!.." Nate, staring back defiantly. Then, remembering.. ".. 'n my Uncle!.. He's the one that turned me on to it!.. So..." pausing for a response. But, not getting one, he returned to his guitar and strum along.. like, as if, he didn't want to discuss it anymore. Blanking him out

At last.. "Whatever, man!.." Buzz, turning away and surrendering to his room.

Nate, mumbling to himself.. "Yeah.. whatever.."

Several of the Rolling Stones had been arrested for possession of drugs (or 'hemp', as the Brits called it!)... and Nate had clipped-out a picture from a magazine, showing them standing outside of the courthouse, having a cigarette, during their hearing in England. Hanging it up on his bedroom wall, it came to his mind now, as he rode along with Buzz to work, early Monday morning. Having missed his alarm (and the bus, as a result), his room-mate had offered him a lift to help him get in on time. One of the songs from the current Stone's album was playing on the car radio. It was Nate's personal favorite.. "Sittin' on a Fence" .. and it immediately brought Lana to his mind somehow. It rang in his ears, as he unloaded himself now in front of the press room. Thanking Buzz, he made inside for yet another day of yearning and torture.

Before he could get too far, Buzz yelled out…

"Nate… Don't forget.. Tonight we're suppose t' go t' my Mom's for dinner!.." Coming back quickly, "Yeah.. ok, man.. " then turning and hurrying off.

Pure yellow mashed potatoes! Drenched with butter, through and through! Nate had never experienced anything like this before! Black-eyed peas.. Fried chicken, so spicy and succulent.. Hey, it was truly a total 'epiphany' for him, of just what could be done with such basic and common foods! This was 'soul food'.. for, although Buzz was a mulatto, his Mother was a full-fledged black woman.. And as loving and kind a woman as he'd ever met too! As he sat chewing now, he considered that Buzz's Dad must've been just one, ol' difficult white man! Considering the trouble that he knew his friend beside him to be 'so capable of', and the absolutely sweet disposition of his Mom, well.. it had to be that! No wonder they were divorced! Made perfect sense!

"Nathan, would you like some more chicken?.."

"Yes, Ma'am.. I'll have another piece.." lifting his plate up, that she might take it from the other side of the table and put it on. "Thank y', Ma'am.."

"Well, Nathan.. Buzz tells me you're quite a blues guit'r picker!.. That true?.."

"I dunno, Ma'am.. I mean.." Nate, becoming uncomfortable.. " Well, I try t' be.. 'n, well.. I dunno?.. 'guess some people like it."

"Well, you should be proud of that.. So many people just WISH they could PLAY, but.. well, it's.. it's very HARD!.. Did you take lessons?"

"No, Ma'am… I just taught m'self… " Then, remembering… "Well, actually, I did take a couple of lessons at a music store in Davis Square once.. Real long ago!... But, I quit after the second, 'cause he wasn't showin' me anything I didn't already know… That 'n, well.. he just kept asking me stuff that had nuthin' t' do with guitar at all.. Y' know, things like, if I'd 'gone to the beach lately?'…or whatever!.. 'n I just figured he was tryin' t' kill time.. Y' know, so's the hour'd go by 'n all.. So, I only went twice…But, no.. just pretty much taught m'self"

"How old were you, when you started?.." She, still curious. That, or more likely, just making conversation.. for prior, Nate had been friendly and cordial, but real quiet and removed, in the same. But, now he was opening up!

"Ah.. 'bout ten…. 'least, seriously, anyways!.. My Dad had this little tenor guitar, that I used to bang around on, before then.. Y' know, when I was small .. He even tried to show me a few things on it, ' couple 'a times.. But I wasn't able to catch on, so I think he gave up 'n just left me to do it on m' own… I didn't have much patience, back then.."

"Well, what was it that inspired you?.. You know, to want to play music in the first place?.. Can you remember?"

"Sure do, Ma'am!.. Hank Williams!.. Yeah, I just loved Hank Williams, when I was a little kid.. He was like my absolute hero, then…" Buzz, looking disgusted at the mention of this, but Nate was rollin' now…

"My Mom had this Vanity table with a big mirror.. and I used t' put my 45 record player on its sittin' bench.. Then, I'd put on my Hank Williams records, strap on m' Dad's guitar and pretend I was him. Y' know, in the mirror."

Nate pausing in thought now and blushing some, realizing he'd just let out a 'deep secret of his life' in the outpouring. Then, to try and hopefully retrieve himself.. "Sounds silly, I guess.. But, well.. that's what got me started.. All 'n all, anyways.." Then, shyly recoiling back into his meal.

Buzz's Mom trying to comfort him.. "I don't think that sounds silly at all, Nathan!.. It's really quite an interesting story.. You should be very proud of yourself…"

"Well, thank y', Ma'am.." Glancing up at her, then at Buzz quickly, and back to his food.

Zack had remained steadfast and loyal throughout.. And had been no trouble, all along.. And as well, supported Nate in his arguments for not bringing Johnny into the already-large-enough band. And even greater, he was the 'true innocent bystander' of the faltering-now band.

Having been "in the area" of Nate's job, late day Thursday, he'd called the pressroom and, ironically enough, gotten through (Despite Brennan's objections!) and was waiting on the front steps, when the boy made his exit.

Tramping through the start-of-dusk (to the continual clicking sounds and echoes of their footsteps, upon the tightly enclosed street), they, at last, reached the busy little square. Trying to hear each other's conversation with the onset burst of commotion, they moved a bit closer together and focussed more sharply, in so, as they crossed through the avenue's backed-up traffic. Picking up speed in it…

"Did y' ever call Gordon, Nate-o?.." (The owner of the Studio and Record Label that they'd been signed to).

"Yeah, but he says he's only interested in Tim.. Not the rest of the group.."

"Y' can't be serious, Nate-o!.. Y' goofin' me.. Right?"

"No, man.. I'm dead serious!.. Really, Zack.. I wouldn't be foolin' with y' on sumethin' like that!.."

"Tim?… Damn, man.. That's crazy!.. Pure crazy!.."

"Yeah, man.. he says he'd only want to keep him.. Should we break up 'n all.. 'thinks he's got some kinda sex appeal that all the girls would love.. Y' know, thinks it'd sell!…"

Zack was silent now.. truly dumbfounded by the thought of it. So, Nate continued..

"Yeah, man.. that's the way it goes!.. We split-up, it'll be all done f' us… 'least, with that deal, anyways!"

Zack held his quiet.. Then, at last, looking at Nate…

"Willie tells me you're doing a sit-in thing f' Wally, this weekend.. with Kev 'n them guys.. Y' thinkin' like leavin' 'n joinin' up with them?.."

"No way, man.. Whatever gave y' that idea.. Willie?"

"No, I just got t' thinkin' like maybe, with all that's been goin' on, y' might be quittin'.. 'n.."

The railroad tracks came up and as they made their way onto them..

"You been thinkin' too much, Zack-a-roni.. 'sides, I ain't goin' nowhere's without you, man.. Whatever I decide t' do, in the end!.. Y' can rest-assured on that!"

Zack peering back and smiling at him in this, with a look of relief and reborn confidence. Nate returning it and continuing.. "That's unless y' decide that y 'd rather…"

Before he could finish.. "Hey, Nate-o.. I'm with you, man.. all the way!.. Whatever y' decide t' do, y' just let me know.."

Nate smiling back with the same look of relief.

Walking along the awkward rails, they held silence for a bit; internally relishing their kinship.. and, as well, the pure and simple beauty of the sky and its setting sun beyond them. Then, typical of Zack.. he removed a harmonica from his pocket and began whining-through some sedating blues riffs. These, echoing back off of the engulfing-them, brick buildings. This, and the auburn sunset.. bringing a deeper feeling of inner peace, despite all of the falling-apart-'n-down-quick darkness upon them.

Nate had performed 'where alcohol was being served' before (Taverns, where under-age band members were allowed in, but not served... As well as, at private college parties, many years past now, where they HAD been SERVED!... And, in so, he'd surely experienced and witnessed a lot in his short time!); but this was TOTALLY different!.. Super sleezy and flat-out tough! Gangster-like! A real dive.. and a very uncomfortable 'eye-opener' for the boy! 'Southie' was notorious for joints like this, but he (having never played the area before) was getting his first nerving-racking glimpse and taste of it now.

Ad-libbing along to numbers such as "96 Tears" was no fun either! Most of them were songs his own band wouldn't touch. Or even consider! But Kev and the band were used to them .. and they sounded full enough for that.. So, it made Nate's job easier.

In between sets, they'd run over songs for the next... In the back's makeshift dressing room, full of its boxes and beer-crates. This was likewise the first time Nate had ever worked with players other than his own band. Still, all and all, it sounded pretty good.. and he was happy for that! But only for that, for the club itself was truly scary! And in his scans about, here and there, he'd inwardly tremble for it.

During the third set, he couldn't help but notice (in all his efforts to ignore it!) that several of the Go-Go girls (caged on all four corners of their dance-floor-level stage) were 'eye-ing' a few members of the band. One was flirting-ly dancing for Alvin, the lead singer.. and, in the same, Nate noticed several men in the audience seething for it. He immediately figured them to be the girl's boyfriends (or 'want-to-be' boyfriends?).. and, with that fear-tinged realization, knew instantly that they were in for some trouble. Yeah, major trouble too! For.. as the set wore on, the heckling and threatening-looks got worse and worse.. And, as fate would always have it, soon enough these men had the entire bar (Who were all, no doubt, longtime drinking buddies!) enlisted in the 'war party'!

By break-time, it was obvious that everyone else in the band was aware of the lurking doom; and as they filed back stage, Kev made straight for a lone walled-phone in the back corridor. Calling the police (as quickly and quietly as possible), Nate made passed him and tried to lose himself (as deeply as he could manage) into the tiny, tight back room. It was comin'!

Within five to ten minutes, the nightclub was surrounded with police cars.. and cops began entering from all sides. This was probably all 'pretty routine' for them, in that section of town.. as they surely had it all down to a fine art, no questions 'bout it ! Nate breathed a slight easier now. He was never so glad to see 'the law' in his life!

Creating a sort of human barrier between the heated crowd and the musicians, they told the latter to pack their gear and load up, as quickly as possible. In a flash, it was done! And before too long, they were winding their ways through the Southie streets; looking back (all the while) in their exit, for following-them cars. But other than the cruisers (Which 'Thank God'-fully tagged them to the city limits!), no one seemed to be tailing them. Nate breathed another deep sigh of relief. And it wasn't until then that he was clear-minded-enough to notice that one of the go-go girls was in the car's front seat. 'Man, these guys are pure crazy!', he thought. Looking back out the rear window, on and off, he kept expecting the appearance of speeding-towards-them headlights. But, they never came.

By the time they reached the apartment, he was, at last, settled enough to give it up. Now in the rear's dark parking lot, they were well-hidden and un-trace-able. They'd made it! A quick shiver and bolting tremble shot through him, as he lifted his guitar case from the trunk. Yes, they'd escaped. Thank God in Heaven!

Sitting around the parlor now, they all recounted the story to Buzz. This, until Nate realized that it was all just becoming another of the 'many parties' that his room-mate enjoyed hosting. So, at last, he retired to his little room, as inconspicuously as he could. Willie (their regular 'flopper', by now!).. within-five-minutes-of-Nate's-departure.. trailed him under and through the makeshift curtain door.. bringing with his entry, a strange 'burning' odor that followed from the just-beyond parlor. It, being.. like nothing Nate had ever smelt before! He wondered (in the moment) if it was some kind of dope? Either way 'n whatever.. He was just too tired and aggravated (with Buzz) to even care!

In the same now, it was obvious to Nate (in seeing Willie enter) that his friend was in another of his depressed and melancholy moods. Trying to hide it though, he offered…

"Hey, Nate.. sounds like y' sure had a close call there!.. Really glad you're ok!.."

"Yeah, Willie.. way too close!.. 'n well, thanks!.. I'm sure glad too!.. For one thing, I surely ain't into fightin' no full-grown men!.. Especially over no.. go-go girls!.."

"Yeah, well.. I think th' one out there's got her eyes on y' .." head-swinging back over his shoulders.. and, in the process, sort-of rolling his eyes in the party's direction.

"A-huh.. yeah, I kinda noticed that m' self.. Either way, she can just keep 'em right there in her head!.." silly-frowning Willie as he proceeded to get undressed for bed.

"Hey, Nate-o.. Can I talk with y'?.."

"Sure, man.. What's up?.." as he removed his clothes.. throwing them in the corner, hopping into bed and under the sheets. Willie plunked himself on the wall's-side far-end of the mattress, as Nate punched the pillow and (re-swinging-forward) banged his head back down on it.

"Well.. D' y' think if a person kills themselves, they go t' Hell?.."

There was a pause. Then..

"Willie, man.. Why y' asking me that?.. I mean, I dunno!…

Damn, man.. I've just been THROUGH HELL m'self.. 'n.. well.." frustrated momentarily, then catching himself for the look on his friend's face.. "Sorry, Willie.." knowing how crucial and important (though, terribly mis-timed!) it might all be to him.. "Listen, I've heard that people who do that… Yeah.. they go to Hell.." hoping that the confirmation might thwart any of his friends' further thoughts (or possible notions..) on it.

"What if someone just missed a person that they really loved? .. 'n that they needed real bad? .. 'n y' know, they just wanted t' be with them?.. But, they'd been taken away.. 'n..."

Before he could finish…

"Willie… Listen, man.. you been drinkin'.. huh?.."

"Yeah, well.. a little… But…"

"Whenever y' do, you get like this.. I mean, I don't mind.." trying to make him not feel uncomfortable.. "but, y' know…" pausing.. "Well, f' one thing, you can't commit suicide… 'cause, if y' do, I'll never speak t' y' again!.."

Willie, in a moment, getting the joke and cracking a slight smile in it.

"Seriously, Willie Boy… you're my best pal.. Y' know that!.. 'n I don't want y' t' die… Ok?.." Willie, being touched and softening now.. "I mean it, man.. You just get that out'a y' foolish, little head.. y' hear?.."

"Ok, Nate-o.. but, I wasn't thinkin' about… " pausing.. "Well, y' know, I was just curious what y' thought 'n all.. Y' know, if that was true?.. 'cause…"

"Willie.. I ain't God.. I dunno know all'a that stuff!.. But I do know this.. I don't want y' to do that!.. Or even ever think 'a doin' that!.. Yeah, that I do know, f' sure!.. 'k?.."

Willie nodding his head. A silence.

"So.. we square on it?.."

"Yeah, Nate-o.. I wouldn't…"

Cutting in.. "Promise?.."

"Yeah, I promise.." sadly consenting.

"Good.. Now, I'm goin' t' bed.." turning in a swing to do so.

Simultaneously, Kev entered the room. But, Nate refused to acknowledge him, pretending to be asleep. It was of no use though, as Kev had just caught the end of their discussion. Willie, in this.. "..'night, Nate-o.. " and leaving promptly. Kev (not getting the message) sat himself down on the bed's outer edge….

"Nate.. Thanks for helpin' out t'nite… Sorry we didn't get paid 'n all, but we really didn't…" Realizing that his 'fake sleep' wasn't working, he responded like 'half asleep' with still-closed eyes… "Yeah, Kev.. That's cool.. No big deal.. But, I'm really kinda tired 'n.. yeah, I'm really beat, so…"

"Yeah, I understand.. " though still sitting there and continuing on. Nate listening for a few more minutes, then blanking out for total exhaustion.

Kev started showing up at the flat, quite frequently now. Pretty much every night that Nate would come in from work (to the 'always-dark, sparingly-lit' apartment), he'd be there.. Listening to the Jimi Hendrix Experience with Willie and Buzz, most times. The latter, having become absolutely and totally obsessed with the "Are You Experienced" LP. Nate liked it too, though it was a bit 'hard-edged and weirder sounding' than he was use to. But, Buzz.. well, he was quickly becoming 'Jimi personified'; despite the fact that he couldn't play the first note on a guitar! But, hey.. What did that matter?.. His natural skin-tone and facial characteristics were truly 'close enough'!.. And with the gradual addition of the flamboyant clothes and similar hairstyling, it was really becoming increasingly-harder to tell the difference!

Either way, the JHE and Cream were the 'power trios' of the day.. and Nate was taking note of both. More agreeably, the latter though. Still, the Dylan thing and folk music were avenues he saw as a possible future.. But, at this point, only as a 'much greater and far-off future'. No, he simply wasn't ready for being a complete soloist... Not to mention, his innate shyness! That 'n.. well, he just really wasn't musically, nor emotionally secure enough to venture forth alone!.. Regardless of his 'still occasional-jaunts' to the coffeehouse 'hoots'... Which truly-'n-only seemed to tax his nervous system!.. That, and all of Willie's nagging-on-him about it! .. No, he needed more time with all of that! It was just.. way too early yet, to even consider going 'solo'!

So, this 'trio' thought was starting to work on him. For after all, his first real Rock & Roll heroes and inspirations were Buddy Holly and the Crickets.. and hey, they'd been a trio! And.. when Nate had just started thinking about creating a band.. or being in one, either way.. it had been because of them! Yes, Holly had been the very reason Nate had switched from acoustic guitar to electric, all 'n all! Then, of course, along came the Beatles (Who were obviously influenced by Buddy; not to forget Nate's second-in-line- heroes-when-growing-up, The Everly Brothers!).. So, it seemed to make perfect sense! Yes, it was becoming a very possible avenue for him to consider. And, when at last, Kev suggested to him (at one of these early evening JHE listening sessions).. "What'a y' think, Nate.. You, Me and Zack?", Buzz (of course) immediately chimed in with.." Yeah, Eric" (his of-late new 'nickname' for Nate, in reference to "Eric Clapton"!)

".. Y' should, man!"

"Yeah, well.. it's a thought, Kev.. Let me think on it some… Ok?"

"Ok… but, man, we could do it.!.. I mean, we'd cook together, f' sure!"

" I don't doubt it, man.. But, still.. just give me a little time.. ok?

Willie (sitting in the far corner) raised his head and started to say something.. But, was promptly thwarted by Nate's waiting stare.. And in so, held silence. His 'words of agreement' didn't need being said. Nate already knew!

There-after, Kev started befriending Willie.. knowing fully-well, it was one of his best ways to get to Nate. And with Willie being the 'Poet in Residence' at the apartment, by now.. it was never really hard to find him! And, per his naturally 'insistent way', Kev worked it like a 'fine craftsmen'! Nate knowing this by Willie's increasing change-of- tune from 'folksinger' to 'trio' talk (Very unlike him, and all too obvious!). And Zack.. well, even he was soon echoing the same. Yeah, it was apparent!.. Kev was not going to let it rest, in the least! Still, Nate hung in with the belief that his band would come around.. and that (eventually) things would get back in order. After all of these years, he just couldn't bring himself to end it. His loyalty wouldn't allow him to break the chains.

Regardless, the negative situation persisted. That, and Stephen's continuing insistence on bringing Johnny into the group. And now, Tim had become his 'all of a sudden' advocate.. Whether for 'true desire to have the organist and that sort of sound'.. or just simply 'out of defiance' (for the furthering loss of Nate's attention and camaraderie)?.. It was hard to tell! But, their once alliance and mutual control of the band had very noticeably diminished and disappeared into a sort of cold war and increasing alienation. The apartment.. Buzz.. Willie.. Kev.. and so on, taking more and more of Nate's time and attention than he. Once 'the best of friends' and co-authors of all the band's original music (in the years past).. Now, it had all bottomed-out into an absolute nothingness. And as much as both of them tried to pretend otherwise (when they did practice and perform together..), the truth was, it was gone.. Lost in the natural progression of time. That, and the typical adolescent transitions and ever-changing stages of relationships, etc., that people of that age group experience. It was inevitable. Regardless (and again), Nate refused to give it up. He always hoped it would just 'work itself out'.

Even-greater was the problem of Ben, as well (Who was now beginning to totally 'lose it' on all levels.. both personally and, as well, with the band). He had always been hanging on by a thread.. At least, since the alliance of Tim & Nate.. But of late, there was something much greater affecting his life.. And, in so, totally 'spacing him out', when it came to showing-up and actually contributing to the music. So, all and all, Nate was ending up in a 'trio'-type unit, whether he liked it or not. At least, instrument-wise! And with the frustration of Tim only mounting (compounded by the whisperings of Kev, Willie, Buzz.. and yes, even Zack now!), it was all starting to have a real impact on him. Still, he'd wait and see!

One weeknight, coming in from work, Nate found two full-grown men in the flat with Buzz. Having purchased beer for them, he made no complaints... Though, he did think it truly odd that his room-mate would allow characters of this 'questionable-a-nature' up in the first place. They, being real greaser types, looking pretty scruffy and like they'd been on a binge for about a week. Unshaven, stinking and pitifully coarse! But, either way, Nate was beginning to accept that his friend was an uncontrollable 'party maniac'.. And that, in sharing the apartment with him, this was just going to be 'part of the package'.. Whether he agreed with it or not! So, why bother complaining? Still, these 'two' were really evil-looking types.. Super Shady!.. and Nate had an initial bad feeling about the whole thing from the very start!

Sure enough, as the evening progressed, they all ended up quite drunk. Though, Nate (for fear of them) purposely held back on 'too heavy a consumption', the further it went.. Again, somehow sensing trouble was brewing in the air. And he surely didn't want to be 'too inebriated' to deal with it, when it came. And, sure enough, too.. into around the eleventh hour, it arrived.. Rearing its ugly head, as surely expected as it was!

Having spent the last hour in Nate's little room (the four listening to records and talking), Buzz and one of the two slugs left for the back of the house now.. In so, leaving the other sitting on the end of the bed with his back propped-up against the wall. And, Nate perched at his pillow. Through-out all of this time, the latter.. had been getting up, on occasions, to change the discs.. But, in this move to the player now, he.. hearing behind him...

"Y' know, you're kinda cute.. "

He fearfully turning in this.. "Huh?....", like not believing his ears.

Giving Nate a queer look, he slurred out a very suggestive comment regarding a certain part of his anatomy...and, in so, eyed it sinisterly . In this, the boy (Realizing that he was still in a stooped position for the record change) straightened up immediately, and nervously fumbled the 'John Mayall & the Bluesbreakers' LP back into its jacket (Despite that he'd never actually put it on the player yet). There-after, quickly re-seating himself on the pillow (in a blurred and frightened haze).. Looking downward and not at him. Just waitin'.

"..' you hear me, boy?.. "

At last, Nate trying to look at him (Though, not staringly).. "Yeah.." hoping the truer 'fear in his eyes' wasn't showing.. "Yeah, well…" ..but, then, totally losing it for the threatening, perverted-looking and drunken-stare of the recipient… "Listen, I dunno if I told y' this, but my Dad's a cop 'n..." A pitiful lie.. and a desperate one at that!

"Yeah, 'n what of it?…"

"Well…" truly lost for what to say.

Regardless, before Nate could blurt-out another stupid utterance, it happened. Buzz (like an absolute lunatic) came running up to his bedroom door, sticking a long kitchen knife into its outside frame... Screaming and hollering.. and just acting totally crazed! What had happened in the back rooms? Whatever!.. His roommate was absolutely out-of-control now! This.. completely thwarting any and all further advances from the idiot in Nate's room, who immediately (in so) jumped up from the bed for the weird excitement at hand.

The minutes after were a total haze. Buzz was having a convulsive-like fit of some sort.. and in it, he ran out into the apartment's hallway, hollering, banging and crashing everything in sight.

In short order, the lady upstairs (probably thinking a murder or something was going on!) yelled down a threat.. bangingly slammed her door closed, in so .. and proceeded to call the police. 'Was this an act?', Nate wondered. Whatever 'n either way, it was working!.. For soon enough, the cops appeared, taking (in the outcome) Buzz off and away, in a promptly-appearing ambulance for the hospital.

Afterwards, the police returned to question Nate.. But, all of this, having (in the turmoil and process) cleared out the two men.. for their fear of being arrested and dealt with accordingly.

Quickly locking the door with the exit of the officers, he prayed the 'two' wouldn't re-appear with their departure. Fortunately, they didn't. Still, he (alone now) spent the remainder of that night awake and fretting.

At last, in the early morning hours, Buzz was returned.. Sedated and incoherent.. and in so, led directly to his bed.

That next day (after what-was an awful, painful and sleepless day of toil), Nate returned to the flat, totally blurry-eyed. Absolutely exhausted and spinning!.. But despite it all, he.. staying up long enough to hear Buzz out about his 'fits'. These, of which, he had never been warned-of or even aware-of prior. Either way, as scared as the thought of them made him, Nate was grateful for, at least, one of them! But, he also wondered now if they'd ever come back.. The fits and/or the two men, either way! And, even greater.. he wondered just what he'd gotten himself into, by rooming with this wild friend of his!

The parties continued and only got bigger, despite any and all of Nate's objections. Every Friday and Saturday night. Weeknights, too, now. It had become an endless stream of intruders. Yes, the word was out and spreading! Nate, often times, secluding himself in his room. But, with only a curtain for partition, it was nearly impossible to keep people 'at bay' and have his peace. It was all.. really and truly becoming taxing!

Fortunately, mid-Summer, the flat directly across the hall became available again.. (A resident coming and going in a wink.. And, probably with good reason!).. So, with Buzz's negotiations with the landlord; soon enough, two of their friends (Bernie and Bruce) took over their 'original' apartment.. and he and Nate moved into the new one. It being pretty much the exact-opposite lay-out (as Buzz had once noted), only with an extra room in the opposing hallways' rear.. One with a wooden door.. And a lock! Nate immediately (and insistently!) claimed it.

Now, at least, he could keep them out. And, that he surely did, finding solitude weekends (..and whenever!) from his long days and nights at the Pressrooms. The craziness remained; but now he could, at least, escape when he wanted to. And he was content for that.. Practicing his guitar and listening to his records without distraction, most times. But, again.. with Buzz's friends inhabiting their former residence next door, the parties only became twice as big now.. Two flats with the doors more-often-than-not propped open for full-scale madness (Despite the third-floor neighbors!).. And, with the 'Summer of Love' in full swing now, "Strange Days" had truly found them!

The Road to Hell

The Road to Hell is paved with good intentions

Things we thought we'd do, but never did

The I-should-have's and I-could-have's.. that, one day, return

to ne'er forgive

The wishes, much too late to fill

That plague and haunt the mind

Yes, the Road to Hell is paved with..

Good intentions, left behind

The chances that we had.. to give love.. when

our hearts did over-pour

But, we held it all inside.. whatever deeper

Reasons for

Yes, the Road to Hell is paved with good intentions

Turned excuse..

That twine by twine was fastened..

In a self-created noose

Soon after getting settled in, on a mid-week early evening, Nate was quite surprised when he answered the apartment's front door to find his Father and Mother there, waiting in the hall. His Dad had returned from the hospital now and had wanted to visit him. And, as well, to see where he was living 'n all.

Leading them back to his bedroom (after a little 'look around'), they all sat awhile on his bed. Nate feeling somewhat uncomfortable now for their un-announced appearance. He was, of course, glad to see his Dad .. and to know that he was back home, at last (And, in the same, that it was a totally quiet night, considering the becoming pretty-much normal 'mania' that prevailed!).. But, still and somehow, there was just an awkwardness about it all. And he wasn't exactly sure why.

"When I was in the hospital, someone in the Rec Room kept playing the Everly Brothers records that were in there.. It always made me think 'f you, Nate.."

He smirked a smile, then looked down without responding. Nodding some in it. He knew his Father was trying to say he really missed him.. and that he was, likewise, trying to reach out.. But somehow he couldn't respond accordingly. He regretted that, but....

"Y' know, Nate.." His Dad still trying.. "The Blue Angels are comin' soon.. ' think y' might wanna go?.."

"Nah, Dad.. I.. I can't.. Really!.. Workin' a whole lot, these days, 'n..." He knew he probably could've, but.. And also, that he was being un-cooperative and a bit cold.. But he just couldn't seem to help himself. He was just truly burnt-out on going to the air shows, the airport and all'a that now. This just wasn't the time.

"Ok, Nate.. I understand.. You're on y' own now.. 'n well...

Listen, Son.. we didn't mean to barge in on y', like this... but, I..."

"Nah, Dad... It's fine.. I'm glad y' came.."

"Well, we better get goin' though.. " looking at his watch and then at Nate's Mom momentarily... " But, listen.. if y' ever need us f' anything, you..."

"Yeah, I know, Dad.. Thanks.." cutting in.. "Sorry.. I'm just kinda tired tonite..'n.."

"Sure, I understand, Son..." Though Nate, totally not; regarding his own behavior. Glancing up towards his Dad now, he noted in the same, that Willie was coming down the hall in their direction. Buzz must've let him in.

"Hi, Willie.." Nate's parents turning to greet him, as he entered the room. The addressee responding with a kind of wave. "Well, we better get goin'.."

This time, Nate conceding.. "Ok, Ma and Dad.. Thanks f' comin'.." and rising to see them out. Willie flopping on the bed, as they left. And Nate seeing them to the door.

When there, and as they made their ways down the hallway stairs...

"See y', Ma and Dad... Thanks f' comin'...". They turning in their descent to wave. Nate quietly closing the door and waiting at it a moment, in deep thought. Putting his head and brow on it in sadness, he rested a second more. Then, removing it, he scuffed back to his room. Willie was waiting anxiously, knowing there'd be 'things to talk about'. He'd sensed the dark mood. And who, better than he?...

"Hey, Nate-o... How y' doin', man?.." trying to show compassion and concern.

"Ok, I guess..." truly sad. Sitting on the edge of the bed, he soon jumped up to find and put on a record by the New Animals. Somehow now he wanted to hear it. Singling out a special track from it, he scratchingly located it with the needle. In this, Burdon sang..

"For you, my Son, I would do anything.."

Sitting back on the bed, he cupped his forehead in his hands.

"Nate-o..." behind him.. "What's the matter, man?..."

"I dunno, Willie.." breaking down into tears.. "I really don't know.."

"Ah, man.. Nate-o.." moving in closer and putting his hand on his shoulder..." don't cry, man.. please?..."

"I can't help it...." spinning away and falling back across the bed into a semi-fetal-like position.

"C'mon, Nate-o.." Willie, trying to comfort him.

"It's all right, Willie.. I'll be alright... Please, man, just let me be alone.. ok?"

"Sure, man.. I understand.." patting his trembling back and slowly getting up to leave.

As he began through the door, he stopped and looked back. Then, snapping off the light, he wandered down the hall to Buzz's room.

The Big Picture

I've wandered down that country road.. must 've

Been a million times

Smelt the flowers in the air

'n soft fragrance of the pines

Then, ventured up the yonder hill

Where the barn rests right on top

But, every time I reached it..

I had to make my stop

For nothing goes beyond it..

Only paper and the wall

And when I hit it, face to face..

My emotions make a fall

And I remember it's just a painting

That I escape in, here 'n there

'cause, truth is, I'm imprisoned in..

this boredom that I bear

"Sitting by the Window" by Moby Grape was playing on the record player. And Nate sat now doing exactly that, sitting by the window (on the radiator encasement and up beside the sill) listening to it in the background. This, in the first flat's back bedroom.. or better, Willie's 'crash' room. A really odd feeling was covering and controlling him now.. and a very alone and 'weird' feeling it was!.. Like as if he'd been sucked into a place 'high-above and away' from everything somehow, and into this sort of vacuum of his own. He'd never felt like this before in his entire life! There was like a thick smoke ring lingering around his head.. clouding everything!.. And, the even-stranger feeling of a tiny seed being caught in the very back of his throat. One, that he'd actually pictured (in his mind) bouncing its way back there, earlier!.. Like in some kind 'f cartoon! This was.. just.. all.. too weird!

Surrounding him in the further-and-beyond apartment were a number of partying people wandering about; but none near-effecting, nor coming into his deep solitude and silence. Yes, it was a typical Saturday night!.. But somehow now, he felt so 'away' from all of that confusion, lost in this 'strange outer-space' and eerie, ecstatic 'far-off-ness'.

Sporadically, he'd glance down through the glass at the closed car lot below.. And, its dead-stillness.. Then, out-'n-up further beyond it, into the black-and-endless sky. There-after, returning and scanning back down to the blurry-lit avenue.. And, at last, back into the room surrounding him. Willie wasn't there now.. Somewhere else on the floor, he assumed.

Back out the window he returned again, considering in this 'enhanced state' of his.. "Where am I?.. " And, this.. (pertaining-to and meaning..) in regards to.. 'the big scheme of things'. Yes, the vast Universe and his very tiny place in it! He felt so 'small' now.. and like some fascinated toddler.. Lost in the thick-and-blinded 'emptiness' of innocent ignorance!.. Somehow, totally removed from all of his normal logic and reality now.. Yet, still.. oddly and reasonably comfortable, despite. And at perfect ease. And, likewise.. just so distant from (..and 'above') the behind-him confusion and noise going on, all about.

"Nate-o.. You ok?.."

Turning through the 'smear' now, he saw Willie entering and nearing. Trying to collect and focus himself, he responded softly...

"Yeah.. I guess... Just thinkin'.."

"..'bout what, man?...." Willie sitting on the floor.. a bit away, but close-enough for conversation.

"I dunno... Just like.. well, how'd we get here?.. Y' know, in this life 'n all?.."

"Man, Nate-o.. Why y' thinkin' 'f stuff like that?.. Geez, no one can fig're that out!.. You oughta know that, by now!.." What a strange reversal of roles, this seemed!

"Yeah... But we all do though.. sometimes.. right?"

"Sure, man.. but it's impossible to ever really fig're it out.. so?.." Willie, smiling.

"I know.." turning back out the window.. "Still.. I was just thinkin' 'bout it, y' know.."

"Sure, I understand.. " Then Willie re-iterating.. " You ok, though?.."

"Yeah, I'm fine enough .. " Not looking back.. Just further contemplating.

Willie returning to his truer self now... "Y' know, if y' really want t' know, I guess I could tell y'.. Y' know, 'least what comes after all'a this, anyways.. Yeah, y' know.. Life!.... 'n all!.. 'least, well.. that much I could!...

Y' see, I was talkin' with my Mom, this week.. Well, I didn't tell y', 'cause I know it.. " pausing briefly.. " Well, y' know, I realize it sounds kinda strange 'n all.. but…"

All of this bringing Nate's focus back into the room; and then further, into his friend's half-sad/half-happy, smiling face…

At last, he verbalizing, whisper-like.. "Y' did what?.. Y' mean like.. y' had a dream, that y'..."

"No, Nate, it wadn't no dream.. Not at all.." almost whispered too, but accentuated with a slight facial twist of sincerity.. "I really talked with her!"

Nate unsure of what to think.. "Well, what did y' talk with her 'bout then?.."

"Heaven.. Y' know, what it's like 'n all.." he, totally sincere and confident-appearing.

"Really?.." Nate trying to detect facetiousness.. But, being so 'spaced' now himself, becoming anxious and caught-up in the 'belief of it', as well.. " Can y' tell me?.."

"Yeah, 'f course.. " Willie's face melting into a glowing-like aura of wisdom.. "Well, f' one thing, it's super beautiful, Nate-o!.. yeah, I mean SUPER BEAUTIFUL!..

See, God made this world.. and He put some of Heaven's beauty here.. Y' know, into our world.. But, only a real little!… Y' know, just enough so's we can get used to it slow-like!… Otherwise, we wouldn't be able to handle it!…" getting so lost in his own conversation, he unthinkingly moved himself up and in closer to the window now, and to an even-nearer seating… "See, Heaven ain't like clouds and castles 'n stuff like that.. No, it's just like here,

Nate-o!.. Only, our minds are happier and at-peace… 'cause, there.. Well, all our sorrows and fears 'n stuff like that are gone.. So, it's almost sort 'f like.. the same place.. but, different!.. Y' know, in a way!"

Nate was becoming a bit more un-nerved now, for the almost-spooky, 'seeming-double-talk' of it all.. That, and Willie's increasing intensity.. But, he held tight, to hear it all out… nodding his head, to clarify his understanding (Though, not exactly sure that he did get it).

"Y' know, someday, Nate-o… a real long time from now, you 'n me are going t' be talking just like this.. Only, we'll be there!.. Yeah, it'll just be a different 'moment'.. Y' know, 'in time'!… Everything's just 'one moment', Nate.. So, it'll be exactly the same!.. Only, y' know, it'll be THERE!.. in Heaven!"

Nate didn't say anything, just gulped and smilingly nodded agreement into Willie's intense face. Then, the latter concluding…

"..'n y' know, what, Nate-o?.. We'll be even greater friends then!.."

Nate (still speechless), at last, gulped and nodded his head again. Willie, seeming content now, lifted himself up and began out.. "I'm gonna go check things out.. Catch y' later.. 'k?"

"Yeah, sure.. ok…" Nate watching him leave.. Then, turning back out the window for a immeasurable time to think about all of this. In a way, it did make perfect sense!

At last (after 'however long?' ..he wasn't sure !), he got up (in this lingering trance) and wandered through the 'confusion' back to his room in the other flat. People were talking to him en-route, but he not hearing them clearly.. Nor, responding in any way. Just continuing. Totally spaced-out and numb!

Locking the door behind himself, he flopped on the bed.. and laid there in the 'rushing thoughts' and dark haze, until he slept. Or, at least, he thought that he had, the following morning. He really didn't know!

It was early Sunday morning .. and, in Buzz's car, they drove along through the nearest main square. "Ode to Billy Joe" was playing on the car radio and Nate listened to it through the on-going talk of Willie, Kev and Buzz.. Focussing in on it and noting it's stark simplicity. Acoustic guitar, bass and these strange-sounding strings. He really liked it. The production was so pure and real! And the song, something he'd wished he'd written himself. It was just so.. 'mesmerizing'!

Still sort of 'spaced' from the previous night, he remained a good bit disconnected.. Introspective.. and, in the same, removed from all the activity and conversation about him. Going for breakfast, though he hardly felt hungry. Still, this was an event of camaraderie.. Something they'd do together, here and there.. And today was no different. So, he'd complied, easily enough.

Willie, at last, turned from the front seat…

"Nate-o.. y' gonna talk t' Katie f' me?.."

"..'bout what?.." glancing up and over.

"Y' know, man… 'bout her going out with me 'n all?.."

"Willie.. I've told y' before.. it'd be no use f' me t' do that!.. I'm her brother, man.. She hates me!.. I'm the last person in the world she'd ever listen to!… You need t' ask someone like .. like Puddin'.." (One of his Sister's oldest friends, who she might actually take some advice from!) "..Yeah, he might be able to convince her!.."

Willie still looked at him.. but, it was obvious he was inwardly contemplating it all... Then, very noticeably and mentally agreeing with its logic, sort of nodded in so.. There-after, turning back forward to finally give it up. It's funny how things, one day, finally dawn on us and, at last, settle in.. Even though we've heard them hundreds (if not thousands) of times before! Eventually, they stick! And somehow, in that moment, Nate just knew he'd never ask him to do that again.

Nate was pensively cleaning nixes at the stone, when 'Brennan' appeared out of the office; interrupting Roger, to let him know that there was a shortage today of help on the Bindery's stapler. Over-hearing it, the boy grimaced, knowing fully well what that meant.. He would be enlisted! Damn, he hated it when that happened! Why always him! Well, on second thought, yeah.. he knew!.. Still, he just loathed the thought of having to be up there again!

So, the remainder of his day would be that.. worse bored, frustrated.. and having to listen to all of the prating going on about him. The only good thing on the horizon, being a lunch-break with Willie; who planned to drop by, after his initial enlistment-board physical that morning. Nate sat now on the stapler's line, flipping-up pre-creased sheets (..and fuming!); remembering (in the same) his own military 'probing' and the 'discomforting episode' there himself, just prior.

When his temporary escape (..at last!) came, Willie was just entering down Carleton (in the direction of the shop) with Nate's simultaneous release. As they, soon enough, converged…

"Hey, Willie Boy, how'd it go?…"

The addressed, giving a gloomy look…

"I dunno, Nate-o.. Not s' good, I'm thinkin'!.."

"Well.. don't go jumpin' t' conclusions.. " At this, Willie pivoted, and they made back for Main. Both, not speaking now. Still in his sulk. Reaching the cornering barroom, they made a direct left; and in this, Nate facetiously looked over at him and offered…

"Here… Have a piece of Blackjack… " lifting the pack of gum in his direction.. "This oughta pick up your spirits!.." smirking snidely in it.. " Hey, it always brightens MY day!.."

Willie, lightening up for the silliness of it… and in so, nudging his friend's shoulder away. Nate, initially losing his balance for the sudden-and-unexpected impact. This, until recovering quickly-enough to catch his friend off-guard with a darting comeback.. There-in, grabbing his neck in a wrestling-like headlock. But this, only jokingly and with a half-strength. And, for that.. Willie not responding negatively.. Instead, surrendering without a fight… "Ok, ok.."

Nate (in so..) lightened up on his squeeze, as they continued to walk along together.. There-after, leaving his arm up and around him; and gradually letting it fall to his shoulders. This, until they, at last, reached the Diner's stairs, about a half block away.

As they entered inside the narrow eatery…

"Man, Willie.. you must'a RESERVED a seat.. " as they slid into the closest booth, right by the door.. "Every other time I been here, it's always packed!.. That's why I usually go t' the Sandwich shop!.. You got connections here 'r sumethin'?.."

Willie just smiled.. Then, he further offered..

"Well, me.. I want a real meal t'day!.. Startin' t' get a little beer belly.. 'n that's the best way y' can get rid 'f it!.. Y' know, eatin' right 'n all!"

"Really?.. I didn't know that… " Nate responding (Though thinking, all the while.. 'if anyone needn't be worryin' about gettin' fat, it was Willie!')

After the waitress took their orders and began away, Willie got intimately quieter, moving in across the table some…

"Nate-o.. I got sumethin' t' tell y' .. 'n I hope y' won't get upset with me.. but…"

"Shoot, man.. What is it?.." Nate focussing now.. "What's on y' mind?"

"Well, remember awhile back, when you recommended me talkin' t' Puddin'.. y' know, 'bout Katie 'n all?..."

"Yeah.."

"Well, I took your advice.. 'n, y' know what?.. " Trying to act casual now, but obviously getting a bit nervous.. " Well, Katie said she would!.. Y' know.. go out on some dates with me.. So..." a pause, expecting the worst.

"Yeah.. So?..." Nate confused.

"Well.. I was thinkin' like y' might be upset with me.. Y' know, like y' always say.. y' know, 'bout, if I was ever t' become your Brother-in-Law.. 'n.."

"Willie, man.. " Nate, cutting in.. realizing that he'd been taking him too- serious.. "Why.. if that ever happens.. Hey, man.. I'd be.. y' know, just real happy!.. Yeah, I'd be SUPER proud t' have you as m'.. " pausing.. "Heck, man.. why you're already my Best Bro, as is!... right?.. So...." Then, remembering his initial point...

" Y' mean t' tell me, that you really thought I was going to be... mad.. 'r sumethin'?.. Hey, I was only kiddin' with y', man.. Just kiddin'!...

Yeah, man, I'd just really think that was great!.. I've always hoped you'd end-up bein' my Brother-in-Law!.. Really!.."

"Wow, Nate-o.. Really?.. That's a relief!.." Willie smiling now.. " Well, y' know, it's kind 'f early now t' be talkin' 'bout marriage 'n all.. But, anyways, our last date.." the truth spilling out now.. " I took her to the Capitol t' see 'The Good, The Bad, and The Ugly'.. Y' know, with Clint Eastwood 'n all?.. Yeah, they were showin' it again, 'n she said she wanted t' see it.. so.."

"Cool... " Nate (smiling in response).. all the while, diggin' through his britches for some change. At last, locating a dime, he slid over closer now and began flipping through the booth's jukebox selector. Finding a title he liked, he put in the coin and punched the numbers. While it was searching-out the title...

"What'cha want to hear, Willie Boy?.. There's another play.. You pick it.. " moving back and away from the machine.. Allowing room for his friend's head to move-in and search. While he was engrossed in it, came…

"She would never say.. where she came from..

Yesterday don't matter, if it's gone.. "

The old farmhouse came into view, per usual.. as the cars made their way up the hillside's crest. It, being their landmark that Stiles Pond Road was nearing. Nate sat on the passenger side of Buzz's 'machine' with its owner at the wheel.. and Kev and Zack, back-seated. Willie would've been with them too.. But, this time he'd weasled himself into the vehicle ahead, carrying Katie. All the 'apartment' and 'avenue-hang-out' gang were making a 'day of it', with a string of cars following behind one another now. Some, being.. 'friends of friends', that Nate hardly knew, if at all!.. But, most.. he'd, at least, met a time or two. Yes, it was Sunday, early afternoon.. with a picnic and swim planned.. Yeah, a 'big time' was in the makin'!

"… it's comin' up, Buzz… " offered Kev (the backseat driver!).

"Yeah, I know.. Chill out, man.. 'k?..'' returned the driver.

"Just try'na be helpful.." Under the breath and left un-answered.

At last, swinging into the gravel road, they hurriedly made for the boat rental and beach area; looking like some 'dying-of-thirst'-caravan in pursuit of a near-at-hand-oasis. Pulling into the parking lot and shutting off their engines; each car-full suddenly burst forth and out, looking like a pack of rats jumping from a burnin' barn! It was sheer pandemonium!

All of the girls aboard began immediately for the picnic tables (under the trees, by the waterline); while the boys instead just gathered about the cars, stretching their legs and talking. One of the latter (A fellow that Nate had never seen prior) turned out to be a soldier 'home on leave' from Vietnam.. An MP (named Bob), it turned out.. and a seemingly 'nice enough' guy, as well.. with a 'story to tell'.. And, (soon enough) all were gathered, intent and listening. It was a pretty graphic account of a battle he'd been in.. And, at the conclusion of it, to prove his validity (as he wasn't in uniform, etc.), he motioned all to his car's trunk, opening it up to show (-off!) his wears.

Reaching in and removing a blackjack.. Then, a pair of handcuffs.. he passed them around, so the boys could get a personal, up-close look and feel. Everyone was really getting off on it.. So, in this, Bob took out a rifle.. But, not offering that around. All getting the message, that he didn't plan to, either.

Then, one of the boys (Hal) pointedly noted (in the trunk) a bunch of uniforms, hats, and other military garb...

"Hey, Bob.. Can we?.." (meaning 'try them on?')

"Sure, man.. here.. " reaching in again, and handing a few of them out to him and the others, near at-hand... "Go f' it, guys!.."

So, the addressee.. along with Zack and Willie (closest in line).. got the 'first dibs' on the 'dress up'.. While, Stephen (Who forever saw 'his moment'!) offered...

"Hey, let me get m' camera!.." running off, back towards the car that he, Ben and Tim had arrived in. Billy Donald (a very early childhood neighbor and playmate of Nate's) had 're-appeared' this day, like out of the 'nowhere past' .. and come along with the previous, in the same vehicle, as well.. And, it was an odd and startling discovery to see him there now.. after all of the years!

By the time Stephen returned for his shots, the 'first dibbers' were fully arrayed. So, coaxing them over to a nearby shed, he made his first click..

There-after, Tim, Billy and Ben fought for their turns.. But, the latter, losing out to 'The Ham' (Zack!), who refused to cooperate and 'give it up'.. weaseling himself into the second photo shoot, as well!

The novelty had worn thin, by now.. and everyone started drifting off. This, too.. because of the pond (.. having been 'the backdrop' for the final shot..).. And, in seeing it again, all were reminded of 'why they'd come'.. and began off to get 'suited' for a swim. And, this (the latter).. feeling somehow 'odd' now for the Stiles'- 'late-night-ers', who'd grown more-accustomed to just 'dippin'..'! But, hey.. what, with the daylight, girls 'n crowd all about.. There wasn't much choice, in the matter!

As dusk began to set in (after the long day).. and 'the party', pretty-nearly 'pooped-out' now.. everyone decided to take a final swim. Willie had spent most of his day trailing Katie about; but with her refusal to go in 'one more time' (As well as all of the other girls, who were put-off by the heavily-increasing darkness), Nate had swayed him away to join the gang and come along. Y' know.. It was one of those 'manly' things y' do.. to prove your 'fearlessness' to the ladies! A good few beers hadn't help the situation either!

So, off they all tramped down to the shore.. Sharin' a toke or two, as they went. Touching toe, it was colder than they'd expected. But, not to falter (in the eyes of the world!.. Let alone, each-other!), they all (finally!) made their way in.. heading, in so, for the raft, a good bit out.

Reaching it, they all made upward for the planked (..'n drier!..) surface in speedy climbs. The ladder rattled in repeated use. This, until all were 'shook-off ' and seated, facing outward in the all-fours. Off-like, they began talking to their near-at-hands. Nate turning to Kev, on his right…gasped out..

".. 's cold, huh?.. " Then, further teeth-rattling and shivering-out.. " Geeeeeez!.. "

"Yeah.. Wadn't s' bad, this afternoon.. But, man.. changed pretty quick.. Huh?.." responded Kev.

".. y' ain't kiddin', man!.. " Nate agreeing… "Brrrrr…"

A silence fell on their quarter of the raft. Mumbling conversations from the others could be heard, behind them.. But, faint. The night was falling quick, and a full-moon was looking down on them.

Nate glanced over to his left, seeing Buzz seated and slightly panting in recovery. Then, having a creeping-in, unsettling thought and odd feeling (due to the smoke!), he swung back around… scanning the other three sides. He didn't see Willie's back with any of those lined and seated. He knew, fully well, that he'd been with them, swimming out!?.. A sudden, overwhelming and dreadful terror hit him, just as he returned-face to his side of the square. Yes, something 'internal' told him (in a flash, and in that splitting-moment) that 'this was going to happen'!.. Yes.. like, it had been 'meant to be'.. or 'predestined'.. that Willie would drown there! In a natural reflex, he instantly jarred his face to the left, trying to cast it off. But, the paranoid thought wouldn't leave him! He started to tremble for it and the surrounding-him cold. Immediately and without-any-further-ado, he spit out..

"Hey, where's Willie?.. "

Kev looked at him.. "I dunno?.. Was he with us?.."

"Yeah, man.. Don't y' remember?.. he was!.."

Then, swinging to Buzz.. "Where's Willie?.. Y' seen him?.."

"Nah, Eric.. don't think he was with us.."

"Yeah, he was!.. I know, f' sure!.. He was right beside me, when we started out?.." with this, Nate swung a look back over his shoulders..

"Hey, anybody seen Willie?.. "

All talking stopped. Every face showed blank and suddenly tinged with fear.

"Where's WILLIE?!.." Nate (to himself) pivottingly hopping up.. soon to be followed by everyone else. Afoot, all began looking about themselves, in a quickly mounting confusion… And then (in their frantic despairing), all about-and-out towards the chilling-and-black-now waves surrounding them.

"Willie!… WILLIE!.. " Nate began yelling out over the rippling, cold water.. Then, turning back to the others on the swaying terrible-now raft.. "Oh, man… I think he's…" stopping short, as not to even voice the thought.. He felt an overwhelming urge to break down and start crying.. But, what good would that do? Re-swinging back out, in a dart, he yelled again…

"WILLIE!… WILLIE, CAN Y' HEAR ME?.. C' MON, MAN!.. WILLIE?.."

Nothing came back. It seemed like forever.

Then..

"Yeah?.." came a soft 'matter-of-fact'-like gasp, just below him.. on his side of the raft. Followed by… "Yeah, I can hear y' .. What's up?.."

Nate looked down.. seeing Willie holding firm to one of the underlying and bobbing barrels, supporting them below.

Willie cracked a smile and softly gasped-out a slight laugh (As to show, it had only been a joke.. 'n that he'd been there, all along).. But, seeing his friend break down now into tears.. and witnessing (face to face) the pain and anguished it had caused him, he knew (within seconds) it had been a very unfair one. He hadn't meant it to be!.. But, regardless, it was all too obvious, in the outcome.. and he started looking regretful, in the same. Wishing he hadn't done it!

Angered and embarrassed for his 'show of emotion'.. and his start-of-tears (in front of the other guys!).. And, as well, for having been 'tricked', in the first place, Nate tangled-out..

"Willie.. That wadn't funny, man.. Wadn't funny at all!.. Y' really freaked me out!.. " wiping his eyes (quick-like) and turning away (to try 'n recollect himself)..

"Nate-o.." pleading-like.. "Man, I was just.. just…"

Before he could finish, Nate dove in and swam off for the shore.

Katie met him, just as he came aground..

"Nate.. I heard you calling Willie out there.. 's he ok?.."

"Yeah, he's ALIVE 'N WELL!.." shot her brother (in a voice she immediately recognized as being his 'extremely angry'- one!), as he stomped-off 'n away. Knowing not to pursue it any further, she slowly walked back towards the group, wondering what had transpired.. sporadically watching him tramp off, as she went.

Being trapped there at the pond (..until all would come ashore), Nate began for Buzz's car to waited them out. He didn't want to see Willie, who he felt certain would be returning home, via the car that he came in... So, knowing that was somewhat of a relief! Maybe he could dodge him, for a while.. 'Least, 'til he could calm down and get himself together some.

Fortunately, Buzz's doors were unlocked. He figured they'd be. So, he got into his original seating. About fifteen minutes passed, when (all of a sudden) he noted (across the lot) what-looked-like Willie's silhouetted-image coming. In this, he put his head down (into his right hand, with his elbow supporting it on the door's handle), hoping he wouldn't notice him. Maybe he was en-route to another car?

At last, hearing the driver's-side door open (and glancing over, in so..), he saw Willie slide in. He turned away, out his window.

"Nate-o.. Listen.. " A slight 'breathing-in' pause.. " I'm sorry, man.. I really am!.. I.. I didn't mean to do that!.. It was real stupid of me.. I had no idea it'd turn out like that... I just.. " It was sincere and honest. And from the heart.

Still refusing to look at him, (before he could finish..) Nate asked, through his cupping-his-mouth-loosely, lowered-now hand..

"Did the others know?.."

"No.. they didn't.. It freaked everybody out.. not just you.. 'k?.. " Willie sounding truly ashamed of himself.. "Really, Nate-o.. I'm awful sorry!.. Will y' please forgive me?.."

A silence.

At last..

"Yeah.. 'f course.. Y' know I will.." Nate surrendering.. and, in this, glancing quickly over at him, then back away..

A pause. Then...

"Man, Willie.. Y' know, sumethin' told me, back there... in that moment.. that you had..." he stopped.. refusing, again, to speak it aloud.

"Well, I didn't... So.. " Willie, sensing what he was going to say...

"No, but.. Well, there's sumethin' more.. y' don't understand.." Nate turning to him now, despite his still-smeared eyes and face.. trying to make a further point...

"Y' just don't.. No, Y' don't know what I.. "

"Nate-o.. I'm ok.. Alrite?.. " Willie (Not hearing!.. Or, maybe better, not wanting to!).. "You can see me, right?.. " pausing.. " Hey, I'm ok!.. "

"Yeah.." giving it up.. knowing he'd be unable to explain what he'd experienced and felt, either way.

"Still my pal?.. " Willie, offering his hand.

"…'course.." Nate shaking it briefly and letting go. Turning away out the front window, he added.. "… always.. " (Like to himself, but shared) . Then, returning his attention back inward.

"Me, too.. " added Willie with a smile " ..'n I promise.. I'll never, ever do that to y' again.. 'k?.. Yeah, 'n that's a head-t'-head promise!.."

"Good.." Nate offered (in a half-toned- 'sigh of relief'.. with a 'tad' of humor intended..), as he momentarily returned back out his window.

"Well, Nate-o.." Getting a bit antsy now.. " I gotta get back.. Y' know, t' Katie 'n all.. I don't want t' miss m' ride .. Y' know, goin' back with her 'n all .. Y' understand ..Right?.. "

"Yeah, sure.. I know…" looking over, smirking facetiously.. "Go ahead on.."

"Ok.. Thanks, Nate-o.." Willie, tangling with the door.

"Sure thing…"

When he was gone, that odd feeling that Nate had had (on the raft) returned.. and he fought with it, inwardly. It, at last, bumming him out, so bad.. that, in mental retreat, he thought to get out of the car.. For some air or whatever…

But, just as he reached for the door-handle and started, Buzz, Kev and Zack all began piling in. The 'sudden, entering voices' and 'the re-focussing of his attention' made the inner 'negativity' disperse quickly-enough for him to stay put. So, that he did. And soon enough, it had totally vanished from his mind.. Gone, like all of the many other 'crazy and fearful thoughts that we have' from time to time.. Yeah, just a total bunch of nonsense!.. And a 'bummer' that he'd refuse to entertain, ever again!

I'm Just Here from Then 'til When

I'm Just Here from Then 'til When

I go, as I have come

No death's ever stopped the world

Not but a single one

Just a memory remains

Of even yesterday

'cause, it died in the morning, when

the darkness faded 'way

Life has no greater purpose than

To reach the final end

To go home to our Father

And be happy once again

'cause, nothin' here's forever

it's a temporary state

things that make us happy, we

appreciate too late

So, I'm just here from then 'til when

Whenever that might be

The deadline that the Lord has des-

ignated just for me

Then, all my steps will disappear

Like footprints in the sand

'cause, I'm just here.. from then 'til when

I sink back in the land

One rainy, mid-Summer's Eve, Willie sat Indian-style on the lower end of Nate's bed; while the latter sat playing his guitar on the upper. During one of the musical pauses, Willie whisperingly blurted out…

"No one's ever going to remember me.. Y' know, like you, Nate… Y' going to be real famous, one day.."

"What'a y' mean, Willie?.. " stopping and turning in his direction.. "Hey, y' going to be a big-time poet, someday, too!.. Y' know that!.."

He looking down, sadly. At last…

"I dunno, Nate-o… Sumethin' tells me not.."

"C' mon, man.. y' know y' will!.."

Looking up, still distraught.. "I don't think so, man.. Sumethin' tells me I ain't gonna…"

"Willie.. " cutting in.. "You're ridiculous sometimes.. Y' just feelin' sorry for.." stopping short of 'yourself', not to offend.

"No, I'm serious, Nate.. I'm just gonna come 'n go, man!.. Y' know, like trillions 'n trillions of other people do!.. But, you… well…"

"Willie.. don't be silly, man.. Y' just… Well…"

"Nate-o.. if anything ever happens.. " getting melancholy and darker than prior.. "Will you remember me?.."

".. 'f course, man!… Y' know that!.. I'll never forget you.. Yeah, Y' know that!.. 'n just why y' sayin' stuff like that, anyways?.. "

On this, Willie started to tear-up. Then, in the same, he turned aside and coiled down into a huddle, upon the lower bed.

Impulsively, Nate looked out of his door, to verify that no one was about and in the hall to witness it (embarrassed for his friend's sake.. and, too, for what he himself wanted to do, but thought someone else might mis-interpret).

Feeling it more important now that he act, he slid his guitar aside and moved in.. putting his hand on his shoulder, squeezing it lightly and trying to console him…

"Willie.. Listen, man .. nuthin' bad's gonna happen…" Thunder and lightning broke the night's silence outside, distracting and un-nerving him for a second. Turning back..

"But, hey.. even if it ever does.. y' can count on me.. 'n just know, I'll do everything I can to let the world know just how great a poet y' were!.. ok?.. But, really… nuthin's gonna happen.. So…"

Willie was too upset now to respond.. Still whimpering on to himself.

"It's gonna be alright… Really, man!... C' mon, now.. you're just makin' y' self sick .. 'n there's really n' need for that.. S', c'mon… 'k?.."

He still remained silent.. At last, just seeming to drift off to sleep in his huddle. And Nate, in this, finally leaving him there on the far-end of the bed for the remainder of the night.

In the morning, he awoke to find him gone. Whatever had happened to him was a mystery. But, one of no great concern... For he felt pretty sure that, middle of the night, Willie had just awakened and taken off for his own bed. Yeah, he'd be all right.

Angels in the Dirt

As the Angels play in dirt

Soiling their robes of white

The darkness creeps through deep

Devouring the light

As inevitable as Sin..

Birth, the moth-like breath

Seeks and flies, compulsive..

Directly into Death!

The rug on the flat's parlor floor was worn thin, with a good bit of dust and dirt imbedded. Willie sat on it now, rolling another smoke and licking its glue-edging, anxiously. Nate (sitting directly opposite of him) watched; noting (in so) the huge, old heater propped there behind his friend with its crusted-filled vents. Thinking, in this.. 'come late Fall, what an awful filthy blow-out that's gonna create!'. That, and just how pitiful and monstrous a clunker it was, t' begin with! Either way, it served well enough now for a decent 'jump-up' seat!.. 'Least, that had been its sole purpose, to date! To tell the truth, he'd never really paid it much mind, until now.   Weird!

At last, after their second smoke…

"Wow, Nate-o.. Am I hungry!.. You?.."

"Yeah.. starved, man!.."

"What'd y' say we hit the Sub shop?.."

"Yeah!.. Ok!.. Sounds good, man!.." Nate, hopping up in this.. But, in doing.. too quick for his own good.. "Yo-o-o-w, man.. Whew-eeee.. Am I Dizzy!..", literally spinning and swaying afoot. Willie.. raising himself, as well.. moved in to assist him. But, he, ultimately.. none the sturdier!

When, at last, both seemed reasonably stable.. "Man, that just caught me totally off-guard.. Wasn't expectin' that at all! " Nate breathing somewhat freer now. But, in this, Willie finding an 'odd humor' in it.. and bursting-out into uncontrollable laughter. Nate, instantly following suit.. Into total hilarity! And, then.. sheer hysteria! This, for what seemed the longest time! The two.. inwardly-tangling to regain their sense of composure throughout.

Then (like two sleep-walkers on auto-pilot), they awkwardly began out into the hallway and started down to the street. With their staggered exit (out and onto the sidewalk), the sudden burst of sunlight and 'open-air of the day' seemed to instantly clear their heads. And likewise, seemed to bring back 'some sort of sense of clarity'. Between that, and the intuitive knowledge and realization that 'the world could see them now', they forced themselves into a 'upright' semblance.. At least, enough to behave somewhat-accordingly.

Then.. like children lost in play, they ran out unthinkingly between two cars that were parked together on their side of the street.   In this, Willie grabbing the back of Nate's shirt and pulling him to a sudden stop, as an MTA bus shot by. It, nearly swiping him, in its unconcerned and continuing flight.

"Man, Nate-o… Y' gotta FOCUS, brother!.." still gripping and holding his collar.

"Hey, Willie Boy.. I saw it!.. " light-hearted-like, with a glazed-smile.. "Man, I was just gonna grab hold 'f the back 'f it and ride!.. That's all!.. Y' know, man.. Flyin'-like!.. Yeah, just like in them cartoons!.." trying to share his split-second's-prior imagined-visualization.. But, with Willie's frowning grimace, trying further.. "Y' know, like a flag.. on the back?.."

"Nate-o… That's crazy!.. Man, you gotta chill-out some!.. Y' gonna get y' self killed!.. C' mon.." letting go of his shirt, and instead putting and securing his arm around his shoulder, leading-like. Then, slowly away, they more-cautiously crossed.

Reaching the opposing curb, Willie finally gave up his hold on him.. and they began leftward, in the direction of the next intersection. There, on the corner, the 'Take-out' sat. Between numerous distractions and their resulting delays, they (at last!) entered.

Relieved now, for their arrival and the safe-haven-like 'containment' of the shop, they worked their way to the counter. Putting in their order, Nate then wandered-off to secure himself a drink from the waist-high, soda cooler. Willie.. seeing him in his search through it, called out..

"Nate.. Grab me a Coke.. 'k?.."

"Yeah.. Sure.. " Nate, momentarily surfacing up and out of its lid.. Then, resuming back down in, for the near-empty-now findings. But, somehow (in all of this) becoming totally 'lost in it'! This.. until Willie tapped on his back, snapping him to..

"Nate-o?… Whatcha doin', man?.. " whispered-like.

He, slowly appearing… Then, with the utmost earnest of looks…

"I got lost, Willie!.." This, causing another 'convulsive-like' outburst of laughter! Only difference now (from when 'in the apartment'), it.. being 'less loud' (for their location)! The two.. (pretty-nearly splitting-their-sides for the ridiculousness of it all!) fought desperately now to contain themselves! But, it was no use! They just couldn't stop! This, until..

"Hey, guys.. What's goin' on over there?.. Y' want these subs 'r WHAT?.. "   The sandwich man obviously not finding any humor in their 'whatever' nonsense!

"Yeah… yeah.. "   Nate and Willie, calling back earnest-like.. finally coming to their senses and beginning back.

After paying and starting out, they noted (in their door-closing departure) that the countered guy was still 'eye-ing them up'. Sensing something wasn't right. Outside..

"Y' don't think he'll call the Cops, d' y', Nate?.."

"Nah!.."   He, suddenly seeming to be the one 'more in control' now.. "Don't worry 'bout it, Willie Boy!.. He's just freaked, man.. That's all!.. C' mon.." squeezing tighter the brown-bag's top and picking up speed. Willie, in the same, following suit.

After scraping the Lino slugs and placing them on the stone, Nate moved to the storage shelves, to collect a chase. Then, placing it down on the work bench, he bent for the furniture rack, grabbing an estimated few of the metal and wood blocks from the shelf. There-after.. cam quions and the quion key.

Organizing the set-up, he grabbed the planer block, flattening all.. and then, tightened it into the lock-up. Hauling it over to the Platen, he, at last, clamped it in and put an additional slab of ink on the rollers. But, this was all automatic and mechanical. Not thought out. For he was lost now in a deeper thought. Of a girl. One, that kept 'appearing' at the apartment every weekend to pester him for entry into his room. And this, not for anything greater than conversation.. That, of which, he was in no great need of.. preferring to be alone and with his guitar only. But, her persistence and sad-looking eyes always seemed to prevail; gaining her entry, when none others would've ever made it passed the locked door. But, she was never 'interrupting' there-after, so Nate let her have her way and sit on his bed listening.

Despite the innocence of it all, there was something deeper going on here though; and Nate was not so naïve as to miss it. There was no doubt, that she was interested in him. And he, not reciprocating, in the least. Still, he was intrigued by her.. and her gentle quietness and bashful-like approach; so he always gave in. And now, in his toil, she played on his mind. Somehow or other, she had become an ongoing daydream of his, of late. And Lana.. Well, the rumors were starting to have a much deeper affect on him now. Yes, of-late, it wasn't only coming from Willie, but too many other sources. Too many to not be true! Not that he ever doubted his friend.. Quite the opposite!.. But, now, the 'spot'-ings (and resulting-gossip) were 'making-way' back to Nate's ears with increasing frequency. Obviously, the situation was escalating. But, then.. they weren't married!   Going steady.. Yes.. and that meant something! Either way, there was no spiritual or religious commitment between them! Yet and regardless, he had grown super tired of the 'word' that was always working its way back to him. And, this new girl… Well, she just seemed so much more sincere and devoted. At least, to 'showing up constantly', for one!   This, of which, Lana hardly ever did. And, Lord knows why, too?.. Where was she, all the time?

So, Nate didn't feel all so guilty in letting her in. Besides, at this point, it was quite innocent. Just friends! So, why not?

Regardless, it all seemed to be playing on his mind a lot, these days.. and momentarily, it was no different.

"Nate.." Roger, over his shoulder, and catching him off-guard a bit.. "How's it goin'?.."

"Oh, yeah.. fine, Roj…" jolted out of his introspect.. "Yeah, I .. I was just about t' bring a proof into Brennan.."

"That's great!.. Y' comin' over to th' North End with me tonight?…"

"Yeah, I guess.. I mean, If y' need me.."

"I really do, Nate…" Roger, sounding desperate.. "got a pressin' job I need t' finish over there by t'nite.. 'n well, if y' don't, I'm truly gonna be up the creek.."

"Sure… " Nate sensing his sincerity.. " Yeah, I'll go.. Sure thing!.."

"Thanks.. I really appreciate it!"

"Yeah, ok.. that'll be fine" and back into his work.

Willie sat on the parlor rug now, looking up at all of the circled-about and above-him (standing and seated..) party-ers, relaying a story to those listening…

"Well, me 'n Kev 'n Wally went over t' the cleaners across the street yesterday.. 'n we met this woman named Vera.. " focussing in now on Nate, who was squeezed into the filled-up couch.. "Y' remember her, Nate-o?.."

"Yeah, well.. Prob'ly.. I mean, 'least if it's the same one I'm thinkin' 'bout.. Ain't seen her in ages though!.. She used t' work at a dry cleaners, down near my Grandparent's apartment-house… Geez, man.. that was years ago!.. " he, truly caught off-guard and curious now. "Well, what about her, man?.."

"Well, she said she remembered you from when y' was just a real little kid. She said y' used to serenade her, out in front of her shop, with this little guitar back then.. That true?.. 'n she also said she knew y' Grandma real well too"

"Yeah, well, I gotta be honest.. I really don't remember that!.. But, I dunno?.. Maybe I did.. Nah, I just really don't remember ev'rything, back that far!.. 'least, not doin' that, anyways.." though he was inwardly tickled by the thought of her (and Willie..) saying that, either way. It somehow brought a validity to his claims of being involved in music from a real young age (at least, to all those at hand, now!).. But, truth being, he really didn't recall the incident. Fact of the business was, he was 'pretty small' back when he lived at his Grandparents'.. with only very-scant memories (..if any!) of those times! Still, Willie's recounting of this to everyone now was giving him a sort-of 'kick'.. For true or no, who cared!.. Sure sounded good enough, either way!

"I asked her about y' Grandma, too.. " Willie continuing.. "..'n she said that she was just.. such a real sweet lady 'n all.." This, bringing a sudden sadness to Nate, that he fought hard to hide from everyone present.. Ending in a spark, his momentary 'glory'!

"Yeah, well.. she's right... " stopping to slightly clear his throat.. ".. my Grandma was a.. an angel.. 'least, I think so.." gulping sharp now, hoping not to sink into the deeper inner vacuum of sadness. Then, to try to thwart the overwhelming tug of it, and quickly change the subject...

"Yeah, well.. I'll have to drop over 'n see Vera sometime.. She's sure a nice lady.. Didn't know she was working there.. "

"Yeah, Nate-o.." Willie, realizing he'd touched a soft spot.. " she told me t' tell y' t' come by soon.. Y' know, 'n see 'er.."

"I will.. yeah, I sure will"

Why is it, that…

You give a man a badge and a stick

And nine times out of ten..

He'll use the stick!?

Nate wobbled out of his back bedroom in just his briefs, rubbing his blurred-'n-sleepy eyes. Waggling further down the dim-lit hall, he reached up and ran his fingers through his jagged mop. Having got in from work totally exhausted, he'd literally zonked-out immediately upon removing his work clothes. A late-nighter, the previous.. (and only mid-week, in that!), he'd had the roughest of days for it.. and now, had paid the price.

Pausing at the hallway's end and turning in towards the parlor, he saw the beginning of a crowd. They, all stopping and seeing him. Little had he known another party was going on! Yes, he'd heard the loud music.. but, thought it only Buzz! His gut-response was to cover himself.. But, too tired and aggravated to care and react accordingly, he just stood there staring back in.

"Lord of the Flies, it's ERIC!.." shot Buzz (referring to his rough and starkly appearance!).. ".. 'guess YOU'RE ready t' party!.. HUH?.."

Nate felt to respond negatively (for the unwanted surprise, at hand), but didn't.. just stood there, silent.. taking it all in.

"Hey, Eric.. what'a y' think 'a this album?.. It's called 'Freak Out'!.. Yeah, it's a new group called the 'Mothers of Invention'.. Wild, huh?.. Cool stuff!.."

"Yeah, whatever.." Nate mumbling with a slightly-sarcastic-smile and accompanying-head- nodding.. Then, in the same, he.. re-swinging back to return to his room for his clothes.

When there, sliding into his 'infamous' torn jeans, he exhaled to himself.. "Man, another freakin' party!.. I really can't take much more 'a this!.. I mean it!". Slipping on a tee shirt and some sneakers, he began back out.

Not even halfway down the hall in his return, he heard a banging on the apartment's back entry (the door right next to his room).. and stopped in a cringe to verify what he'd heard. It came again, only harder. He wondered in this, as no one ever used that doorway?.. Everyone always entered from the front? Maybe it was someone new.. 'n just not familiar with the regular routine? Geez.. more people!

Aggravated for that, he turned and walked back. Then, opened it. Two police officers were standing there.

"Hello?.. " He said. They, starting in without a word... "Hey, you got a search warrant?.."

Shoving Nate aside, the first .. "We don't need one.. " and the second following with a similar arrogance, as the boy just wobbled out of the way without another word (Not wanting any further trouble).

Looking about and following the sound of the music and chatter, they reached the parlor door, entering it with.. "We've had complaints about a party going on up here?.. Who 're the renter's here?.."

Nate hearing (as he tagged them slow-like) Buzz answering.. "I am.. Me, 'n Eric.. " Then, correcting it with.. " Ah, Me 'n Nate.. over there" as the noted, at last, reached and entered the room.

In the sudden and following silence, the formalities were heard. The threats were made and all were evacuated accordingly there-after.. The 'two' being warned that the landlord would be contacted, and they best put an immediate end to 'the nonsense'!

When, at last, they were gone.. they breathed easier.. and (Buzz..) swore off the "parties".   But, within a week, that was all totally forgotten.

The Winds of War

The Winds of War

Are a bitter, shaking breeze

A cutting deep..

For the very soul to bleed.. its heart out

Its tears.. and mortal fears

Yet, through-out mankind, they just never disappear..

The Winds of War

For men.. are only men

With inbred earthly fault

With their hearts in chains..

'n tightly bolted vault.. Loving only

their immediates

with wrath to show for all others.. expedient.. with

The Winds of War

The Winds of War

I tremble in

For the fruits of Death

Have bloomed from sin

Of the greed.. of the pride

Of the so-childlike mankind...

The Winds of war.. so

Violently, they blind

The so wretched scent

It clouds the darkened air

Choking, gasping hearts, whether home-front here

Or there.. for the innocent

Once again must pay

For the very few guilty, always walk away

From the Winds of War

Willie showed up at the apartment, one night around late Summer, telling Nate that he'd joined the Navy and was leaving for Chicago... for 'boot-camp' or whatever?.. And, that he'd be shipping-out in the morning. His Dad, having been a sailor.. a Commander or sumethin'-or-other.. Willie was now going to try and follow in his footsteps. It all seemed so weird and unexpected to Nate, as he'd never heard him speak a single word of wanting to do anything of the like, prior. Not to forget, his so 'sensitive' nature!.. No, it just didn't seem to make any sense at all!   But, then.. The Vietnam War was drafting everyone capable, and Willie (unlike Nate, whose asthma had gotten him a 1-Y classification and a temporary pass) was no longer able to dodge it.   This.. surely weighing and playing into his decision, to just beat his notification and 'ship out' on his own! But, again.. he had never discussed any of this with Nate (in any shape or form!).. So, the whole situation didn't seem 'real'.. or even 'near logical', at the time!

Coming into his back room, that night, Willie stood off by himself in the corner. This, as the 'Fresh Cream' LP spun in the background; and the 'resident' dealt with 'tactfully'-removing a few intruders. At last, succeeding and getting free, Nate focussed-in on his 'waiting' friend, and they spoke briefly of his leaving and departure.

Somehow or other, though (for all of his former distractions or whatever?..), he didn't seem as 'moved' (.. or as 'serious') as Willie obviously had expected him to be. At least, that's what it seemed like to Nate, in the moments later and beyond. But then, (in his own defense..) this truly had all been so unexpected for him! So, 'out of the blue'! Regardless, in the hours and days following, Nate somehow perceived and regretted that. But, at the time, it just really didn't seem to be 'all that big a deal'.

Willie, on the other hand, had been pretty-emotional and deeply-saddened by it all. Obviously, for much greater reasons!.. And, having come to say goodbye, Nate had just seemed a bit 'oblivious' to the true nature of what was happening. At least, he felt pretty sure that's what Willie had thought, in the aftermath.   But, greater and more accurately, (in those very moments) he was truly 'at a total loss' for what to say!

Either way and soon enough, Willie was off 'n gone.. This, along with all of his 'constant support and the tight-knit friendship'..   sucked into the vacuum of 'the past' like a breath of life exhaled away!   But, yes.. in the moment, it just seemed like another.. "Goodbye.. See y' later.." to Nate. Little could he for-see the changes, that the future would have in store!

Beth had a new second-hand Volkswagen; and when she told Nate (that night as she sat quietly in his room.. listening to him practice), he was totally taken back. A car! Wow! He would've never expected it of her. Not that it was so far-fetched.. but, just.. well.. so 'unlike her'!...

"Really?..." Nate, stopping in mid-chord, and turning in her direction.

"Yes, really!.. my Dad just bought it for me... It's outside.. Wanna see it?.."

"Yeah!.." pausing.. "Yeah, sure.."

Tramping down the apartment's back stairwell, they at last entered the dusk-covered, back parking lot. And, sure enough, there it was.. a bit beat-up and slightly rusted on the fenders... but, a viable and 'as cool as ever', little red bug!

"Man, what a trip!.. Cooool!.." Nate was overwhelmed.

"Wanna go to New York City, tonite?.. Annie.." referring to her friend, back upstairs at the 'never-ending party' going on, just beyond the doors of his 'retreat'.. " She wants to go there.. Y' know, with Jimi .." meaning Buzz.

"Yeah.. Well... Sure.. I guess.. " he, not wanting to sound afraid or insecure about it (Though, it all did seem pretty crazy!).. " Yeah, that'd be cool.." but, not said with any real commitment or enthusiasm. It didn't seem to matter, though..

"Great!.. I'll go tell Annie!.." and off she hurriedly went. Nate, following slow-like and thinking 'what 've I got myself into', as he re-tramped the stairs.

The turnpike was bleak and bare; in its late night, road-lit glare. Everything was dead and silent.. and 'ill-looking-ly' illuminated, as they finally pulled off into an upcoming rest stop. Trees look very different, when lit from the side. Ghostly!

It felt like 4 or 5 AM.. but, Nate was unsure exactly; as he'd left his watch behind, in all of 'everyone else's'-hurry to leave. Not having a car himself.. Nor, ever having paid any attention to where he was going when driving with others prior, he was totally lost. And a bit intimidated for it all. But, he'd never express or show it!.. No ways!.. She might think him immature.. childish.. or whatever! No, he'd hang tough... No matter what happened!

Pulling into the parking area, they glided into a space. There were many to choose from, for it was pretty-much vacant. A little 'makin'-out' went on (front & back seat) there-after.. and, at last, someone suggested that they probably didn't have enough cash between them all to make the trip. Nate was gratefully relieved in hearing this.. and when they were finally back 'on the road' for home, he breathed even easier.

Still, something about all of this excited him. At least, in regards to this new girl, Beth. For this was a real eye-opener for him, considering his former image and view of her. And, it oddly-enough only further attracted him. For he had always 'wanted to go places'.. but, was so unsure of exactly how.. And, here was this girl that seemed to be the type to do just that! And, without very much concern either! Or, fear! He liked that.

Plus, she was a very attractive girl, to top it all off! Not to mention, her pleasant nature, in general; the more he'd come to know her. Yeah, it all seemed like a pretty good match, he thought.

A Dove at First Sight

I came upon a white dove

Her beauty struck my eyes

I caught a moments' glimpse.. and was

Completely paralyzed

And as I watched her grace, so soft

I yearned to only near

The thought that she would fly away

My utmost inner fear

And so I moved in slowly, not to

Make an awkward sound

And each step justified the fragrant

Beauty I had found

What if I should want to speak..

Which words are best to choose?

And should I not express myself..

If so, I just might lose

This rapture felt, unspoken, must

Be told, if ever heard

Je T'aime.. but, even whispered

Might alarm this fragile bird

What have I to give, I thought

To coax her closer near

The simple seed of knowledge might be

Small, but sweet and dear!

And so I placed it in my hand

And offered all I could

The dove took it, more willingly

Than I had guessed she would

And as I walked away, it struck me

Maybe I should stay

For she might know a way we both

Might soar and fly away

'What a gawd-awful band!..' he thought.. 'out 'f tune.. and well, just ..for a lack of better words.. amateurish!..   I mean, the album's psychedelic cover looks pretty good, I guess.. But, the music itself.. well, it's just.. PURE TRASH!'

Buzz sat in Nate's room, playing him a new LP he'd just gotten. Of some new San Francisco band. A bunch of losers! Nate wanted to be polite, so he just offered…

"Ah.. I don't like it that much…"   Then, seeing the frown, he added.. "Sorry, Buzz.. it's just.."

"just.. what?.."   he, becoming a bit defensive.

"I dunno.. I can't really say.."   Though, he surely could have! "It just don't hit me, I guess.."

"Really?.."

"Yeah, really!.."   looking at him now.. "But, y' know, if YOU like it.. well, that's all that really matters anyways.. right?..   I mean, music's just all about taste.. y' know!.. All 'n all, anyways"

"Eric!.. Man, I can't believe this!.. I mean, these cats are like the NEWEST THING!.."

"Yeah.. 'n what of it?.. I mean, so was the Hoola Hoop once.. Right?.." said light-heartedly.

"Yeah.. True, but.."   Buzz, thinking of how better to convince him. But, then.. realizing it wasn't gonna work.. "Well, whatever.. I think they're SUPER cool!.. "   and tacking on..   "..'n everybody ELSE does, too.. so…"

"Yeah.. Well, ok.. that's cool!.. That's you.. 'n everybody else.. RIGHT?..

But, me.. I just don't agree.."   Nate, trying to be fair..   Though, he really wanted to say.. 'Now, the Doors.. There's a real group!.. Rehearsed..

- 179 -

Refined.. In tune.. Talented.. and well, just.. Super Tight!.. Pure musical class and finesse, man!.. But, these clowns.. they're just pitiful!.. No matter HOW Hippie-Lookin' they are!.. Hey, that's just all gimmick!.. 'n the FAD, anyways!.. Yeah.. sure, they're foolin' some people.. Those who don't know the difference!.. But, anyone that really knows music, knows better!.. ' .. But, all of this.. he didn't verbalize. And, why?.. only because he didn't want to offend his friend, who (all the while..) believed himself to be some sort of a connoisseur of 'hip music'!.. Despite the fact that he.. only 'listened a lot'!.. Couldn't play a single note, but.. hey, what's that?.. Heck, he had all of the perfect makings for being a future 'music critic'... Pure ignorance and self-righteousness, beyond any sense of reality!

Either way, Nate never saw himself as being one that fell 'in step' with the crowd, just to please them.. No matter WHAT the trend! .. And Buzz, well.. truth be known, he did! Still, Nate wasn't going to 'tow the line' for him or nobody, when it came to music .. or.. t' anything else, f' that matter!

"Sorry, that's just my honest opinion.. " Nate concluded, in the nicest way he could. Even tacking on a smile. But...

At this, Buzz hopped up.. walked over to the stereo to retrieve his record.. and said...

"Ok, Eric.. That's cool!.. " a good bit upset, but trying not to show it, in the same.. "I can dig it!.."

Nate responding.. "Great, man!.. I figured you'd understand.." , though he knew better!

Reaching the bedroom door, Buzz stopped and turned back, adding...

" REAL heads.. Hey, they dig 'em!.. So.." implying that his room-mate wasn't 'hip enough' to appreciate their 'deeper thing' (What-ever, the hell, that was!)! Nate, in this, looked for 'facetious-ness' in his face (Not wanting to believe he'd go this far!).. But, he was dead serious!.. So..

"Yeah, well.. Who'd know that better than 'Mr. Are-You-Experienced' himself.. Right?.." Nate couldn't believe he'd said that! But, in the after-thought, he was glad that he had!

In this, Buzz walked out defiantly.. returning to his own room, only to blast it out, full volume. Nate got up and softly closed his door. The remainder of the day would be a 'cold shouldered' one, he was sure. But, hey.. that was ok .. He'd get over it! Eventually!

In sitting back down on his bed now, Nate began thinking it over. Yes, it was obvious to him that the whole 'Hippie thing' was already starting to become a sort of 'oxymoron within itself'.. Or, a 'catch-22', you could say! Yes, suppose-ably about 'being a non-conformist'.. when, in fact and reality.. ALL ABOUT 'conformity'!.. Sure, a totally different kind of 'conformity' than the older generation and the very society, that they 'railed on about', all the time!.. But, still.. a 'fall in step', 'mob-mentality' kind of thing! Yes, the very opposite of what he'd witnessed, believed-in (and admired-so-much) about the Bohemian 'Beatnik' days (the early '60's Folk Music Scene and the Coffeehouses, etc.). But, now.. it was all somehow turning into this .. a complete travesty of 'open thinking'! An absolute mockery! And, it was just.. truly sickening!

In September, they were evicted. The constant complaints and calls to the police had finally reached the landlord's ears (Or, better yet.. 'leniency'!) and they were gone. Both Buzz and Nate found themselves back at their parent's.

By now, Nate had given notice to his band. Yes, he had, at last, decided to leave and form the new 'trio' with Kev and Zack. The old band would be doing one more performance that Fall; at a local High School Dance, which had been booked quite a time earlier. Then, they would part ways for good and ever. Johnny would be there (with his organ), as well.. and Nate had willingly complied. He, understanding that they'd need to be taking 'their new direction' too. Besides, it really didn't matter anymore, all 'n all. So, who cared.

And when that 'final' night arrived, Nate was in rare form.. Smiling like nothing was going on, in all of the photographs that Stephen (per usual) was documenting it with. Commemorating the event. After all, it would be their last performance together ever again!.. And surprisingly enough, Kev was there, as well.. getting his 'mug' in them too. So, it seemed that all was resolved and at peace now.. Despite all the former negativity. And Nate was greatly relieved for that .. not to forget, his decision to move on.

The performance went so well, there was an overwhelming sense of 'true regret' that lingered in the air, long after the last note of their Rolling Stones' cover, "It's All Over Now" rang out. Yes, things truly were 'all over now'!.... A band that had once started out together, five to six years earlier.... and had experienced just so many things as 'brothers' was now lost and gone. Just a memory! As they silently packed their equipment, all tried to hide their deeper sadness.

A number of handshakes and well-wishes and Nate was off, leaving with Kev and Buzz. As sad and as hard as it all might be though, he was movin' on.

He smelled the mildew. A strong whiff of it hit him, as he rolled open the old file drawer in the basement. Since his return home now, he had lost his upstairs sliver-of-a-room to Katie, next-in-line for its inheritance. He didn't mind though. Sleeping downstairs wasn't all that uncomfortable, either way.. as it was only Fall, and he planned to be out before the cold of Winter hit. And, having been on his own as he had for a spell; this was, at least, a bit more removed from the main family's upper quarters. Not to mention, he could still stay up late, playing his guitar 'n all without waking anyone.. So, it suited him just fine.

Reaching into the lower drawer now, he removed a few of the old art books and drawing pads. His Dad's more 'personal' work.. not the commercial stuff! The damp odor increasingly climbed upward and at-him in this, like some sort of 'historical incense'. He so-loved that smell though, as he especially associated it with these private moments and these special treasures of his. All throughout his boyhood, it had always been the same. Yes, it was more than the scent itself.. But, rather.. all part of 'the ritual and the memories' it conjured up inside of him.

Flipping through the further-browning pages, he eyed the work. The sketches and the finesse of them. The absolute grace, craft and beauty! There was true life in them! Yes, they seemed to live and breath.. and he imagined in this quiet introspect and self-huddle, the models and actual events that had been there and happening respectively, during their very creation. And, too, what lay beyond their immediate reality. The deeper story! From black-and-white stillness to vivid-color and movement in his further mesmerizing study. Yes, he could actually seem to see and experience it.. through his Father's eyes somehow!

With a latch-clicking sound from above, into his warming 'fantasy' came cold 'reality'.. The cellar door was opening!.. And in this, his Mother yelling down to him…

"Nate… it's Willie… he's on the phone.."

"Ok, Ma… I'm comin'.." hurriedly cramming the materials quietly back into the file cabinet.. and closing it quick, but soft, that it might remain his secret.

At last, there and to the walled-phone in the kitchen, he moved deeper into the lower-level part of the stairway, that led up to the second-floor. This, for the quiet and somewhat privacy it afforded..

"Yeah?.. Hello?..

"Hey, Nate.. I called for Katie.. but, she ain't there.. D' y' know where she is?.."

He was tear-choked, but trying desperately not to sound like it. That, and a bit on the inebriated side.. and for that, Nate overlooked his lack of any 'personal greeting' or 'conversational formality'. He was desperate and focussed. And, calling long distance, Nate assumed…. So…

"Nah, Willie.. I ain't seen 'er.. Sorry, man!.. I dunno.. she's just.. y' know, out somewhere's.."

"Nate.. I'm really… y' know, depressed… Big-time, man!.. " breaking down, then slightly recovering .. "I just wanna talk to her.. That's all!.. She ain't really there, 'n .. y' know.. just tellin' y' t' tell me that, so she don't...."

"No, Willie.." cutting his line.. " I know what y' thinkin', man.. but, I'd never do that t'.."

"Y' wouldn't be lyin' t' me, Nate.. Y' know, like 'cause she told y' to.. 'n.."

"Willie.. C' mon, man.. you're my pal.. Y' know me better than that… Right?.." fully understanding his concern, but….

"Yeah.. I guess.." half-conceding.

"Willie!..." firm-like.

"Ok, Nate-o.." and slightly lightening-up further with.. "I know… but, please… Will you tell her I called, when she gets back?.."

" ..'f course, man!.. y' know I will!.. Y' can count on it!.. " hearing him sink further into a whimpering in the background.

"Willie.. Listen, man.. Where are y' ?.."

"I'm in Hell, Nate… Yeah, in Hell"

"Willie, c'mon, man.. Where are y' ?.. You home on leave?.. Maybe we could.."

"No, man.. I don't wanna see nobody… Only Katie!.. That's all… Ok?.."

"Sure, Willie.. but…"

"No, Nate.. I mean it, man.. I can't see nobody… Understand?.." The Bee-Gee's song quickly came to mind (for Willie's love of them); but Nate not wanting to point it out, nor even near question his sincerity now…

"Yeah, Willie.. I do…"

"Ok, then, Nate-o.. I'll just be seein' y' later.." sniffling.

"Alright.." soft-like, but not content with it.

"See y'…" Willie hanging up.

Nate holding the phone to his ear, beyond the resolve.. hearing the deafening and annoying dial-tone enter.. Inwardly cringing, then hanging up.

Kev finished the re-wiring of Nate's old Silvertone Amp, adding another head on top of the first, and offered…

"Now, Nate-o.. Y' gonna get some REAL mean distortion!.. " turning back to his own bass guitar case on the basement's floor, and bending down to get something out of it. Re-swinging back up.. "Here, try this, too.. It's a Banjo String.. Clapton uses one for his high E.. Y' know, so's it'll give it more sustain and better bite 'n all!.."

"Hey, cool.. Thanks, Kev!.. I'll put it on right now.." un-strapping his new Gibson SG and doing so, while Zack continued to bang and tune his drums.

Nate's little brothers, Peter and John, watched bug-eyed from the cellar stairs now.. curiously lost in what this 'new band' was going to sound like. As young as they might've been, they sensed something was going to be different. Yes, different than what they'd been used to, for so many Saturdays prior. And when, at last, everyone was set.. the 'two-some' stopped their 'seating-disputes' to sharply focus in…

"Well, what's it gonna be, Nate-o?.." Zack settling in.

"Well, I been foolin' with this new instrumental thing.. What'a y's say we start off with that?.."

"What's it called?.." asked Kev, still fiddlin' around with his big, red Fender Jazz Bass and all his amp controls.

"I call it 'Death of the Wars'.."

"Cool!.. What key?.." Kev convening.

"Well, it's mostly in Em.. but, then it goes to…" he continuing.. briefly playing and filling him in on the chord changes. Zack, all the while, silent and listening.

"Gotcha!.." Kev, mimicking and following it a bit.. Then.. "Let's give it a try.." and off they all went into the wildest piece of music his little brothers had ever heard. Their faces in sheer awe over it. This WAS different! Yes, totally different from what they were accustomed to! Their frantic applause and excitement proving so, when it ended. And even the trio themselves, being moved by its sound and the kids' responses!.. They all smiling and laughing openly (Despite their efforts to contain it, for their age) in the settling. Yes, this was new territory.. and they all KNEW it!

Dancers

There is no promise.. just a wish

That we can hope to give

A moment's feelings, set to vows

Surrounded cold in 'if'

I was never promised life

It came, but still I know

Uncertainly I travel

For someday I'm bound to go

Who can vow security

And still be found in-debt?

Even when it's guaranteed

It's still a voucher's bet!

Soaken in hypocrisy

Gamble, weigh its' chance

For all can say.. I do, I will..

But, most just like to dance!

Not only had it been a 'year of change' for Nate's music; but in the same, the ending of another long term relationship. That, being.. breaking-up with Lana. It had been coming for a long time (Just like with the band); but having been seeing his new girlfriend, more and more now, it only seemed right to 'formally' end it. This, of which, not being an 'as peaceful' a transition though.

Lana sat glaring at Nate from across the circle of friends, all crouched and sitting 'Indian-fashion' upon the worn-thin oriental rug of Buzz's attic room. And the dark-and-dim-ness of its lighting didn't help or hide it, any in the slightest either!

Since moving back to his parent's house, Nate hadn't been up to Buzz's Mom's until now.. But, with the invite to this "small party", he had, at last, returned.. Along with his new girl. They sitting together now, a bit un-nerved for Lana's strange behavior and evil-eyed stare.. Trying to dodge it and pretend it wasn't happening. But, greater.. wondering why she'd been invited, in the first place.. Or, had even 'showed up', for that matter?.. Rarely having been present at any other of their 'get-togethers' at the apartment or otherwise!.. So, why now? But, then.. she did live right up the way, just a block or less, so.. maybe, that was it? This, or maybe that she had seen Buzz earlier in his travels.. and he (having slipped!) got cornered into inviting her? Whatever?.. she was here now.. and fuming!

Kev and his new girlfriend, Allison were among the handful.. All.. smoking, high and listening to the new Beatle's "Magical Mystery Tour" LP.

All of a sudden and out of nowhere, Nate (having been totally-absorbed in a conversation with Buzz, sitting right beside him) felt his shoulders being violently pushed back .. and simultaneously, felt the pressure of his body being jumped on and thrust downward… Instantly forcing him into a lying position, with his face-up on the rug.

He (as quickly as possible) focussed, in all of the confusion and shock of it.. and, in so, stared (stunned-like!) back up into the red and totally-irate face of Lana, now kneeling on his pinned-down body.

Everyone there (including he himself) was shockingly bewildered by the craziness of it all. The room went 'humanly' silent, despite the continuing background music from the stereo.

She said not a word, just held him there trapped-like, for what seemed 'the longest of moments'.. totally steamed and fumed. Blood in her eyes! Nate waited for what she would say, but absolutely nothing came out. Sure, he could've pushed her off, if he'd really tried.. But, hey.. this was a girl!.. I mean, what could he do? Or, really even say? Obviously, she'd not gotten over their break-up. But, considering her prior 'total lack of concern for him' in all-else-and-everything-otherwise, he figured this had to be.. Well.. all just the result of 'her pride'? It was the only thing that seemed to 'make sense' to him, in the moment! Either way, her actions (..and this pure 'craziness') sure didn't make a 'bit of any', for certain!

He still waited, staring back up at her.. while Beth just sat quietly beside them.. appalled and looking on. And, he was glad for that; as any sort of physical or verbal help on her part wouldn't have made anything the better, in the least!

At last, Lana (in a hysterical flurry) hopped up off of him, and hurriedly tangled her way to her feet in a continuing 'runaway' from it all. Possibly having come to her senses somewhat, she made across the dim-lit room now for the door.. Fumblingly opening it… leaving.. and slamming it shut in a violent bang.

The "Magical Mystery Tour" spun on.. but, no one even heard it, in the least, now. Nate looked about himself at the 'staring' circle. Then, at his girlfriend.. shaking his head and wits down-like for dis-belief. At last, raising his face to them all, he exhaled..

"Man, that was a Bummer, wadn't it?.."

Everyone nodded in agreement… still lost in the reverberating thoughts of it all.

"Sorry, Eric.." Buzz offered, after a moment… "I had no idea she planned t' do that!"

"Hey, man.. No big deal.. Ain't your fault!.." Nate, still spaced, but recovering.. "No, man.. that was HER thing!.. Nuthin' t' do with you!… "

Reaching over, Buzz turned up the record player's volume, only to hear..

"Nothing is real.. and nothing to get hung about.. Strawberry Fields, f' ever.."

At this, he smiled and turned back to Nate for its irony.. and the latter, forced an uncomfortable receipt. And, this.. not in an arrogant or snide way.. for he (like everyone else there..) truly felt embarrassed and saddened to see her take it so hard. And, to such an extreme. For, yes, everyone of us (at some point in our lives) have done things like that… Just simply lost it! We all are human, and we all suffer in each other's shame. This.. if we have any kind of heart at all within us!

Later that night, when finally alone together .. and walking away from the party and the house…

"You don't think Buzz had anything t' do with that.. Do y' ? .. I mean.." Nate, hating to even suggest it, but figuring Beth his confidant.. ".. That was just.. all too weird t' be.."

She, cutting in.. "No, Nate.. I think you're just being a bit paranoid.. "

"I dunno, Beth.. "   momentarily stopping and looking at her, as they started their way onto the Walden Street railroad bridge.   Then, resuming verbally.. and in their walk, as well..   "There's sumethin' goin' on between me 'n Buzz..   I can just feel it!..   He's got some kind 'f a bummer about.. " stopping short, not to speak too soon and be misunderstood.   But, having to conclude it somehow, now that he'd open the 'can of worms'..   "Well, Beth.. I just kinda think he's got a problem.. about you 'n me.. Y' know, somehow I can just tell!..   It's in the little things he says 'n all..   Well.. I've known him a bit longer than you, 'n yeah.. I can tell..   'n I'm not just sayin' that either!"

There was a silence. At last…

"Well.. maybe.. I mean, you'd know that better!..   But, still.. I don't think he set that whole thing up" (meaning Lana's attack) ".. No, that was her!.. Just a classic case of

'I don't want you.. but, no one else can have you either'.. No, that was all her thing, Nate!.."

He thought on it a few seconds..   "Yeah.. ok.. that prob'ly IS the deal with her.. But, still.. sumethin' weird 's goin' on with Buzz, these days!..   I dunno what it is?..   But, I can just FEEL it!…"   A pause.. Then adding...

"Whatever.. I'd still like to be friends.."

"Well, then.. just be one!.. as best as you can!.. 'n if he chooses not t' be.. then, hey.. that's his fault!.. Right?.. Y' know, then you can't blame yourself!"

"Yeah.. ok.."   soft-like and thinking-away now..   "Yeah, Beth.. I'll try.."

"There's been some talk 'bout a lay-off comin'..." Glenn offered in a half-voice, as he paused in his return from the john, for the stripping room.. Inquiring, in the same.. "You heard any word of it, Roj?.."

"No.. Sure ain't.." heard Nate, as he curiously moved-in closer to them now, from his slightly-further-position at the composition room's stone. Roger, resuming.. "But, then.. Y' know.. Thing's 've been getting' awful slow, lately.. It's sure possible!.."

Bill, stopping now.. looking up from the Linotype.. and waiting to hear more.

In this, Nate noted the front office's door opening behind them (for someone's entry..).. and for that, whispered out in warning.. "Guys!.. ". Then, turning away and moving back (as inconspicuously as possible), he returned to the awaiting job case.

As Mr. Hampshire proceeded in, Glenn resumed his journey.. leaving Roger to converse with him. In so (and out of the range of their business huddle), he brushed-in closer to Nate, in his passing. Then, in a near whisper (mouth-forming the words, all the while, for enunciation and better effect!), he finger-pointingly (..up close to his face) offered... "And you'll be the first t' go, Elf!..".. , tacking-on a teasing and smirky smile. It was all 'in fun'!

So, Nate (in the same) quickly swung back to his work.. and jokingly rebutted by scratching the side of his head and hair with a digitus impudicus. Then, immediately re-glancing back out, he verified that Glenn had received it, in his continuing and further retreat through the doorway. The latter's 'sour-faced-smile' proving that he had!

Not, but a few seconds following.. and into Nate's 'glory gloat' (..leaving hardly any time to relish it!) appeared Brennan. She, coming out of 'her hole' and through the same door as her still-in-conversation Boss. In so, seeming to be 'a totally different being' now.. Smiling as wide as if a falling house had just missed her! Nate immediately noted it, for its extreme oddity!

And, in so, became 'paralyzed into a stare' of dis-belief! What had happened? 'How weird', he thought.

As she continued beyond the informal meeting, her 'new' countenance remained.

It was truly chilling to see! Scary, more than anything else! What was going on? The closer she came, though.. the more he noted a deeper 'snarl' in it (Or, at least, he read that into it!).. and with her sudden eye-contact, he turned away, back to his work.. Waiting as she continued behind him.. Expecting the worse! But, despite all.. she only passed and continued on.. heading towards the back of the building.

Nate returned his scan.. watching her leave.. wondering over this 'strange change' of appearance. Maybe it was her birthday?.. and someone had just given her a brand-new broom! Nah, that was a mean thought (As justifiable as it truly might've been!)!.. But, no.. 'What was going on?'

Just about the time Brennan reached the further-ahead aisle's bend (for the Bindery), it hit him! 'Maybe Glenn is on t' sumethin'!'

"Instant Up!... " rolled off of Nate's tongue, like out-of-nowhere..

"Yeah.. INSTANT UP!.. That's IT, MAN!.. INSTANT UP!"

Kev dead-stopped.. immediately agreeing.. "Yeah, man.. Wow!.. That is IT!.. Yeah, that's sure US alrite!", as they spacingly trooped, side-by-side, opposite-and-passed the Cooper-Frost-Austin House.. then, further up Linnaean Street.. Heading in the direction of the Avenue hang-out. Late day was on them, and falling with great increase.

A name for the new group had eluded them 'til now. They had wanted a great one.. and nothing 'even near good' would come. And, time had been running out, as they were planning on debuting the band soon at the Unicorn Coffeehouse's 'open-mike' night. So, this had become the 'main issue', of late. And Kev had brought it up again, only moment's before, in their briskly jaunt.. Then, sure enough, it just 'came'!.. Like a gift from Heaven!.. Weird!

Yes, and they both 'instantly' knew, that Zack'd love it too! They were sure of that! There was something 'magical' and 'just so fitting' about it, that they hardly expected otherwise. No, this was it! Yes, and it was agreed upon, in that very moment!

Just as the candle-lit windows..

With a flickering warmth

Speck the darkening hour of dusk

The streets, wet and smeared..

With sparkling reflections

Bring a chill to our bones, robust

Yes, we shiver inside..

And tremble a bit

And somehow recount and replay

The way we've been blessed..

By even just knowing

These scenes and the truths they convey

Kev lived just down the road from Nate's parents', in the nearby 'projects' with his Mother.. And, Nate and he, presently (.. with Zack tagging behind some, for the lugging of Kev's reel-to-reel recorder) climbed the 3-story brick-buildings' cement stairs, reaching the 2nd floor's dismal entry. Their 'practice' at his folks had just concluded.. and Nate felt a bit un-nerved now (for the darkening-of-day and the bad reputation of the immediate area). But, with Kev's seeming unconcern (or, better, familiarity..) of the surroundings, he persevered-on, as if totally 'un-moved', as well.

Word had it that Willie was home 'on leave' now for the Christmas

Holiday and planned to possibly drop by, later that night.. So, all were somewhat excited. They'd spent the afternoon recording a number of new originals (plus, a silly, little ditty that they'd written about him) and were anxious to have him hear it all now.. And, not to mention, to just 'simply get to see him again'!

In through the door, they fumbled.. entering what-immediately-seemed-to-be a very 'homey', little parlor. One, with just enough furniture and seasonal ornaments to give an immediate 'warm and comforting feeling' from 'the uncaring world outside' and its seconds-before cold .

As Zack entered and Kev shut the door behind them, Nate scanned to his right.. in through the rectangular living room with it's small-and-cornered Christmas tree; and then, to the further-beyond-it kitchen. In the latter, he saw a very kindly, older woman.. Her white hair and old-fashioned dress-style immediately verifying that assumption. She, finishing up 'the dishes', he assumed.. For, in the instance, she was drying her hands with a towel and coming forth..

"Mom.. This is Nate.. " Kev putting down his guitar case, and swinging his arm in the-noted's direction. Then, in a further slight-spin.. "And, this is Zack.." in so, noticing the heavy recorder still in his hands, and moving in now to retrieve it.

"Well, hello, boys.. Kevin has sure told me a lot about you two!.. ' says you're just some of the area's 'top-rate' musicians!.." They, just seeming embarrassed in this.

At last, Nate mumbling out..

"Well, I dunno, Ma'am.. but, well.. we sure try.." looking nervously at Zack, who was, in the same, noddling.

Their continuing silence and awkwardness, causing her to round-up soon..

"Well, it's nice to finally get to meet you.. but, I do need to be getting to bed now.. It's been a very long day for me.. and tomorrow's church 'n all, so.. " a slight pause.. "Well, I guess I'll just turn in early now.. and leave you boys to your music.." She, noting that Kev was (all the while) setting up the recorder on the adjacent cornered table.. and sensing he'd want some privacy and time alone with his friends, she began away…then, briefly turning back..

"Kevin, remember.. not too loud now…ok?.. and you be sure 'n lock up and turn off the lights, when you're all done, too… Alright?.."

"Yes, Mom.. I will.." they watching as she returned the towel to the kitchen counter.. Then, continuing in her departure into the leftward and un-viewable, slight back-hallway. Nate thinking to himself in this, how 'each one of them had been blessed with such sweet and saintly Mothers'.. So kind and understanding! For Zack, likewise, had such a 'peach' of a one, as well.. Truly sweet and loving! He wondered in a resuming thought what Willie's Mom must've been like.. She, too, had probably been really swell; considering all of the pain her son had expressed, since her passing! What a deep 'hold' Mothers have on their boys! No wonder Willie seemed so lost without her!

"Well, throw your coats over there.." Kev pointing to the sofa's top that ran against the right-hand wall, just beyond the door.. "..'n have a seat, guys.." and they, flopping accordingly.

Hooking up the recorder to his stereo system and shutting off the parlor light (which was dim to begin with), Kev began the tape. "Sweet Shameless He & the Minuet Company" rang out.. and sounded just so good in the dark. It amazing them for the chance to really hear it happening, without all of the toil and effort of performing it. It was truly good! I mean, really good! Different.. and original.. Not like anyone else they'd ever heard! Zack's lead vocal was superb.. and the music itself.. Man!.. Were they on to sumethin' or what!

Next came "I Am I".. a piece Nate had written and sang himself. Totally different type song, but just as 'good-and-mind-blowing' as the first. They were ecstatic!

The instrumental "Death of the Wars" was next; and by now, they were 'flying' (in both meanings of the word)! They couldn't believe themselves! But, before it could finish, a loud knock came on the door. Their first (..and mutual) thought was 'the neighbors.. complaining'.. Or, worse, the cops! It showed in their impulsive and sudden fearful looks at the door. It came again.. a bit louder! Still, no one moved. Until, at last, Kev snapped off the recorder and began in its direction to answer. Opening it, Nate (sitting in a chair directly in line to see..) swingingly saw...

"Willie!..." jumping up to greet him. His head was pretty-well shaved now, but there were no questions about just 'who it was' that was wrapped-up inside that P-Coat! Zack (sitting on the sofa and unable to see) hopped up too.. as Nate moved in to give 'their sailor pal' a welcoming hug (as Kev had already done, being the closest at-hand). Zack, followed suit, and they all (in the excitement), at last, took seats, talking like crazy. It was just so good to see him! In all of their 'musical introspect', they'd totally forgotten he might be coming!

After much conversation, they finally settled in to playing him the little song they'd composed about and for him. He was truly touched. It showed in his expressions. And they were all glad for that.

Rewinding back, they played him the other tracks, and he was genuinely excited about it all..

"Nate-o... This is some really cool stuff!.. I ain't just sayin' that, neither.. Y' know, just 'cause y' my friends 'n all.. " looking about now at the others, as well.. " No, I really mean it!.. This is truly far-out!.. Y' guys are gonna go so BIG!.. 'n I mean, BIG-TIME, man!.. yeah, BIG-TIME! "

It was truly encouraging to hear that from Willie. And when, at last the evening passed and they packed it in to leave, Nate and Zack tramped along with him (back to the main avenue, a mile or so) to see him off on the bus for home.

Along the way (..and after passing Nate's parent's), as they worked their way through the tiny square…

"Nate-o… Katie?.. How's she been doin'?.. I mean…"

"Willie.. Listen.. Katie's been datin' some other guy.." hoping to spare him the 'word on the street'.. " I don't really know him, all too well.. but, I met him a couple times.. 'n I don't think it'd be a very good idea for you t' be messin' with him!.. I mean, sumethin' tells me it'd be better that y' just let it all be… Y know, 'n stay clear 'f it.. That's just my thoughts on it, man.. You'll do as y' see fit.. Y' know.."

"Does she love him?.."

" I dunno?.. I really don't, man!.. Y' know, she's my Sis.. but, hey.. she don't tell me stuff like that. I really can't say.."

"Man, Nate.. What a real bummer!.."

"Yeah, I know.. Sorry t' have t' be the one t' tell y' , but…"

Zack interrupting.. "Willie, if I was you.. I'd just go find someone else.. Man, there's lots'a other.."

Willie cutting in.. "No, Zack.. I can't, man… Y' don't understand!.. It's much more than just that t' me!.. "

"Well, ok.." Zack, backing off.

At last, reaching the bus stop on the mainway, they stood there in the cold, pacing.. Not saying a whole lot. Just waiting. Until, reasonably soon-enough an oncoming bus appeared.

As it rolled in closer… "Whew.. Thank God, they're runnin' late t'nite .. y' know, with the holiday 'n all, I was a bit worried.. " Willie, making conversation.. and looking down at his watch, in the same.. Then.. "Hey, that reminds me.. 'Merry Christmas Eve', you guys!.."

"Hey, yeah.. you're right.. it is, ain't it! …Well, technically, anyways! " realized Nate.. "Well, then.. same to you, Willie Boy!.. 'n Merry Christmas too!.." as the bus swerved in now, and the door flapping-'n-flutteringly opened. Zack chimed in too, with the like.. as they all did their quick hand-shakes. Then, he was aboard and gone.

They stood watching the transit disappear north.. Into the blur of the distant street lights. Not looking at each other, for their still stare and meditations. At last..

"Man, Zack.. it was sure hard telling him that!.."

"Yeah, Nate-o.. but it's better that y' did.."

"I guess.. I dunno?.." looking at him now.

"Yeah, well.... " Zack concluding.. " I guess I better get goin' too.. Got me a long walk, so.." starting off.. then, turning back in it.. " .. well, you have a Merry Christmas, Nate.. 'n we'll talk soon.. 'k?.."

"Yeah, you too, Zack.." starting back now, as well... "..'n yeah, I'll call y' .. Prob'ly Tuesday sometime"

".. Sure thing, man.." and he re-swinging forward in his lanky and speedy jaunt.

THE THIRD RING

The Ripples of Life

The Ripples in the Pond of Life..

From Pebbles that we throw…

Disperse, distort, the further that..

The waves move out and go

Making what was once so clear..

And sharply, so defined…

Now vague and blurred and lost in meaning..

As letters left unsigned

Stephen had a flat now with his newer and younger friends.. And for that, a combination 'New Years'/Apartment Breaking Party' was being held to celebrate. Nate attended, along with Kev and Zack. The foremost sat talking now with the host..

"Well, I don't think the new band's gonna work out, Nat.. I mean, we've been trying to keep it together, but I for-see it goin' down ultimately..

But, y' know, really.. t' tell the truth, I don't care that much!.. I mean, I'm gettin' more 'n more into my photography and film stuff now, anyways.. so, it's really no big deal…

Did I tell y', I'm gonna be putting a dark room in here soon?.. That 'n.. I'm lookin' into some grants now too?.. Y' know, t' make a movie!.."

"Really?.. Wow! .. Well, no, y' hadn't told me, but yeah.. I know you've always gotten into all'a that, so...." Nate, not really that surprised.. "Hey, anyways.. what's the movie gonna be 'bout?.."

"Me.. growin' up here in America.. " Stephen pulling in closer on the sofa's edge, for the increasing party volume all about them.. "Y' know, bein' first generation 'n all!.. 'cause, well.. my folks.. they came here from China.. Y' know that, right?.."

"Well, I dunno?.. I mean, y' mighta told me 'bout that 'first generation thing' before .. but, well.. if so, I forgot. Either way, y' know, they do speak pretty good English!.. ' really wouldn't never 've thought that, but.."

"Yeah, but.. well.. they're still pretty 'old world' though!.. I mean, all 'n all.. Y' just prob'ly never noticed it.."

Nate conceding.. " Yeah, y' right.. ' never really did!…
Hey, not t' change the subject, but you still gettin' into that ole Animals stuff?"

"Sure, Man.. Y' know me.. 'course!" Stephen smiling.

"Yeah, I know you!.. " Then, Nate confessing.. " Well, I gotta say.. I been getting' into the Beatles alot, lately!.. Never really took them all too serious before, I'll admit.. But, Kev.. well, he's been turnin' me on t' them over his place. That, 'n well, their newer stuff's just really been makin' me take note, thcsc days!.. But, hey, like I said.. I gotta admit, I just never paid that much attention t' them before.."

" Yeah, you 'n all'a that Folk, Blues 'n Old Country crap.. I know!.." Stephen facetious and smirking.. "Hey, by th' way.. how's Buzz been doin'?..“

"I dunno?.. I ain't really seen much 'f him, lately.. I'm thinkin' like the last time I saw him was in the Fall… or maybe even November.. or whatever!.. What with the band, my girl.. 'n well, just everything.. I just been too busy!.." Nate pausing.. Then.. "..'heard he's got him a new place down near Central though.. I applied for a printing job down that way, 'n it's lookin' like I might just get it.. So, if I do, I'll probably drop by sometime and see 'im.. Y' know, after work or whatever!.. I did tell y' I got laid-off from my old position in Kendall .. Right?.. "

"No, man.. when was that?.."

"Just a couple weeks back.." Nate becoming a bit angered now.. " Yeah, they let me 'n a few others go.. 'n right before Christmas too!.. Man, there's no mercy in the business world!..

Me, I don't personally care, s' much.. But, y' know, some 'f those guys had been real 'company men'.. showin' up even the very day after they'd gotten their fingers crushed!.. 'n even one 'f them guys, right after he lost one!.. 'n still, after all 'a that, they just let him and the others go, regardless of their families and the Holidays!.. Heartless, huh?.. Man, that oughta tell y' sumethin'.. "

"Yeah.." Stephen agreeing.. " Well, y' know, it's all about the Almighty Dollar, Nat.. Hey, Y' know, that!.. it's the bottom line, man!.."

"Yeah, well.... " Nate, disgustedly jolting his head to rid himself of it.. " Anyways.. No, I ain't seen Buzz in a good while though... Sure seems like that, anyways!.. But, I figure he's still gettin' along ok enough .. Ain't heard no bad reports, so…"

Just then, there was a ruckus in the next room, that thwarted any further talk or concentration. It seems that one of the boys.. One of Willie's old schoolmates.. had gotten a bit too drunk and out-of-hand.. and was now jokingly dancing a strip-tease in the far-end hallway and extension of the larger living room. Whatever had inspired it was a total mystery! But, everyone standing about (guys and girls alike) began gathering around him now, clapping and cheering him on.

Nate felt a bit embarrassed for him, as he sat watching.. while, this kid began throwing his clothes off and looking way too 'inebriated and trampishly effeminate' in it all. And, worse.. It was just truly sad to watch the crowd 'playing him' like they were. Yeah, sick, more than anything else!.. And, flat-out cruel!

He glanced over at Stephen… who was by now, likewise, becoming more-obviously disgusted and aggravated, the further it went on. Being one of the hosts (and feeling obligated to..) he, at last, jumped up and interrupted it.. putting it all to an end in short order. And just in time too, for the boy was nearly nude.

The dawning of this 'sudden sanity' brought tears out of the 'caving-in-now' dancer, as Stephen (after collecting his clothes) proceeded to lead him away and into the back rooms. In this (the boy's crying), made it all, even sadder to watch.

There was a very obvious 'stench of guilt' that permeated the air..(as well, as the remaining mood of the party-ers) for a time after. And, rightfully so, Nate thought. But, with Stephen's, at last, return to the festivities.. and his…

"He's ok, now.. I put him t' bed..",   everyone slowly regained their composure and conversation; and tried to act like it never had happened. But, Nate and his crew wanted out now.. and as soon as they were able to accomplish it (without offending Stephen), they split..   For (short of their 'host' friend, who they knew to be 'real'!..) this sort'a crowd.. with its artsy-fartsy 'scene'.. Well, that just wasn't 'for them', in the least!

The new job was in a much bigger factory. One, further west on the same river as the previous; only, closer to the college area and its Square. A building with five massive flights. This, with a huge chain-linked-in parking lot and a mote-like, sprawling lawn.

By this point, Nate had finally figured out one of the most crucial 'no, no's' of searching out a job.. And, that being.. to never, ever put 'music' (or anything even near-related to it!..) on your job application in the 'other interests/activities' space. This was instant suicide!

Now, might I say, in the same.. (as he'd often witnessed, in the past.. But, better realized since!..) Had he been a 'college student'.. or someone focussed on a more 'legit' and 'serious' aspiration or trade.. And studying for it, etc. (And, in so, 'late' or 'absent' on a few occasions, here 'n there), there would have been 'great exceptions' made for him (and his erring ways)!.. Yes, things would've been totally different! .. Everyone would've bent over backwards for him!.. And, likewise, they would have had all of the 'understanding and compassion in the world' for any of his misgivings. But, with Music.. No sir!.. No, 'cause that was 'a hobby' (as Brennan had so verbally denounced it to be!).. .. Hardly comparable to a 'real career'!.. Hey, after all, isn't that the very reason why they always say.. he 'PLAYS music'.. Sure!.. Like as if it were some kind of a 'child's game'! Damn, did Nate just HATE that stinkin' terminology!.. 'PLAYS' music… RIGHT! Whatever! But, that was a whole other story..

Either and any way, he had 'returned to the Bindery' now, in accepting this job. But, this.. only in agreement to it being a 'temporal' placement.. Yes, as a 'shoe-in' for future pressroom employment. A position he really hated accepting (Actually, loathed!).. But again, there was an ultimate purpose. And, another incentive being.. that this printing firm ultimately paid much more for its press-room help! So, he was simply biding his time now. Plus, with it being located a whole lot closer to his new residence (on the other side of the river now), traveling would also be minimalized and less expensive, in the outcome.

But, this new Bindery was no different than the old. At least, in one way, f' sure!.. Yes, and that, of course, being.. the cantankerous, old women.. with their evil-hearted cattiness!.. Complaining and gossiping their ways through the long, tedious days! Miserable ole cluckers!   Yes, Nate's former-observations and inner-disgust over it all, only proving to be all the truer and more accurate (..and sickening!) than ever!

These were some sad people! Yes, he'd admit, there was always the one or two exceptions… But, all 'n all, these types were 'the norm'!   And it only made his draggy and dreary days, all the more uncomfortable and unhappy! His only relief and escape, being the cracked-open (in warmer weather) windows.. These always being, miserably-dirty and smearingly-hazed to begin with.. Yet, still, what lay beyond them (the sounds.. the circulating air.. the smells..) brought cherished thoughts of 'freedom', despite all else at hand.. making his life 'at least bearable' on certain occasions.   Yes, and likewise, they fed his weary, gasping soul, here and there!

On and on within the confines, the boring collators and stitching machines repeated themselves (like Chinese water-torture!), as he (in the process) repeated himself in his 'responding-to-them' labors.   That, and the frequent 'clock' glances.   Listening, all the while, to the gnawing 'cackles' of the surrounding-him hens.   He didn't know which was worse!..   Or, more aggravating!   It was a true contest!

With the, at last, momentary shut-down of the line now, came…

"Nathaniel.."   He, turning in this…   "Do you have a girlfriend?.."

He, not responding..   for detecting the insincerity in Margaret's question. And this, better.. for the sinister-like smile of nearby Joyce, who was jogging a small paper load, before placing it in the binder-feed.   At seeing this, he simply turned back and away to his work.. Ignoring them, but still aware.

"What about a boyfriend?.. "   she continued..   "I've seen you meeting some nice, young fella outside, after work..   Is he.. y' know.. you're boyfriend?.."

Nate, not turning, but answering just loud enough..   "Well, he's a boy.. and y' know, he's a friend.. so, I guess y' could say that.. huh?"   sarcastically giving in some and playing along with their nonsense. Peripherally noting in this, that both Margaret and Joyce were cupping their mouths in mock-like astonishment and childish-belief.. So, who was to be laughed at more here?

"You two go t' the movies and stuff like that together?.. " Joyce, recovering her mouth with her cupped-hand, thereafter.

"Nah, not really.." he still physically ignoring them, but conceding to their game verbally.

"Just stay home and watch TV a lot?.." Joyce persisted, re-mimicking the mouth-covering, yet again, for Margaret's sake.. Then, adding.. "Y' know, together?.. Like close 'n all?.."

"Yeah, sure… whatever y' say.." still refusing any eye contact.

"Well, that's no answer, Nathaniel!.. "   Margaret re-entering.. "C' mon.. What do you and your boyfriend do together?.. " hoping to embarrass him for his known shyness. This, of which (to these types), being 'immediate incriminating evidence' of sexual deviancy. Shallow minds have shallow reasoning!

Nate (having had enough) turned and looked at them defiantly, scanning back and forth between them… Wanting to scream out.. 'Grow up, you two.. Will you please GROW UP!', but he didn't. No, he held tight. For.. that's exactly what they wanted out of him! An outburst. Hoping to upset him and further ruin his day! Yeah, just simply to drag him down to their miserable level. Yes.. These two were just 'devils with pitch forks'.. True demons!! And he wouldn't allow them the benefit of it all.

So instead, he just turned back to his work, simply refusing to acknowledge them any longer.. All the while, thinking how he'd believed he'd finally rid himself of these kind of childish 'suggestive' accusations, back in High School. But, things really never change, do they? They just simply 'grow up' and get bigger! And to think, this was all 'just because of his long hair'!

How ridiculous! It just frustrated him so deeply.

Internally, he tried to calm himself. Between the women and this ongoing 'incarceration', he thought he'd surely explode. How much more of this could he take? Would it ever end?

SPRING COMES 'A BLOOMIN'

Ulysses

Ulysses…

Mounted in your armor

Rusted in the rain

And stuck upon the mountain

You always look the same

As frozen as a statue

In a Prussian winter's cold

Unable to release the grip

The razor sword, you'll hold

Until you're stiff 'n lifeless

You'll shiver in this shell

Cramped up, even sleeping

In your metal prison cell

"Curse this cage of armor..

and the 'liengance I defend

that led me to this frozen doom

this paralyzing end…

What could be worse, than this

Disaster I have found?.."

Then a violent wind blew in

And swept him to the ground

Face down in a heap of snow

There's always something more

And sometimes if you ask for it

You'll get what you asked for!

Nate's music and love life were better than ever now. Despite all else. The new band was getting tighter and busier.. And, well.. they even had two 'roadie' friends now, that drove them about.. and helped with the loading and setting up of their equipment.

Bruce and Bernie had been their old 'apartment' pals.. The latter, having a total obsession for the Doors and (more particularly..) Jim Morrison. Both were bigger and huskier than Nate and Zack.. and much more 'harder-edged' than Kev (who was a more 'mellow-er' version of their equivalent statures).. So, having them accompanying-and-about on shows was a true relief at times. Especially for the bar gigs, where 'lives hung in the balance'!

Bernie had a Ford Econoline Van that was pretty beat-up.. but, it ran just great.. So, he was 'top-dog' of the two. But, Bruce was really just 'more of his friend', either way.. So, he really didn't care all that much about any 'status'.. and quite honestly, had only started coming along to hang-out with him, in the first place. So, it was all pretty comfortable a situation and "co-pasetic" (as Bernie would always say!), for all concerned.

Heading south to Rockland now, they were all jammed in as tight as sardines.. listening to the radio.. and enjoying the fresh air of Spring blowing in on them from the front-side windows. Nate had brought Beth along, this time.. as they weren't supposed to be using their own amps or drums on this show, and he thought there'd be some extra room.. Though, not fully considering, the actual 'seating' situation.. and how 'very limited' it was, all 'n all! So, still.. quarters were close. But, everyone seemed pretty content and happy-enough; and, for that, he was presently at-ease-enough for having taken the liberty. The concert they'd be performing that evening would be outside (if the good weather held up, which it seemed to be doing!) in the town's park.

Bernie (getting Mother Nature's call) yelled back...

"I'm gonna stop up ahead here.. ' need t' take a leak.." putting on his ticker, and slowly edging over and off the main highway.

When settled into the dirt pull-off, they all got out for an arm and leg stretch.. While Bernie, in the same, headed up for the tree-line and gradually disappeared. Bruce (having his camera handy) suggested..

"Hey, Nate.. why don't you 'n the band climb up there on that ledge.. 'n I'll take a few pictures?.." pointing to a huge granite mound, near at hand.

"Yeah.. ok.." enlisting Kev and Zack to start up the side embankment towards the huge rock's top . A glacier of a rock it was, too!.. bordering the highway.. and obviously, cut out and trimmed especially for its passage.

When, at last, to the peak.. the three gathered out on a ledge and stared back down, as Bruce took a few frames. But, upon returning, he warned Nate that they had looked 'pretty tiny' in the shots, for the greater distance of it all.. and it probably wouldn't be 'very use-able' in the outcome.

"It don't matter, man.. " Nate consoled him.. "they're not for publicity or nuthin'.. So, no big deal!.. Y' know.. "

Then, in they all packed again.. and away they rode.

It was a basketball court.. chain-linked-in.. with a makeshift stage in one of its corners. This tarred area.. centered into a huge, surrounding-it grassy field. The crowd was massive, packing its entire inners.. With pretty much the same as a carry-over, outside and around the stage's fenced-in enclosure. Nate (armed with his guitar now) kissed Beth, then started out of the van for the stage. But, Kev, grabbing his arm, stopped him before he could leave…

"Nate-o.. I got a surprise f' y', man !.. Here.." digging into a duffel bag, that likewise housed chords and other band equipment.. "It's my Dad's old Marine Jacket!.. " putting it forward.. "Cool, huh?.. It won't fit me, s' why don't y' try it on?.. It'd look really cool onstage.."

"Hey, Far-out.. Yeah!.. Sure!.. " taking it from his hands, putting down his instrument and swinging it on.. "Shoot!.. Fits perfect!.. How's it look?.."

"Man, y' look like sumethin' off'a Sergeant Peppers!.. Wild!.." as Nate buttoned it up and grabbed his guitar again.

Then, through the outlining crowd they all made.. Beth watching from the Van's open side. She could see the rear of the stage well enough from there, and didn't want to fight her way through the pitiful masses.

Dark was starting to fall heavy now. In around the fences' corner, they worked their way.. coming, quickly enough, to the near-opening and gate. In they all went for the stage.. Bruce and Bernie helping and leading them through the crowd.

Up the rattling back-steps of the platform, they hurried.. as, all the while, the emcee began introducing them. Plugging into the furnished amps.. then quickly adjusting the mike stands, Nate and Kev began strumming random notes to check their tuning. All was well, and Zack was now seated and banging away, so (without further ado) in they began with "Death of the Wars". This always first, to get adjusted.. and, as well, to show-off their musicianship and playing ability, right up front.

Not but two songs in.. and before the third could be kicked off.. came a screaming and yelling voice from behind them in the crowd. Yes, beyond the chain-linked fence to their rear. Nate turned to look, but had no idea what was going on.

Bruce (all the while, to the front of them now..) was in the crowd, taking pictures with his camera. Hearing the commotion (even from his further stance; and ironically-enough, above the surrounding crowd's rumble!), he quickly snapped his shot and began in, towards the platform's rear.. Sensing something was going to happen. That, and for in his camera's view, he could likewise see a young man climbing the fence, directly behind the stage. And this being, the very same one cursing and yelling at the band now.. and he (in the same, for the masses all about him), taking the quickest route he could find to get to the players.

Reaching the staging area.. and forcing his way to its back, Bruce caught the kid just as he 'touched toe' and hit ground on the court's tarred side. Tangling with him, Nate and the band (Not ever starting their next number) watched concernedly.. wondering exactly what to do. The entire crowd was more focussed on that, either way.. so, they all just held tight.

The kid was screaming something about Nate's wearing "The Colors" on stage.. and how that was "sacrilegious" 'n all! That (dis-respect), being the absolute 'last thing' on Nate's mind, when he'd put it on and worn it. Quite the opposite! But, then.. with Vietnam going on.. and all of the protesting and so forth, maybe the kid had thought it was intentional or whatever? Still, he was flat-out wrong!

Meanwhile, Bruce and he were starting to swing at each other now. And in so, Bernie came running up to the platform's rear, yelling to the band to "C' MON!.." .. And, they, doing so promptly.

As the fighting between Bruce and the young man followed them, they all worked their way through the crowd and back (at last!) into the still-opened Van.. Finally, slamming the door violently with Bruce's hop-in entry.

Immediately locking it!

Bernie had worked his way to the driver's seat now, and was 'warning-ly' reving it up. This, for the crowd had started to encircled it; and were, in so, starting to rock and shake it. In the gradual process of hearing and seeing what was going on, they had ultimately sided with their town-mate.. and were now, starting to try 'n topple it over! Nate pulled in close to Beth .. and Kev offered (out of breath)..

"Thank God, we weren't using our own equipment!.. " Then, further (for being in the enclosure).. "Man, they 're CRAZY out there!", as the Van rolled and swayed back and forth. Bernie got angry in this..(for the way they were treating his vehicle..) and floored it backwards. In this, swerving an extremely-awkward turn. Being in the back of the cab, no one ever knew if he hit anyone! Or, worse.. ran over someone! But, they assumed not. And, with things as 'dire' as they were now, no one really cared to ask, either way!

Then came the shower of rocks as they straightened-out, jolted-forward and began away.. Banging and loudly crashing on the roof and the back doors!.. None fortunately- enough hitting the rear windows!

Bernie picked up speed now. Then, the banging stopped. Everyone was so tense and freaked out! Still expecting the worse! Like sitting on eggs!

Then.. (in the aftermath) as they made away, further and more distant now.. into the apprehensive-and-chilled silence came a just-audible-enough whisper...

".. 'guess that's why they call it ROCKland!.. Huh?..." Zack, nervous and slightly-smiling up in this.

There was a deathly pause. Then.. like an avalanche.. absolutely everyone burst out into an uncontrollable laughter. Total hysterics! The tension had been so high and tight.. and the release so needed, they simply couldn't help themselves! Yeah... Leave it to ole "Ringo"!

The word was that he had been 'found tied-up and trapped inside of an old, discarded refrigerator'. One, with its handle removed.. and laying in a small and overgrown, wooded lot. Undiscovered until now. Suffocated. And, this.. somewhere right in the area of the old apartment too! The coroner had estimated he'd been dead for close to a year now. Which was, ironically enough, just around the time Buzz and Nate had moved up there! Yes, Ray Bolger. Yeah, his good, ol' high school pal, Ray-Man!

When Nate was first told, it took a minute for the name to sink in. Usually, when we hear such reports, they are about people that we don't know, in the least.. So, it sort of goes 'in one ear, and right out the other'. And so it was, when his Dad had 'spoke it aloud' (while reading the account in The Chronicle; as they sat together on stools, at the counter in Verna's coffee shop), it took a good few seconds to 'register'...

"Did you say 'Ray Bolger'?.. Let me see that, Dad..." as his Father complied, moving the opened pages in his direction. Nate had, over-anxiously, hunched-in-and-over to read it now; nudging and cramping him awkwardly, in the doing...

"Here, just take it, Nate.." to allow for some breathing room.

He, hurriedly doing so. Re-spreading the pages in front of himself, he focussed in on the article.. unthinkingly sipping his coffee throughout, spellbound by the discovery.. Peering back and forth (throughout and in-the-process) between the story's text.. and the smiling, 'Graduation Book'-photograph of Ray. Then, head-spinning towards his Father...

"Man-o-man, Dad.. This guy.. Why, he just drove me CRAZY in school!.. Real BULLY!.. Super Violent 'n... Well.. Just plain CRUEL!... Yeah, him and his knucklehead buddy, Brad... " pausing in this, like introspectively recalling.   Then, in remembering (and mentally picturing..) the latter of the two, he meditatively returned to his Dad.. "Man, ' wonder what Brad thinks 'f his BIG, TOUGH HERO now!.."

"Well, Son.. Y' know, there's an old sayin'.. If y' look for trouble long 'n hard enough.. well, eventually.. y' find it!.." Then, in a second breath.. "Or, better yet, like the Good Book says.. 'Seek and Thou Shall Find'.. Yeah, 'n that works both ways, I guess.. huh?..

Either way, I can't help feelin' sorry f' the kid… Terribly hard way t' learn a lesson!.. " pausing to take a bite of the donut he wasn't supposed to be having!.. Then, adding.. "And, as f' that other fella.. Yeah, that friend 'f his.. Well, just maybe some good 'll come of it all now, 'n he'll change.. Y' know, before HIS time 'n luck run out.. Yeah, that's all y' can hope for!"

Nate found all of this 'wisdom' and 'good will' a bit unfathomable. I mean, it did make some kind'a sense, he figured.. Y' know, if y' thought on it enough.. But, still 'n despite.. his facial look now showed the exact opposite. And, he just couldn't help it! No, somehow.. he had to admit, he was truly glad. Yeah, flat-out 'contented with the outcome and realization' that Ray had finally 'gotten his'! And as for Brad.. Well, he was only hoping to get word of his demise, as well.. And, just as soon as possible, too! Hey, these guys were creeps!.. Evil-hearted thugs.. who only saw good, genteel and kind-hearted people as LOSERS! Yeah, WEAK 'N IGNORANT!.. And perfect bait for their wickedness! No, Nate wasn't sorry. And after re-considering all of this, he turned to his Father with a smirked smile (implying.. 'Yeah, Dad.. but, I don't agree'). And, for this…

"Well.. it's all still kinda sad, Son.. 'n maybe someday, you'll see why.."

Nate turned forward and away now. Re-hashing it in his mind. Nah!.. No ways!.. He doubted that.. Yeah, he really doubted that!

ANOTHER SUMMER

My Dream is Forever

My Dream is Forever

It's not fickle, it won't change

Though it comes upon detours

It is steadfast and remains

Big hands, little.. reaching out

And I just can't turn away

Still My Dream is Forever

Dawnin' fresh with each new day

My Dream is an Endless Stream

Flowing from my heart

Winding 'round the obstacles

To make its many starts

Yes, as long as there's another day

'n I don't dam it, but endeavor

It will reach the Golden Valley.. 'cause..

My dream is Forever

The million tears.. of mine and theirs

They only make it deeper

'n faith sometimes gets pulled below

'til I jump in and retreive her

But, the Laws of Nature, yes, the Laws of God

They shape it for the better

And when I come to see that

My Dream is Forever

Yes, My Dream is His Endless Stream

Flowing from His heart

Winding 'round all obstacles

Ever making starts

Yes, as long as He'll grant another day

'n I don't dam it, but keep faith

I will reach the Golden Valley.. 'cause..

My Dream is Forever

Nate saw shacks imbedded and specked into the deep Southern cotton fields, sporadically distributed upon the vastly stretched farmlands. They, exactly as he'd always envisioned them to be, when listening to Lightnin'. Yes, Lightnin' Hopkins! "Hello Central.. Could you please give me two o' nine?" .. rang in the ears now of his travelin' mind.

And, then there were the stories that his Mother would always read to him, as a little child.. of Brier Rabbit.. 'n so on.. 'n Uncle Remus!.. from "The Song of the South"!.. Yeah, they'd sure painted a pretty picture in his mind!.. of a place he wanted to be!.. 'n it was all right 'before him now'.. in Technicolor!

Farm-hands would occasionally dot the passing view.. He'd wave to those close enough. It was like being on a riverboat.. or a Huck-Finn-type raft, gliding along through it all. Wandering free.. watching, smelling and hearing the rippling waves now so close at hand. The latter of these, now awakening him to his truer senses. Yes, the water sounds (Not to mention, the creeping smell of its pollution!), rudely bringing him back to himself . This, and to the greater truth of where he was... On lunch-break from the new Factory. Walking along the nearby river. He disappointingly remembered now, how often-times he would escape like this (from his former job, further down stream), carrying his brown-bagged sandwich & soda, to dream of his future and say a few prayers. Yes, that God might help him succeed and do good in his music. That and to someday .. just get away! But now, more than ever, he was growing itchy.. Yearning so badly to make his move and just leave this place. Yes, this nowhere town!

Often he'd hike along the river's edge, thinking the like. But, today.. well, somehow he had just gotten so lost in it all! It seeming so vivid and real that, when he came to, he was actually shortened of breath.. Uncomfortably tense and apprehensive. It was all becoming unbearable! When would he make his move? The waiting was only creating more and more anxiety in him! He needed to act. He knew that! But, 'thinking about something', and actually 'doing it', are two very different things!

Willie had returned now. Having come back in June with a Military 'Dishonorable Discharge'. Kev had told Nate that he had seen him, when he and a few of the 'old gang' had attended the Jimi Hendrix concert downtown.. and they'd all taken the public transit in together. It seems Willie had been doin' a bit of ranting and raving about his "unfair" judgement, en-route.. And in so, emotionally exorcised it all by angrily bending his dog tags in half and throwing them on the cement floor, as they left the train station. Kev (being behind him in his exit, at the time) said he'd picked them up; as it didn't seem right, Willie throwing them away 'n all.. And, that he'd probably want them back someday, when he'd simmered down a bit.

Either way, now.. with the apartment being 'long-gone'.. there was no real gathering place anymore for the old crowd. No, that had (as a result) pretty much dissipated. And Nate's life, too, had changed so drastically, since then.. Living in a town away now, across the river in his own apartment. So, there was really no place for everybody to congregate anymore. And Nate was surely not going to host any of the craziness that had caused the fall of the apartment. Besides, it had always upset him to begin with!

Willie, in so, gravitated to the younger crowd.. and found a roommate in an old school chum (Tad) from his hometown, and they were now sharing a flat, near Porter. Before Nate had taken his new residency and was still staying at his parent's in the interim, Willie had continued to call there, on occasions. But, as always, it was in search of Katie.. and, too, more-often-than-not, he was (in the same) drunk, upset and crying. Nate would, of course, always try to comfort him. But short of this, and a few more visits that Willie made (on a few rare occasions) to Kev's house to listen to tape recordings of the new band after their rehearsals, their friendship and once-close-ness was now sadly wanting. Losing touch. Nate felt awful about it; especially considering his friend's continuing-to-spin-downward life (Which was made all-the-more devastating by his Father's 'kicking him out of the house' at the news of his discharge). But, time and things had moved on now, and it was really out of his control to help him anymore. His new girl and he were always together, for one.. and, between that and work.. and the new band, it just truly 'ate up' all of the free time he had to be spending with any of his old friends. It was just the way life had evolved!

Despite, Willie wasn't prepared for the changes as they were. Having been away, he (probably..) felt that he'd missed a lot of things.. and, in coming back now, he'd expected it to all be just as he'd left it. But, fact was.. everything had changed!

And worse than that, his persistence with Katie (Who was still dating this 'other boy', at the time.. And, a real violent one without any mercy, he was!) only amounted to his getting beaten-up pretty bad, as a result. Nate truly couldn't believe his eyes, when he saw Willie, a short time after the incident. Just so facially battered and bruised! What an absolute 'bronze-over-brains'-thug this jerk was! And, whatever Katie saw in him was absolutely beyond Nate! But, then, Katie had always been so different than him on a personal level... So, he just chalked it all up as another of the many 'brother-sister'-chasms they'd known!

All the while, Willie (staying with his friend now) only seemed to sink further and further into depression and bouts of illness, in these times. And, on one occasion, Nate even being 'publicly chastised' by Willie's roommate, Tad, at the shopping center store (near their apartment). This.. for not being more concerned over his friend's failing health. But, then.. Nate hadn't even been aware of it prior! Still, even if he had, what could he do?.. He was absolutely in no position to fix anything now! It surely wasn't that he didn't care; it was just that he was too busy and removed now to do anything that would truly make a lasting difference!

Meanwhile and soon after, Willie started dating Lana. Word of it came to Nate.. but, of course, by then, he couldn't have cared less. Their relationship was over for good, at this point. He only hoped in hearing it though, that she would be good to him.. And, for him, ultimately. He needed someone desperately.. Someone sincere and concerned. Someone he could cling to. Nate wasn't so sure that she'd be 'the girl' (Knowing better of Willie's 'true love'!), but just maybe this would work, in the meantime. Y' know, to help him through the hard times that he was experiencing?.. Yes, just maybe, everything would be okay now?

Pryers

Beware of People who pry..

Starting each sentence with "why"…

Loose conversations, tongue transportation..

Watch for the schemes they contrive

Barging their way in your life..

As if they can lighten your strife…

Boosting your ego, eargerly they go..

Piercing your guard, like a knife

Gaining your trust, patting shoulders..

Conspiring with magnetic ears…

Preying mantis.. Judas.. then, kiss..

Gossiping off 'Paul Reveres'.

Running his hands along the skid's stack of glossy stock, he got it! One huge paper-cut. Whew, did that hurt! Damn! Putting the bloody wound immediately to his mouth, he cringed in pure anguish. Oh, how he hated Bindery work! He'd thought he'd rid himself of it.. But, here he was again! Not to mention, the boring, tedious and monotonous day's worth of constant repetition. Pure Hell! Short of his lunch breaks (when he had even 'weathered' the outside bitter cold of winter, for just a moment's freedom .. Not to mention, the on-going 'witches' back-biting!), it was truly never ending. The absolute curse of mankind!

Still licking the blood from his dry-chapped, dirty-grated hand, he felt the beginning of its throb. 'And, these things take so damn long to heal too!' He felt to cry. Between it and the general depression caused by his situation and surroundings, it seemed momentarily unbearable. Only good thing being, it was on his right hand.. Otherwise (like so often, in the past..) he'd have to suffer worse with it, for his guitar fingering.. Which it effected for a 'seeming-endless-time' there-after.

Feeling an even deeper surge of depression now, he fought his immediate inclination to escape.. Even if it would only be for just long enough to recover.. But, he knew, too well, if he left (and the assembly line had to stop), there'd be 'hell to pay'. Yes, when he'd return (as he'd done, in the past) the crew's disgust-filled and evil-eyed looks would be worse.. and even harder to bear. So, no.. he'd suffer it. Somehow! Stopping only for a few seconds to quickly go and rip off a piece of brown hand-wipe to wrap it in, he returned.. Then, he resumed the jogging.. Trying to pinch the towel's end between his next-of-finger, in the process. This, for he knew (all too well) that his partner (on the other end of the pile) would be as unforgiving and impatient as the rest of them, further down the line. And, likewise, in the same.. he, not mentioning a single word throughout to even 'suggest' the other's understanding or concern, let alone 'sympathy'! For this fellow was an older, impatient and generally miserable person; who's only 'one-ness' with him was in the very task at hand.

And he being, as well, one of the 'witches' allies!.. So, the boy's conversation with him (as before the incident) was totally void.. Yes, the man's 'acquired'-hatred and his 'venom-filled'-eyes were piercing-and-blatantly obvious enough in themselves! And this, too.. from the very first day they'd met. So, any assignments together were always.. 'purely duty'!

Victor was his name. And, that truly said it all!.. For he always had to be 'over' everyone he dealt with. Yes, the control freak! Or even better, the 'conqueror'! And, this.. at all and any costs! And, that, too, in itself.. was more noticeable than the cruddy, un-brushed and broken teeth that filled his mouth!.. For at least they stayed hidden, most times! But, this 'look' of his.. being constantly definite and un-disguise-able!

Out of nowhere (and as if to almost be reading Nate's mind), he literally spit out..

"You're a musician.. right?…"

It was a prod, and the boy immediately sensed it.. But, to give him the benefit of the doubt, Nate offered.. "Yeah.. How'd y' know?.." for he, himself, had never disclosed that to a single soul there.

"..'cause, you musicians all got that look.." snidely said.

"What'a y' mean?.." Nate, still half focussed on his injury and trying to play dumb.

"Y' know.. that.. WEIRD look!.. " Victor smirking, and making a strange facial gesture.. "like.. y' know, thin and pale.. that starvin' artist thing!.. like you never eat nothin'!.. With the long hair 'n all, too!.. 'n, y' know, real skinny.. like you're on drugs or sumethin'.." period-dotting-it with the sourest of sneers.

Nate stopped fooling with his makeshift bandage now, and just looked at him like 'what'a y' talkin' about?'. Or, better.. 'Are you f' real?'.

Sensing the 'thin ground', Vic tried to sweetened it with…

"Ever play with any 'f them big groups?.. Y' know, famous?.."

Nate (wanting to put him in his place) said, as matter-of-factly as possible...

"Yeah.. 'bout a month back, me 'n my band opened up for Procol Harum.."

"Who 're they?.."

"Rock group.. y' know, from England!.. They do that song 'Whiter Shade of Pale'.. Ever hear it?.."

"Oh, Yeah.. I heard that!.." Vic, seeming a bit uncomfortable now. Then, re-composing himself.. "Well, hey, man.. if y' so damn good, then whatcha doin' here?.." .. responding just as all ignorant people do, when attacked with any facts they can not dispute or compete with.. Yes, the old 'go for the throat' approach!.. Like any rat would do! Or, more on a human level, 'simply ridicule, when losing!'.

The boy felt to come out swinging. But, it'd be no use. How could he ever explain to a knucklehead this dim-witted, what the music business was like?.. It'd be a total waste of time.. and energy.. and, fact was, this loser wasn't worth another minute of either!

So, instead, he swallowed his pride, and just returned to the fanning.. pinching another load from the stack, and thumbing it upward into separation. This, forcing Victor to comply. But, now he was 'Victor-ious' and gloating.. And, almost struttin' in it! 'That's cool..' Nate thought.. 'Let him enjoy it!... He'll still be stuck in this factory.. or one just like it.. for the rest of his miserable, shallow life!.. Me, I got much bigger plans!..'

The Procol Harum 'opener' led to another 'golden opportunity' at the 'Psychedelic Supermarket'. The club owner had been impressed enough to give them another gig with the San Francisco group, Moby Grape. Likewise being fans of theirs (as with the former), Nate and the group were 'high flying' now.. and excited in the hopes of 'just meeting them' (Let alone, getting to perform on the same show and before them!). They all had been big fans ever since 'the apartment' days.. so, this was a real treat!

Nate stood center stage now on a protruding-outward platform.. Kev on another, running parallel, along side of him. Zack, in the connecting-them-together back. Using a new Dual Showman Amp (placed to his immediate right and rear), the volume was biting and intense now. 'Too intense', he considered in a moment. Then (as if it had almost been a sort-of premonition or something!), his right ear went deaf! Yes, totally deaf! He gulping in this (Despite his continuing-regardless performance). Then, again.. attempting another swallow.. to try and make it pop (like as-if, coming down from a higher altitude).. hoping it would bring it into submission. But, nothing happened. The hearing (in that ear) was gone! Maybe he'd broke an eardrum? There was deathly, ringing silence in it!

In his mounting fear (which the 'earlier and routine tokes' enroute, weren't helping, in the least!), he thought to conclude somehow.. But, he knew he couldn't. No, this was just 'too big of a deal' to take a chance on 'pee-ing-off ' the owner like that. He'd just have to hang in there. 'Maybe it'll come back?' He tried to focus in on the set instead. But, the anxiety it all was causing him was truly freaking him out! Why now? Damn it! 'Ain't life just like that, whenever things are goin' good?.. Sumethin'.. yeah, sumethin's just gotta come along and screw it up!'

He did make it through the entire performance.. But, wondered how it all might've sounded in the aftermath. Beth and everyone else assured him, that it had been 'just fine'.. And no one had even noticed anything different. Still, he felt un-nerved and totally 'spooked' now by the whole incident.. Like it was all.. some sort of 'omen'!

Slowly throughout the remainder of the night, his hearing did start to slightly re-surface .. And, he was truly grateful and relieved in that. But, he still couldn't help but worried over the future.. and of the possibility, that 'the episode' might return again.. And, maybe.. just maybe.. next time, 'the sounds' would never come back? It occurred to him, in a moment of this, that.. 'Maybe Willie was right?.. and I really ought'a have considered just doin' Folk Music, all 'n all!' ..That, and 'this crazy Rock lifestyle' itself were starting to 'flip everything around backwards on him' now anyways.. and it was all truly beginning to take a toll on his mental well-being! Yes, the 'highs' were all starting to become very scary 'lows', of late! Yeah.. freaky, uncomfortable and far-out bummers!

Trooping towards the dressing room's entry, they all marched along now.. Only to be stopped by the bodyguards, that were manning it for 'The Grape'. Having just come off stage, their 'openers' thought it would be a good time to attempt entry. This, before they had the chance to leave or whatever.

Kev pleaded...

"We just wanna meet 'em.. That's all!.. We were the openers.. Remember?.."

"Yeah, 'f course!.. But, y' don't understand.. they're havin' a bit of a tiff back there right now.. 'n we got word t' not let anyone in.. Sorry!" responded the biker-lookin' guy. But, there was really no reason to explain.. For it was all too obvious (even from their location now) that a literal fist-fight was going on inside. They could see it themselves. The band members violently pushing and swinging at each other in the back room.

"..C'mon, let's go.. " mumbled Zack, as they all agreed and began away.. heading back into the auditorium-like cavity of the nightclub. On the way to their seats, Nate offered, sarcastically.. "So much for that 'be sure and wear some flowers in your hair'- crap.. Huh!.." and all, getting a good, little chuckle out'a that.

They hoped that (later into the evening) the opportunity might arise again. But, it never did. The tension stayed notice-ably the same.. and each attempt was thwarted.

Either way.. as good as everyone had said their own performance was (that night), Nate (himself) felt it all had been 'a real big downer' in the end. . A truly, weirdly- negative and disappointing night too, all 'round! And, one that he never really wanted to re-live again! Especially, in regards to that 'hearing' thing!

The town's Common was the site of a weekly concert series and (what the Hippies called..) "The Love In". Instant Up had performed there, on several occasions.. and had had another date booked for the end of July.. And, it finally had arrived.

Kev had become good friends with Stephen, at this point.. and they were both fooling with their mutual Bass Amp set-up's now, on the back side of the park's makeshift staging area. Behind them, on the nearby street, passersby (on foot and in their cars) were taking gawking peeks at the oddly-dressed "weirdos", that were assembled in masses, just beyond this closer-to-the-road, propped stage. Kev (per usual) had talked Stephen into the use of his equipment to 'add to his outdoors sound'. They, both, trying to be as quiet and inconspicuous as possible, for the near-them 'presently-performing' entertainers (..These players, further in towards the park.. And, facing the crowd).

Nate sat on the grass (on the directly-adjacent-to-the-crowd, left-hand-side of the stage area, beneath the trees) with Beth and Willie, pensively watching John Compton & Robin Batteau doing their regular folk music set. As John introduced "Pascal's Paradox", Willie nudged Nate..

"Man, these guys 're great, huh?.. Y' know, Nate-o.. Y' really oughta still consider.."

"Willie!.." Nate cutting him short.. " How many times y' gonna press me on that?"

"Sorry, Nate.. I won't, n' more.. ' k?.... Promise!" dropping his head. Then, returning quiet-like, with a slight smile.. "I just can't help thinkin', that..."

"I know.." Nate, facetiously staring him down. Then, conceding .. "Well, f' one thing.. I must admit, I really do dig that violin work!.. I mean, now there's sumethin' I'd really like to use with my stuff too!.. Man, that guy's great!.. and Compton, well, hey.. what can y' say about his material!.. Super writer, huh?"

Willie just nodding.

After a momentary pause and listen, Nate swinging back to him…

"Hey, where's Lana today?.. Thought you two were goin' out now?…"

"Yeah, well… she couldn't make it.. Gone somewhere's with her parents.." Then, noting Beth's attention being caught up in the performers… " Hey, speakin' 'f that, Nate-o.. y' ain't upset, in any way, that I'm…"

"No, man… Y' know that!… Don't be silly…" Nate, sincere-like… "…'sides, even if I was t' care.. Hey, 'n my opinion, she couldn't 've picked a better guy!.. Right?"

Willie raising his slightly embarrassed smile to greet his.. and the latter, reaching over to lightly shove his shoulder away. Willie, complying in a mock-'fall away'.. lethargic-and-goofy-like; but very-obviously and innerly-pleased for their momentary-and-still closeness. It showed in his aura. Old and 'genuine' friends are like that.. They just 'take-up' where they've 'left off'!.. No matter how much time they've been apart! What's 'real' is 'real'!

At this point, Zack (behind his drums now) sideways-ly called out and over to Nate, that they were "on soon".. and he hopped up to go. In this, Willie called his name, as he started off.. and he returned, anxiously, with… "Yeah?…"

"I'm gonna go watch y's from out there.. 'k?.. " looking off towards the crowd.

"Yeah, sure, Willie boy.. " Then, pausing quickly.. "Hey.. You ok?.." having detected a beginning-and-odd sadness in his look and eyes.

"Yeah, Nate-o.. I'm all right... Hey, If I don't see y' later, you take care.. 'k?..."

"You betcha, man.. You, too.. 'k?" Nate truly concerned now.. and holding still, despite his greater need to hurry.

"Sure thing, Nate-o.." smiling, but forcedly..

There was an uncertained, uncomfortable pause. Then…

"Hey, gotta go…" glancing back at his waiting and anxious band-mates.

Willie.. "Yeah, break a leg, man…"

"Ok.." Nate taking off.. then, grabbing up his stand-held guitar.. strapping it on.. turning towards the audience.. and awaiting his cue to enter; as Zack's introductory beat began the piece off.. All the while, he being innerly perplexed over Willie's behavior.. 'What was with him?' It made him feel so uneasy now.

Searching about the audience, throughout the beginning of their set, he couldn't seem to locate Willie. And, the more he looked, the more that odd feeling that he'd felt at Stiles, the Summer before (.. on the raft) returned. Remembering it now.. and feeling it mounting inside. He fought with it.. This was hardly the time to be entertaining thoughts like that!.. 'Hey, maybe he'd just left?'.. 'Nah, he said he'd be watching from somewhere's out there'. But, there was just too many faces now!.. and just too much activity and confusion! One big blur of excitement. So, at last, noticing that his concern and search were distracting him from his performance, he instead forcingly gave it up to concentrate on his work. He'd see him later. 'No sense in bringing back that stupid head-trip 'n bummer!.. Yeah, especially not now!'

After loading up their equipment, Nate asked Beth if she wanted to 'hang-in' and enjoy some of the festival.. Then to (later) take a walk around the boarding square.. to do some window-shopping.. And afterwards, maybe have a bite at their favorite restaurant, Pewter Pot. But, greater and more-truthfully, to possibly locate Willie, who was still lingering and weighing on his mind.. Though, Nate.. expressing only 'the formers' to Beth (In that she might not understand his concern and worry).

So, with their 'goodbye' to the rest of the crew, they made back into the madness. And yes, true 'madness' it was! Everyone.. young and old alike.. looked stoned out of their minds. The smells of burning marijuana and patchouli filled the air!

At one point, in their tangling through the 'cloudy' masses, Nate caught sight of a young, mesmerized girl (She couldn't have been 13 or 14 years old!), dancing about in a cotton, loosely-fitted, flower-patterned maxi dress.. doing head-stands.. with no underwear on. Her parents.. sitting nearby on the grass, huddled over a pipe.. totally unconcerned and 'Doin' Their Own Thing'! Their daughter.. meanwhile.. exposing herself to the entire crowd! Weird! Or, better yet.. Sad!

Wandering back to the stage area (with still no sign of Willie), they heard the introduction for the next band. And, Nate (having heard of them, on a local level) stopped Beth, that they might 'check them out'.   In their performance, he noting to her, the identical clothing and 'copied'-stage-antics of the Rolling Stones. It was truly uncanny!.. Could've been the 'real thing'! Only, it wasn't!.. So, the couple left after a few numbers.. and made for the square. Nate, offering in their walk away..

"Either way, they're real good at it!.. I gotta say!.. Yeah, just as good as the Stones' Live!.. " He, having seen them numerous times. . " Only, y' know.. No one's ever going to be them again.. So, why?.. I mean, why bother?"

At last, entering a paraphernalia shop on the far-end of the square, they wandered about, looking and pulling at the racked clothing. But, this.. more for Beth's sake than his.. as he always refused to purchase any of this 'over-priced garbage'! No, that and.. in his mind, this was the absolute 'commercialization' of Hippie-dom!   Yes, the 'materialized' beginning of the end!   And, just furthering proof that it had all become a 'cultural masquerade'! Pure 'n flat-out 'capitalism' with a new hairdo! Yes, it all just seemed to be getting.. so full 'f crap anymore!.. And so 'unlike' the original Bohemian 'Beatnik' days (that he'd witnessed, only a few years prior..) with its black-'n-white turtlenecks, chinos, P-coats and other more sedate apparel.. Now, the blaring, obnoxious 'full color'-explosion of the Flower Children! Hey, Peter Max must've been pocketing zillions upon zillions!

And as-if to only further disparage 'the fakeness of it all'.. and even greater, 'prove his point' of the 'fall in step' mentality that had 'taken over'; as they left the shop, who did they run into, but...

"Buzz!.. Hey, man.. Longtime no see!.." Nate, truly excited and trying to be friendly.

"Hey, Eric!... "   Then, Buzz.. not-so-excitedly adding.." .. Yeah, 'n hello there to you too, Beth.."   This, because (in his mind).. she, in fact, being the reason that Nate and he were no longer rooming and hanging together, among other things. Total nonsense!.. But, we all need a scapegoat, now don't we?

"Well, what's been happenin', man?.." Nate, trying to ignore the obvious.. "How's the new flat?.. You're out near Central now, rite?.."

"Yeah, man.. It's a cool pad!.. 'n party-time, ALL the time!.. " Buzz trying to impress. But, noticing it wasn't working, he went for the throat instead.. " We're having us a Veggie-Acid party t'nite, man!.. But, hey.. I know you ain't.. Well.. Y' know.. in t' all'a that, these days.. so.. I really couldn't invite y' .." Then, the dagger.. " Y' know?.. You just wouldn't FIT IN!.."

"Yeah, whatever, man.. No big deal.." Nate, still trying to dodge it.. and seem unconcerned. And, fact being, he truly was!.. Unconcerned, that is!.. And, not at all interested in attending any such party. Still, it hurt, just knowing Buzz's intentions! But, then too.. how ridiculous a concept was that, to begin with!.. Vegetables (to stay healthy!) and Acid (to destroy your brain!).. What a bunch of hypocritical baloney!.. Only further proving the kind of 'diluted thinking' drugs had created! No, Nate didn't care.. But, it was just the attitude and arrogance underlying it all now. I mean, whatever their 'differences of opinion', they still could be friends.. Right? Wrong! Not in Buzz's mind. Nate was just out of his 'SUPERIOR mystical loop', these days!.. Yes, one of the 'un-enlightened'! And, yeah…things had sure changed!

"Well, we best get goin'. " Nate grabbing Beth's arm, and starting off.. "We gotta get us sumethin' t' eat.."

"Yeah, well.. Sure, man.. See y' 'round.." Buzz .. Then, adding comically (but, intended 'seriously') .. "Don't choke on it now.. Alright!…"

As they walked away, and were far-enough-off to speak privately, Beth said..

"Boy, Nate.. is Buzz ever loosing his hair!.. Geez, it looks terrible.. Huh?.."

"Yeah, well.. that's all'a the speed I hear he's been takin'… Catches up with y' 'ventually!"

"What's wrong, Nate?.. You look really depressed.. " Beth asked across the table, as they buttered their steam-burstin' blueberry muffins. "You ain't lettin' what Buzz said, bother y' now.. Are y' ?"

"Nah.." Nate, settling back to his chowder.. "Nah.. not at all!.. " pausing to spoon a sip.. and take a bite of the muffin.. Unsure that he wanted to get into it. But, then…

"No, it's… Well.. it's Willie.. Y' know, when I was getting up to go perform 'n all?.. Well, sumethin' he was sayin'.. 'n the way he looked at me.. y' know, it just struck me all wrong.. 'n, well, it hung with me!.. That, 'n just this strange feelin' I got from it all, in those moments! ... I really can't explain it!..

.. 'n even after I was up there, it stayed with me, Beth.. 'n I just couldn't shake it.. 'n, y' know, then I just couldn't seem t' locate him in the crowd!.. I mean, I know there was a whole lot 'f people there 'n all.. But, I just got this weird feelin' 'bout it 'n.... I dunno… I did finally rid myself of it... But, y' know, then it came back.. Right after we got off.. 'n well.. I just really can't explain it…" Intentionally dodging the re-telling of the whole Stiles' incident.. Not wanting to go into it all.

"Well, I saw him!.. " Beth, trying to comfort.. "He was sitting a couple 'f rows back from the front.. on the other side of where we were.." meaning from their original seating under the trees .. ".. Yeah, I saw him.. 'n he looked like he was really enjoyin' it!.."

"Really?.. Well, why couldn't I see him then?.. I mean, if he was that close?.." Nate, earnest-like, but still perplexed.

"I dunno?.. Maybe you were just looking in the wrong direction!.."

Then, he.. soft-like.. "Yeah.. Well… maybe.. " realizing now he'd never be able to convey the feelings that he'd had, at the time (Let alone the 'head-trip' thing, from a year prior!)...   "Yeah, I guess he'll be alright.. "

To only further dampen Nate's spirits (regarding the demise of hippie-dom.. and its total 'loss of direction'), who did they see on their walk back through the 'Love-in', but Brad! Yes, good ole Brad, Ray's 'mental serf' from his 'High School Days'.. Now, in shoulder-length hair, tied-dyed tee-shirt .. and totting two face-painted flowers on his cheeks! Nate stopped dead-in-his-tracks, causing Beth to almost fall-back in her 'yanked'-continuing walk. She, looking back at him confused-like.

"See that, Beth?..   That guy right there?.. " pointing to him in the crowd, as he (unaware of Nate's eye) continued in his ridiculousness. And, that of, walking about 'stoned-like', giving all of the 'nearest-at-hand females' in his path the peace sign. It was truly comical to see.. and Nate spit-out a sudden, cynical laugh for it!   Then..

"That guy, Beth.. When I was in school.. Him 'n his buddy, Ray.. Man, they just drove me crazy!.. Constantly threatenin' me, 'bout cuttin' my hair off.. 'n y' know, bullyin' me, ev'ryday!.. Total greasers!.. Isn't that just.. so.. full 'a it!..", as he watched on. Beth listening, though unfamiliar with the history.. and in so, not responding.

Nate resuming anyway.. "Man.. This whole thing.." glancing about himself now..

" it's just become… so.. absolutely FULL 'F CRAP!.."

After a further moment of introspect, Beth tugged his arm, and they began off.

"I'm gonna fly someday"

"Yeah, Dad… I'm sure y' will.." returned Nate, in a quick sideways glance. Then, refocusing-out on the jutting and rapid ascent of the Blue Angels, he hoped his response had seemed genuine and encouraging enough. Unsure, he thought he'd elaborate more.. and started to turn back in his direction again. But, before his first word came out, he decided not. It would only diminish his second's-before 'vote-of-confidence'. His Dad seeming to sensing it though…

"Well, even if I never do.. God gave me the better portion, all 'n all!"

Nate had no idea what he'd meant by that.. And his facial puzzlement giving that away. In self notice, to try to hide it, he returned to his scan forward.. at the large silver-looking hanger in the near distance. Though, deep inside, truly curious.

"Yeah, God sure gave me the better portion… There's no question 'bout that!"

This, pulling Nate's focus back to him again, for the overpowering mystery of such a 'seeming-totally-out-of-place' comment.

"Yeah, havin' you kids alone.. Hey, that's about as good a gift as anything else God could'a ever given me, in this world!"

Nate's eyes dropped in this, momentarily.

"That.. 'n well, y' Mom.. Yeah, I've been a real lucky man!.."

Nate quickly nodding his head.. but, not looking at him. For truly baffled. But, not wanting to say anything otherwise. As he saw no validity, nor justification in this. It truly made no sense to him.. Just more of his Father's spacey, double talk! Sure, it made some kind 'f sense.. but, all 'n all, it was pretty ungraspable. And a bit lame! But, y' know.. whatever!.. as long as his Dad seemed content with it, why disagree? So, Nate just re-focussed back out to the aerial-criss-crossing jets in the distant sky. Actually, they were pretty cool. Well, at least, a little.. anyways!

It was an August night, when the phone rang in Nate's new apartment. Around 11 PM. He wondered who'd be calling him so late. Picking it up, he heard a frantic voice. It was his sister Katie. Breathless and between deep, gasping sighs...

"Willie's dead, Nate!.. He drowned in Stiles Pond!.. "

Nate went instantly cold. But, catching his breath..

"Geez, Katie.. Don't play with me like that!..."

"Would I kid around about something like that?.. He really did, Nate!.. I was with the kids.. We all went out there for a picnic today.. and to swim 'n all.. 'n he and Lana.. they went out in a rowboat, after dinner.. Susan and Puddin' were in another one, along with them.. 'n I guess he lost the oars somehow, so he jumped in to get them. He went down twice.. 'n the third time that he came up, he said 'Goodbye'.. Then, he went down and never came up again!.. "

"Dear God in Heaven!... " A pause. "Oh, I'm sick!.. " another pause. "I .. I.. gotta go.." hanging up the phone.

Images of arrows came through the walls, piercing him in all directions, as he made for his bedroom. Falling on the bed, face-down, he just layed there for what-seemed an endless time. Pulsating and racing thoughts violently flooded his mind! ...Imagining being there, and regretting not! ' .."Goodbye"...Why would he say that? '.. echoed through his mind. Then, he began remembering.. 'The Man-child' poem.. And, all of the things Willie'd said, throughout the years.. The threats!.. The warnings! He wondered, in an instance.. 'Was he high on anything?... Did he commit suicide.. over his Mom?.. or ..over the military discharge?'.. 'He always made me wonder if... if...'.. But, these thoughts were making him increasingly sicker now.. It was all just.. too overwhelming! He tried to repell them and stop thinking about it all, but it was no use.. 'No, he wouldn't do that.. commit suicide!.. I just know it!... He promised me.. But, "Goodbye".. WHY THAT?'..

Then, the recall of the last time he'd seen him on the Common (at their concert) returned.. And what he'd said, as Nate was going on stage.. The really 'strange way' he'd looked in it too!.. And, that ill-at-ease feeling he had had while performing.. Yes, that odd and weird 'sadness' and 'sense of loss' he'd felt, at the time and there-after. All of this (in the pounding, mental haze and its randomly-returning memories..), at last, bringing forth 'the raft incident' to his mind!.. And, this.. (in its re-surfacing..) hitting him, like a ton of bricks!.. Yes, being comparible and similar in its epiphany and dawning, as to the intense, musical climax-and-finale of the Beatles' "Day in a Life"....with its droning and final note!.. Yes.. in its resonnant settling, 'everything' ..becoming so 'pre-mediatively' clear now! .. Yes.. 'n to think, that had only been just one year before!.. In the very same location!.. He lost his breath, in this, now.

A slow-recovering pause followed..

At last, rolling over and upward to try 'n further retreive himself…he whispered out, in a gasp…

"Damn you, Willie!.. You promised me, man!.. Yeah, You PROMISED me!.." and then, his mind went totally blank.. His heart.. achingly numb. He just truly couldn't take, or even think on any of this.. anymore! No.. he just layed paralyzed and lethargic-like in the dark.. Staring up at the ceiling.. Absolutely and totally spaced.

I do not wish.. Fancy Clothes when I die

No Fancy Clothes.. in which to lie

No, I do not need.. or want them more

Than what each day.. in life, I wore

For what joy be they.. that before didn't bring

No, I much prefer.. a pair of wings!

Lana was the 'weeping widow' at Willie's viewing. Nate thought it all a bit of 'overkill', as he knew better 'who Willie really loved'. This and not to mention, his own 'more intimate relationship' and personal history with her; that was, in effect, playing-into his negative response to her behavior. But, to be fair, he did consider that she had, in fact, been right there and present, during the drowning.. Witnessing it, first-hand! So, maybe this was more of her reaction to (.. and as a result of) the 'trauma of it all'; more than any of the ' romantic implications' that it was sending off. Either way, he was a bit turned off by it.

Having driven out to the Funeral Home with Bernie (along with Kev and Zack) , they entered the wake pretty-much un-noticed.. For all of the friends and family in attendance were completely filling the room and the lobby, and it was all very unorganized. Yes, it was quite packed.. And, the conversation, heavy. Yet, Nate was hardly concerned-with or aware-of his immediate surroundings now.. and too intent on his purpose in being there, to even take much note, either way.

At last, walking up to the casket through the crowd was a hazy-'n-painful ordeal. And seeing Willie laid out was absolutely chilling. Nate had experienced death before, but this was all very different.. For, this time, it wasn't due to natural causes, as in the past. Nor, had it ever been anyone so young or close to him in friendship like this.

Kneeling down in front of the casket, he 'speaking'-like thought...

' Well, Willie.. at least, y' with y' Mom now!.. If anything, at least that.. huh?' trying to mentally converse as casually as if it were in everyday life. But, it didn't seem to help or remove the 'total remorse' and ill-felt-'blackness' of the moment, in the least.. Nor, the sickness and agony it was bringing up inside of him. He felt completely nauseated. And over-hearing someone behind him say.. "He looks so good, doesn't he?.." only further upset and depressed him. He wanted to turn around and say.. 'No, he looks dead.. 'n freakin' terrible!..' .. but, knew better and held it in. The anxiety was mounting.. And hearing Lana further backset with all of her 'weepings and sobbings', he simply couldn't bear the 'circus' of it all. So, he began up.

Glancing back once more at Willie, he broke into tears. But, he immediately tried to thwart any notice of it, by quickly covering his face and pulling tight. Regardless, Zack and Kev (as depressed as they both were..) noted it; and in so, grabbed hold of Nate's shoulders. Grasping them firm-like and supporting him, they led him away. Bernie pulling-in the ranks, as well; to lend them all moral support, as they mournfully proceeded off further.

Collecting himself somewhat-better now for this, he continued out with his friends aside.. Too deep 'in a vacuum' to even think of searching out any relatives for hand-shaking or expressing his sympathy. And, into the early summer's night, they all made.

Driving back to the old avenue 'hang-out' .. and reaching the exiting tip of Garfield street, Bernie suggested they take a spin out to Stiles. Before he could make the swing onto the main-way though, Zack spoke-up from the back…

"I don't think so, Bernie.. I feel sick.. I just wanna go home…'k?.."

"Sure, Man.. Y' want me to run y' there, first?.."

"Nah, I wanna walk.. I'll just get out here.. ok?.. I really need some air.. " Zack, tangling to exit now.

The roads and moods were pitifully dark and solemn. Kev was up front on the passenger side.. Nate, slumped down and somewhat-stretched-across the back clamped-in seat. Yes, the depair clung thick; and the talk was sparse-t'-none for the longest time.

Gradually (a number of miles onto the highway), he could hear Bernie and Kev start conversing up front (Though, it was barely audible for all of the wind and van noises about).. This talk, regarding him (the formerly noted), "sometime" in the future, "possibly singing a few songs with the band". Bouncing somewhat about, in the backseat, he ignored it.. and thought instead about a new guitar riff that he'd been fooling with, of late. A weird-sounding 'Spanish guitar'-like thing.. very spacey and haunting.. that seemed to fit the very mood and moment at-hand. This, until Bernie reached over and snapped on the radio.. in so, interfering with his ability to continue to hear it in his mind. So, he gave it up.

Further up, into the darker and back country roads, the airwaves (at last) rang-out the sounds of the "New York Mining Disaster 1941". Nate's initial response (and inner impulse) being to call-out to the two (up front) to 'Please shut that off!'. But, in hearing it more (as it played on..), he knew they wouldn't understand.. Nor, would they have any of the like-memories that it brought to him of Willie (..and their long-before trip out there).. So, he just held tight. Listening.

It brought tears to his eyes; and he hoped the two-some affront would remain in their propped forward stances and never notice. The static and break-up of the radio was 'like identical' to that long-ago night; and it only seemed to further bring back the sad recalls. As much as it was moving him (As that's what music should do, of course!), he wished it would end.. Trying to dodge it (here and there), by looking over and out the front and ahead side windows. But, the darkness beyond-them only seemed to created 'more space' for it to ring into! At last, surrendering.. he arched forward and down-like, placing his palms on his face. It'd be over soon!

AUTUMN LEAVES

The Fall of Man

Weary 'n worn..

As Winter comes on

The scenes with their coldness

Increasingly strong

It's the Fall of the Fall

Thanksgiving will call

With its bounty 'n prayers

And shared by all.. in…

Unending praise..

We thank 'n share

The gifts of His giving

Yet, fully aware.. of..

The love He imparts

with those in our paths

to show kindness and gratitude..

or in-shamed-ly react

Ironically enough, Willie was buried on his Mother's birthday. How perfectly fitting!

In the days following, tales of the events and its unfolding were passed on. Being that Nate was not there to witness it personally, it was all 'second-hand information' for him. And for that, all of it seemed very mysterious and confusing.

Stephen (Who had been there among the group in attendance on that fatal day..) told of how he'd not actually been at the very site and location of the drowning; but was across the pond when the word of it came back. And then, how he'd fallen asleep in the car on the way back home from Stiles, later that night. This, from all of the exhausting trauma of the day! And in so, had had a dream that he'd seen Willie 'hitchhiking west' on the Turnpike. And, that, along with the true-to-life discovery (a few days later) of Willie's wallet being found (on that very highway!) by the State Police (and on the very same evening of the drowning!) made for all-the-even-greater 'spooky speculation'!.. And this further information, told by Tad (Willie's roommate), who had soon-after been contacted by the officials, trying to locate and return it to its (now deceased..) proper owner.

Yes, there was just such an odd nature about all that had happened. And what with the likewise questionings of these authorities (that were overseeing the case) of 'whether or not' Tad had any reason to believe that it was a suicide, only further fueled the legend. And, yes.. quite a 'legend' it was becoming.. and very quickly at that!

Nate didn't know what to think. Between that and all of the inner grief of losing his friend… Well, it was just totally overwhelming.. And, in the same, scary and hauntingly preying on his thoughts through-out. And, too, with the mystique of the early Fall itself (all about him now), it was only further 'fueled'!

One thing for absolute sure, Nate truly wished now (in the time passing), that he'd been more-attentive to his friend's dire need.. Yes, and that he had 'made the time' to search him out, to try and 'possibly' prevent what had occurred, all 'n all. Which is not to say, that it wouldn't have happened the same, either way, in the end.. But, at least, he wouldn't feel so bad about it all now. Isn't it always like that though, when it comes to retrospective thinking?.. Yes, and when it's truly too late to do anything otherwise? But, then.. life itself is just 'so demanding'!.. And again, even if he did have the foresight, could he have truly done any the better? Well, fact is.. we can always 'do better', whatever the outcome will be! Yet, we don't! And, there is sincerely no excuse! Yes, and it is all.. truly 'to our shame' as a human race, in the same!.. And, a lesson 'best-learned' young too!

Nate was sorting through all of this in his mind, these days.. And, with the Thanksgiving meal and family activities (from earlier that day..) behind him now, he sat on his bed, reading through two of the remaining letters that Willie had sent him, while he'd been away in the Navy. All day long, he had been feeling like he might be coming down with the flu.. Sort of 'depleted', energy-wise and mentally-blurred. It was the 'change of the seasons', he figured. But, either way, he was going to 'turn in' early.

There is a 'spirit' that stays in a letter (or anything else, that we write from-the-heart) and lingers forever there-in, beyond all time. A 'deeper thing' than just the very words themselves! It is 'in the way' they are written and said! And, even 'spaced'! A unique 'voice'!.. Or, is it the 'nature of the person' themselves?.. Possibly a very piece of 'their soul'?.. Whatever.. it truly exists!.. And.. this especially, when we are (or have ever been..) 'on a personal level' with its writer! (And, I'll add.. even if not!.. for, sometimes if we are 'spiritually sincere-enough' and try to 'focus deeper into them', we can actually 'see ' beyond our own senses!)…

And, so it was with Nate, in these very moments, as he read through them again.. literally communing with Willie's 'being'..   and, in the same, experiencing-and-seeing the very- 'physical movements and facial characteristics' that would have accompanied his words therein . It was momentarily-comforting, but extremely-painful, in the same.. And, the latter, at last, took the better-grip of these two emotions.. making him lie back down on the bed for relief. In deep and anguished thought, he struggled with it.

Then, it struck him! Yes, something in one of the two letters!

So, hopping back up and moving closer now to the bed-stand with its yellow-ish light, he found the one; re-reading the short paragraph, that had curiously re-surfaced in his mind…

"… mostly I just stayed in the barracks and thought. I decided a lot of things during my 'period of meditation'. I think I'd like to really sit down and try some serious writing and find out for once and all whether or not I have the talent to make it as an author or not. I've got a lot of doubts but I feel that now is the time to tell it like it is."

Replacing the letter on the stand, he laid back down and stared up towards the dim-lit ceiling. The thoughts of all this just broke his heart! Yes, to simply know that his friend would never have the chance now to do that.. Nor, anything else of-the-like, for that matter!

At last, he awkwardly blurted out..

"Hey, Willie Boy.. an Author, huh?.. Well.. Maybe someday y' can help me write a book?.. 'n, y' know, like y' said… we can 'tell it like it is'!.. What 'a y' think?…"

It was a light-hearted gesture and a pitiful response to a very desperate reality! And it almost sounded 'corny' to he himself, after it came out. But, it was all that he could think of to say now.. and it had just come out so naturally! Yes, and it had most-surely-and-sincerely been from the heart!.. That's all he knew or could say about it!

With moisture rising and blurring his vision, he persisted in his stare upward. At the ceiling.. Like in a trance. For what seemed the longest of time. Between these thoughts.. and the heated, 'flu- like' delirium that he was starting to feel cover his body and entire being, he couldn't decipher which felt worse! At last and finally, sleep overtook him.

The middle of the night, he awoke completely drenched and shivering from an intense fever dream. One, in which he had seen Willie in his P-coat on the avenue (as he had, in actuality, on a previous year's Thanksgiving).. and, in this vision, had been 'so happy just to see him' that he had ran up and began hugging him, gasping-out... "Where y' been, Willie?.. Just where y' BEEN, Man?" . It had just been.. so real!

Awakening in all of the excitement of this now; he laid there, in the darkness.. slowly coming to his senses and realizing the greater truth and reality.. And, in the painful dawning and trembling aftermath, he wept uncontrollably.

Blessed Be the Autumn Leaves

Blessed Be the Autumn Leaves

that fall in brisk descent

leaving trees their nudity

for, with the winds, they've went

Cluttering the meadow's bed

Like corpses from some war

Yes, Summer's death, it's taken toll

As with each year before

Have I, as with the trees, left fragments

scattered 'bout the Earth?

To rot with but no longer use, those

things I knew since birth?

Are some of them still living

or have all, but, blown away?

Will one day I, with rake, collect

each dispersed yesterday?

Yes, Blessed Be the Autumn Leaves

that fall in brisk descent

leaving us our nudity.. in which..

eternities are spent

Nate was driving now.. A hand-me-down Olds '88, that his Father and Mother had given him. In pretty 'good' condition considering! Yes, and 'good' too, in that Nate was hardly the 'mechanic' type!.. Lucky to know even the 'near basics' of car care! Still, it was his pride and joy! His first car.. and (like his Dad and Grandpa before him) he just loved driving! Anywhere! Anytime!

Packing his guitar in the trunk (as he often did).. one evening, he made for Stiles. It was an 'Indian Fall'-like, December night; though there was still a slight and reasonable chill in the air .. And, he had hoped to enjoy it (this warmer burst) before Winter had fully set in.

Reaching the pond just before total sunset (Though, the already-dawned moon, offering fair illumination in spite), he parked on the gravel lot and let the motor run momentarily, as to hear-out the remaining radio-play of "Love is Blue". He just loved that piece!.. And despite the slight static in it now, it truly sounded.. so beautiful!

At last, with its conclusion, he shut off the engine and got out. Looking about, he pocketed his gathered-up-now dungarees into a more-comfortable fit.. reached for his jacket inside, to warm the beginning chill.. and then, began into the tree line, bordering the water's edge. He had often sat there with Willie .. and, quite naturally, gravitated to that very spot now.

Looking out across the pond, he, at last, sat himself down. Remembering a few moments from the past now, several scenes replayed in his mind; carrying Willie's face and expressions with them into a fleeting sight. Happy and sad ones. But, all bringing with them a deep sigh in his spirit. The final one (The raft incident, from only a Summer prior), literally stealing his breath away.. and fighting it now, he swung his head down with. "Geez, Willie... Why, man?.. Why?"

Becoming over-anxious, chilled and 'short of breath' for it now, he hopped-up and started for the grade to go home.. Trembling internally, as he went.. And, the discomfort increasing with each uphill step!

But, at last, catching himself (by the time he reached the car), he instead stopped. This, in second thought. He really didn't want to leave. He'd come a long way! Then, remembering that his guitar was in the trunk, he re-considered. Yes, he would return with it. It would sedate him, he hoped. It always did! So, popping the latch, he removed it from its case.. noting (in so) his old beat-up cowboy hat, that he wore on occasions (these days), laying aside and further back. Reaching for it, he plopped it on his head and began back out across the lot. At last, in the going (to try to distract and humor himself.. and, hopefully 'lighten up' some!), he began somewhat mimicking James Dean from in the movie "Giant", when he was pacing-off 'little Reata'. Yeah, the hat had brought it all to mind! Either way, he was going to deal with this on his own terms!.. And, now!

Re-settling himself on the shoreline, he began playing soft-like.. Looking about and across the rippling waters. The music did help. Fooling with the very 'Fall-like' and haunting minor key riff now (that he'd been mentally toying with, the night that Kev, Bernie and he had come up there, a while back), he played on. Yes, this, the very one that had a sort of 'Spanish Guitar' sound to it. He had been repetitively fooling with it, of late, every time he practiced. This (for one), because he knew his Mom liked that style of music.. and he thought it might impress and please her, if he could eventually master something with it. But also, because it had a kind of 'airy-ness' to it, that seemed to suit his mood and feelings, these days.. That, and its sort of 'folky'-sound, all 'round.. made him feel it would please his old friend, in the same!

All of this was giving him a sort-of spiritual rest and comfort now.. and (for that) he decided (in the moment) to try to write a lyric and melody-line to go with it. So, grabbing his pen and notebook from his jacket-pocket, he began to jot a few lines down, despite the very-increasing dark about him.. Writing without clear enough sight or light to be super-accurate with its legibility. But, it didn't matter.. He'd decipher it all later. Yes, the flow was just too intense now to try and hold it back.. Or, to try to ignore it; despite whatever the surrounding circumstances were!   He must exorcise these demons within.. Yes, all of this overwhelming pain and agony that had been draining him!.. Put it into 'his' perspective!.. And, under 'his' control!   There would be no other or better time!.. Yeah, this was 'the moment or no'! Flat-out!   And.. ' Willie.. you better hear me!'

At last, organizing it all as best as he could; there-after he laid the opened notebook on his knee in front of him. Then, re-crouching over his instrument, he (in squint) ran through it from beginning to end.. Singing and playing it with the deepest emotion he could find.

Finally.. as the last note drifted off into the night-filled silence about him, he laid his instrument aside on the grass, and slowly turned back forward. In this, re-picturing a collage of scenes from the past with Willie's face splattered into them. And for that, a flood of saddened came, that he could no longer restrain. So, he didn't even try.. Just surrendered... letting it go, gushing forth, like as-if he'd opened the gates of a dam.. Releasing it... Letting it escape, like bad blood from an infected wound.

With wet streaks warming his cheeks now, he re-straightened himself up in his seated position, to resume his further stare-out across the pond. In so, remembering again the very night that he had sat there in this spot with Willie.. and how his friend had heard the angels from across the pond. It occurred to him now, that.. that had been the very location where Willie'd ultimately drowned! Yes, across the pond.. on the opposite side. He surely must've been experiencing a premonition at the time! Yes, a 'God-given' warning! And, then.. in the same and in another way, re-considering his own 'premonition' now (from that very Summer before), well.. it just all made it seem like .. 'God must've truly LOVED Willie! .. Yeah, like.. like.. DOUBLE!'

In a Tree Line

In the green of the tree line

Through the mornin's pale haze

There's a silence, un-speaking

Like that heard at graves

An awing, still presence

So there, but unseen

That calls to my spirit

With temptin' serene

In tramp, through shrubbery

To the crackle of stem

I enter in search of

This mystical gem

But, like fool counting leaves

I'm no better equipped

For my arms can not grasp

It, even one bit

Oh, if I could just know

What it is about it

Entrap it, encase it

In a neat mental fit

Then, word it in a work

That others might share

And feel its deep presence

Lurking in there

And know that one day-waitin'

All will be revealed

When into it, we walk

In repose, bliss 'er-sealed

THE FORTIETH RING

ALL SEASONS RETURN

Life disappeared

Come with me.. beyond this tense

Down Garfield Street.. around the fence

Steve lives right there.. Skip, down the way

If you listen, real close.. you can hear them at play

Yes, echoes in the playground.. down by the old school

Haunting spun mem'ries.. unwrap from their spool

With a silence, so clear.. they ring in my ears

Like music, I knew.. yet, faintly now hear

Straining, I listen.. Though it's everywhere here

Like a corpse, still in motion.. it's Life Disappeared

Where did it go?.. God only knows.. Yes,

I turned, in a moment.. and, Life Disappeared!

Come further, don't worry.. no, don't be afraid

The past is a movie.. we often replay

So, follow down Crescent .. 'til just by the curve

Here to Sacaramento… was, once, the whole world

See me playing with friends.. in the yard at the bend

Inside, between the buildings.. of tan and cement

Look, my Father has come.. for supper's prepared

That I might go home now.. at the top of the stairs

Nate walked through the old neighborhood now. It, looking pretty much identical to how he'd left it.. Not much changed at all!.. Only, a lot smaller than in his recalls.

Since his first year of High School, his family had relocated to their present home on the north side of town. Still, a half of a childhood had been spent here.. and walking towards the crescent street now, many memories returned.   These, and the noted other 'points of interest', where something specific and/or monumental had occurred. It felt kind of eerie being here now.. But, having been 'in the area' by chance anyway, he thought it worth a look.

It was early day, the dawning of Fall and very quiet.. For, with school in and jobs to attend, the resident body were totally absent. Having entered from the bottoming-tip of the tiny street's 'aerial J' (actually, the northern most side), Nate made a stop near its connecting-street's corner..   In this, pausing momentarily, to scan over at the first house that they'd lived in as a family. He could scarcely remember anything of it now!.. Yes, his memories were so faded and hazy. Yet, regardless.. it came to him (in this moment) of the 'very first' recall, that he had of 'life itelf'... Yes, the most-'furthest-back' thing he could remember from its very start!

It all had occurred when he had been just 'a tike'.. in an automobile.. rear-seated (or better yet, standing and holding onto the driver's front-seat and its back-cushioning), looking out at all of the city's bright 'lights'! Yes, he still could see it in his mind, to this very moment! That 'dawning' split-second of self-aware-ness and the world all about him! .. And, it seemed in his memory now, to have taken place in a convertible.. (for the overwhelming awe that it had brought to him, at the time!).. But, then.. he truly couldn't remember anyone in his family ever owning anything, but a 'hard-top', that far back. Either way, it had been such an awesome and spellbinding event!.. of sheer brilliance and enlightenment! .. Yes, like an absolute 'epiphany' and 'ecstatical-awakening'!

He remembered further now that some of his Mother's family members (from Vermont) had come in on an airplane and/or a train (This, of which, he couldn't bring back at all).. But, that they (his parents and grandparents) had gone to pick them up, for their weekend stay. And, in the same now, he recalled that following morning, how he and his Mother had gone to the local corner-store (by the poultry shop), to get some items for their breakfast (This, before everyone else had awaken). She carrying him, most of the trip. Yes, this recall.. and then (one more came..) of the-later-occurring 'traumatic-fire', that had forced them to leave that house, a year or so after. In the painful re-surfacing of it (the latter one), Nate took a retrieving breath and moved on.

Making his gradual way into and up-around the crescent's near-at-hand bend, he remembered playing 'army-men' in the still-vacant lot and yard to his immediate left. Then, in a total head-turn to the opposite side of the street, he scanned the old Ryan family's house.. and peered down, in so, through their left-sided driveway. In the same, focussing-in on its widening backyard beyond; where he, likewise, used to play with his friends. In this moment, he recalled the old tree house that they all used to climb up to, that would've been further and behind the next house. But, considering it was private property, he squelched any notions he might've had, to walk down and look.. and see if it was still there. Either way, he knew it was still very much 'there' in his mind, and that'd do fine enough! So, he continued on, further around the bend.

Raising his focus up now and away from his inner thoughts, he viewed the old Donald house, directly ahead. It, still looking identical and like (all else there..) ' in-a-time-warp'. This, momentarily catching him off-guard; and for that, forcing him to clear his throat and mind to his present reality.. Wondering, in the same, if his old friend and playmate, Billy, still lived there. By now, he'd probably be its owner.. and off to work somewhere.

So, walking on a little further, he made for the center and straightening-out of the street. No cars would be coming .. And, even if they did, he'd surely be able to hear them, in all of this stark silence.

Scanning back to his left now in his gradual jaunt, he noted the arched-entrance-way of their old apartment house. This stucco encasement (with its slight staircase).. surrounding the very-and-same, identical door from his early youth (with its, likewise, old-metal '48' numbers-and-lettering still tacked upon it.. Only now, painted-over! .. Talk about cheap and miserly landlords!)

Glancing up (in his passing), he focussed-in on the 2nd floor's little alcove windows. This, immediately reminding him of his Father; and how he'd sit and watch him draw in there, as a boy. It, giving him a sudden, inner tingle. So, to dodge it, he viewed away.. towards the rightward-placed, parlor glass. But, suddenly noting (in the same and the split-second after) what was a quick flash of 'reddish-like' sunlight, bouncing off the previous. In this, he stopped his jaunt.. and shot his eyes back to the alcove; but only just long enough to catch the flickered-end of its shine-and-brilliance. Weird! He shook his head.. and, immediately there-after, looked up to the sky, trying to place the Sun. Yes, to see if its location could've created that somehow! But, it was cloud-covered now and at what-seemed-like the wrong angle, either way. What? 'Now, that don't make sense!'

At last, unable to decipher any logical reasons for it, he glanced down upon himself and at his Father's ruby ring, resting on his lifted-now hand and little finger. "Nah.." he shook his head.. "Impossible!.."

He stood, pausing a moment more. Thinking.

"There's just no way!.. Nah.. just.. No way!.."

He began off. There was no use trying to figure it out! Yeah, just like 'Life itself'.. No use trying to analyze it, in the least!

Nate pulled away and re-surfaced now from his deeper thoughts; and, in the same, ended his formerly-erratic walk. This, for his more-immedate purpose at hand. And that being, his at-last 'find' of Willie's grave. In this, stooping down and in towards its marker…

"Hey, there, Willie Boy.. " he voiced softly.. "Remember me?... How's m' ole fodderwing pal been? ... You still been watching us, from somewhere's 'out there'?... I sure hope so!" gracing further down from his half-kneeling position now, to a more-comfortable sitting-stance on the dying grass…

"Well, it's sure been some time, since I've been by to see y', ole pal.. Yeah, I know!... Life's just always so busy, man!.. But, y' know, always think about y' , here 'n there!... Hope y' liked the song I wrote about y' , awhile back… Been thinkin' about writin' a book about it all too, f' some time now!.. But, y' know, wasn't quite sure how to approach it. I mean, after all this time, it's really hard to even remember 'myself' from back then! ..Let alone, how I felt and thought 'n all!.. Y' know, it's like.. I myself died, somewhere along the line!... Really!..

Anyways, I finally think I got a way t' do it all though.. 'n include my ole Printing Days too.. 'n my Dad.. and well, just alota folks from those times!.. Y know.. like re-trace and record it all into somethin' like.. one big and extended ode.. Yeah, man.. like a 'Book of Odes'!… Hey, that might not be a bad, little title for it too!... What'a y' think?" momentarily relishing the idea. Quickly returning though, and getting serious…

"Y' know, I gotta admit.. you were pretty 'right on' then, 'bout my Dad.. 'n what 'real heroes' are! .. 'guess, losin' your Mom, early-on-'n-all, taught you that! …Still, it was a little bit uncanny, that you had such a good handle on recognizin' selfless people 'n all, that young!.. I mean, 'n knowing what really 'n truly matters in this world! It's kinda incredible, to tell th' truth!" pausing a second in the thoughts of it.

"Anyways, Willie.. y' know, this world has really done a total 'one eighty', since we were comin' up, man!.. Boy, if you've been watching, you gotta know that!.. It's like.. everything we believed in.. 'n worked towards.. Man, it's all gone haywire!.. There's no dignity or respect for nothin' or no one, n' more! Absolutely nothing is sacred! And.. common sense.. well, that's gone down the drain.. along with all or any real or true justice anymore! It's truly sad, Willie-Boy! .. I swear, the Sixties were cool in some ways.. Great music, idealism 'n stuff!.. But, overall, it sure just turned everything totally and absolutely bass-ackwards! Really, man! And what's worse is the way they depict and glorify it, historically speaking, 'n all!... When, fact is, it's pretty nearly the fault of everything that's 'socially screwed up' today!.. 'Least, judgin' from what I've seen!.."

Stopping to collect himself and momentarily glance about at the mystical Autumn daybreak around him. This, for a bit of relief. But, at-last returning in a sigh of disgust…

"Drugs, man!... That's what done it!.. Twisted everything!.. Yeah, 'n that whole 'rock & roll', 'live-fast-die-young' mentality and nonsense!.. We were just.. all so, caught up in it!... 'n.. it's prob'ly, most-likely the reason you're…" stopping.. then, looking away and refusing to finish it. At last, re-swinging and resuming with..

"Willie.. y' gotta help me with this book, man!… I mean, it's real important.. for the sake of the kids comin' up now 'n all!... Y' know, it's just like you once wrote to me 'n said .. Yeah, we gotta 'Tell it like it is'!... No frills!.. We gotta let them know how trivial 'n minute.. and how short-lived that 'coming-of-age' part of life is!.. Yeah, in the 'big picture' of things! .. And, just how easy it is to get sucked into all of that 'death-culture nonsense'!.. 'n narcissism!.. 'n even greater, how much can be lost for it ultimately!... Geez, Willie… We just gotta, man!... "

Pausing to collect his emotions briefly, then looking back …

"Hey.. Y' with me on it?.. I mean, I'm gonna need y' help.. 'cause, some folks are gonna hate me for it!… Y' know, call me all kinds 'f names.. for bursting their 'Flower Power'- bubble 'n all!.. That, 'n for refusin' to be a 'go along to get along' with their 'societal craziness 'n degradation'!" cracking a sort-of disgust-filled smirk here..

"Either way.. it's the truth!... 'n somebody's gotta say it!... 'n be willin' to stick to it!..

Yeah, it's like that ole poem I wrote, back then.. Did I ever show it t' y' ?... Well, now that I think 'f it, I believe you were gone by then.. But, anyways.. it was about 'Trees'.. 'n how they record each year with a Ring… Y' know, on their trunks!.. Well, Willie Boy.. it takes alota 'rings' to make a tree strong.. 'n me, well.. I sure got 'em! " facetiously-laughing, and lightly-patting his stomach in jest for it.. "So, maybe I'm strong enough, in the same!.. ha!.. What 'a y' think?.. huh?.." briefly smiling, then pausing momentarily...

"No, seriously, Willie.. I'm countin' on your spiritual and 'whatever else you can do'- help on this.. ok?... I mean it now! "

A brief silence; followed and accentuated by a stronger-and-moving-now, Fall-like wind that pressed in towards him.. and then further-beyond and through-out the back-set graveyard. Nate, in this, glancing up to breath it in and momentarily follow it.

Turning and looking back down at the stone, he surrendingly whispered, out of his thoughts..

"Well, I guess that settles it, Willie boy.. Anyways, I best get goin'…" arching upward to, at last, stand and brush off the seat of his pants. Then..

"Yeah, ole pal.. we'll see what we can do, 'bout letting this world know y' passed through it too .. 'k?.. No, I didn't forget!.. Hey, y' know, me!..". A pause…

"Heck, even though, ' they' hardly know me.. Or even care t'!.. Still, let's give it all a try!.. 'k?" pausing again slightly, as if awaiting a reply.

Starting away, he had a momentary and very-vivid flash-back of Willie's smiling face that stopped him in his tracks.. And this, in response to all that he had voiced prior. Turning back now (and trying desperately to hold the picture of it, in his mind), he fondly added…

"Well.. Meanwhile, just like ole Jimi said.. 'Meet y' in the next world.. 'n don't be late!'.. ".. Again, having another fleeting vision of Willie's humored smirk. This, bringing a similar-like-one to his own. Now, this.. was the way he wanted to remember his old friend!.. Not sad, but.. happy! And in a good way!

Re-swinging, Nate walked back to his awaiting car. And off he went.

The Pastels of Fall

The Pastels of Fall

Surround and call

Do we stop and behold.. the

Blatant beauty of it all?

The majestic glory ..

Of God's-sending Art

Or are we blindly, so lost.. in..

What this world imparts?

Like silver-dawned hair

On the aged and refined

They, with wisdom beyond.. the

Spring, Summer's mind

Matured in full bloom.. with their..

true colors arrayed..

Yet, paled for soon harvest

Of a cold, winter's day

Ah, but 'round us, they stand

And in whispers, they call

But, does anyone 'er listen..

To the Pastels of Fall?

EVEN DEEPER INTO THE FALL

In Willow Grove

In Willow Grove

Hidden in the shade

The children play with angels

All tears wiped away

In Willow Grove

There's no sorrow

No fear, anxiety

For what will come tomorrow

So, follow me and listen

By the flowing water stream

In Willow Grove, it's peaceful

And Heavenly serene

The foliage was absolutely stunning, as Nate drove up the backroads towards Boxford. It was, in the same, an absolutely beautiful autumn morning. He was still contemplating his earlier visit to the grave; when, at last, coming to Stiles Pond Road, he turned in.

Following the dirt-and-gravel set of tire-tracks that (still..) constituted its through-fare, he soon found himself entering what was (unknown to him, at the time..) someone's private property.

Dead-ending into the house's rear (Its front, facing the water's edge) and the surrounding back parking lot, he promptly noted a kindly fellow (approximately his own age) walking forth to greet him...

"Hello, can I help y' ?.. " stooping down-like to see into the car.

Nate proceeded to introduce himself ... at last, even going so far as to explain why he'd come. Yes, how he'd had a friend that had drowned there, many years earlier and so forth. This, for the gentleman just seemed so warm and friendly, and easy to open-up to. And, oddly-enough and in the same, it was like they had been friends for years; despite the total improbability of them ever having met before!.. Yes, just 'hitting it off..', as they'd say, 'so naturally'!

Nate went on to tell him that he was an author.. and planning on writing a book about it all; and that, in a way (to sort of validate his intrusion) he was doing some research in returning now. At this, the gentleman offered that he park there and take a walk with him, as he was sort of a 'local scholar and historian' regarding Stiles Pond, and might could be of help somehow. Gratefully, Nate did so; thereafter walking along with him through his land.. and, at last, out to where it ended and where the old parking lot had once been (Now instead, just a track of overgrown vegetation and heaps of mounded dirt piles).

The landscape was misty and smeared like a freshly dabbed oil painting. Wet- looking and hazed. This was Nate's favorite time of the year, and he glanced sporadically about, at the brilliant lines of foliage, as they moved through them now, talking.

Further on, the smell of pinecones came, as they crunched over the oncoming needles matted below. The evergreen's above. He breathed it all in deep. This, momentarily easing the eerie tension inside. In the sky, came the approaching sounds of geese honking their 'goodbyes' as they made South, over and pass them.

"Well, Nathan.. I must say, with all I know of this pond, I'm not familiar with your friend.. Nor, with anyone else ever drowning out here, f' that matter.... Though, I'm sure there's been, on occasions, I guess… Y' know, one time or another…

But, I can tell you about the old-timer that once owned all 'f this land, back in the early 20th Century ..” .. and on he went into a very detailed account of this fellow and his local legend. Nate thinking it somewhat interesting, but totally unrelated to what he could use or what he came for. Still, the ongoing conversation helped him to not get 'too-deeply lost' in the 'shortness of breath'-like feelings that this 'revisiting of long-past memories' was causing him internally.. That, and the certain sadness that accompanies such 'returns' as these. Those, of which, being compounded now by the misty-morning haze, drifting up from the pond; and the dreamy-like nature of it all, in general. Yes, a certain apprehension and deep melancholy seemed to be lingering about 'in the air'. So, he greatly welcomed this company and the continuing stories. For the man's very peaceful-and-calm way in speaking them, somehow eased his listener's spirit.. And, in the same, brought a sort of strange 'solace'!

At times, throughout, though.. Nate couldn't help but think it 'odd' just how knowledgeable this fellow was on the history of the pond and the area. That, in itself, was sort of eerie! Not to mention, that he likewise noted a strikingly-familiar- 'similarity' in this stranger's face to someone he'd once known, in certain glances and angles.. But, he (.. not wanting to stare them through for any misunderstandings or mis-interpretations) just tried to ignore it. Still, he sincerely couldn't help but note an uncanny 'facial' likeness in him. Yes, it was really all just.. 'too uncanny', you might say! Regardless, he impulsively rejected any further thoughts on this as being pure 'nonsensical conjecture', when he caught himself believing in anything deeper for it. Yes, at the time, he felt it absurd to even consider. Still, it hung on, throughout and despite.. And, far beyond that, after he'd left, I might add. And likewise, into the much greater distance, as well. No, he never stopped wondering about and pondering over that 'visit' in its aftermath.

WINTEREST

It's All For You

It's all for you.. that I have

Even the air I breath

You who gave me life to live

And sincerely, I believe…

It's all for you.. my battles won

My trophies at your feet

Yes, all for you, inevitably..

For one day, when we meet

It's all for you.. that I have chose

To trust beyond this life

Yes, in spite of all the failing truths

Around me, like the night

Still, through the darkness.. I blindly grasp

your hand, I do not feel

Yet, still believe it's holding mine

Despite what seems more real

Your fingerprints are everywhere

I look upon this earth

'n no matter how much.. wealth may tempt

I do know what it's worth

And even if I gained this world

I'd always know it's true

That, in the end, it'll go again..

'cause, really.. it's all for you

Sitting alone now in the chapel part of the very church that Willie had 'prophetically' pointed out to him, years past.. he contemplated the efforts that he'd made in collecting and recording the events that had occurred then, in the faded-gone Sixties. Yes, what he had accumulated, up to this point... And, all.. for this book that he planned to write! Was it really worth doing?..

Thinking of his own life, he considered just how much his friend had missed. Yes, the many decades! Nate had witnessed and experienced just so much, since then!.. The travels.. the children.. the grand-children.. The just 'so many things' Willie had lost out on! What an absolute tragedy!

He continued into deeper thought .. and to 'his work' (.. in the arts and music), and wondered if it had all been worth it now. After all, he'd never succeeded to the heights that he (Nor, Willie) thought he would. But, then.. maybe he'd never been meant to? Well, for one thing, at least he'd been able to do what was in his heart, all through-out his life!.. As minimal money as he'd made!   Still, he'd done all right somewhat.. I mean, what did it really matter how many people knew him.. or if he'd become rich, like so many of the unhappy-despite-that ones who had!

This last thought, bringing to recall 'Ole Hank'.. and remembering now, how much he had wanted to 'grow up to be just like him'. Yes, and to be able to write things that moved people to what was 'true and righteous'!.. and make some sort of a lasting contribution to the betterment of mankind! Well, that was his only real dissapointment and regret now.. Not having 'reached the masses' that he'd hoped to.. And, in so, not being able to 'share the gift' and 'message' that he had believed God had given him.. Yes, in the 'work' that he'd felt he'd been assigned to do. But, then.. maybe it just wasn't 'the time' for it yet? I mean, God (if He truly did mean for it 'to be'..) controlled 'all time' anyways..   So, who's to say what would come of it?

It occurred to him now, as well.. that, often enough (in his travels), Nate had heard it said.. 'If Hank were to come back to Nashville today, and try to become famous and successful 'n all.. Why, he'd just go nowhere!'.. Well, one thing was for sure, Nate could truly testify to that 'greater truth'! Yes, as he'd sort-of 'lived it all out' himself!   That, and in the very same.. Had Hank been 'raised from the dead'.. and given the chance to 'do it all again' .. a 'second time around'... yes, Nate knew intuitively (as well..) .. that he'd have surely... and positively.. and without a single doubt.. chosen 'his family' (and 'especially his children'!) over all of the superficiality of the Music Business and its 'Meat-grinding/Artist-eating' demands! .. Yes, Hank positively would've 'put it all aside'.. and been with his children instead!.. And, made 'absolute sure', that they received a 'much greater' and 'more stable' inheritance!

Nate was also convinced, in the very same, that .. 'Had Hank actually 'come back'.. and flat-out 'told them' who he was.. Still.. no one would've ever believed it anyways! Yes, just like Jesus Himself, when He had tried to explain to everyone, who 'He' was! And, why?.. Because, it all didn't fit-into the 'normal reality' of their own 'little worlds'!.. and, or even more precisely.. their own 'little minds'!.. And, ultimately, this being the 'very reason' they killed Jesus!.. Yes, for Him.. having simply stated that! But, then.. wasn't it 'He' who likewise said.. "with God all things are possible"? Yes, 'ALL THINGS'!..

So, with that.. (.. and as Alton Delmore of the Delmore Bros. once wrote.. 'Truth is Stranger than Publicity!'), Nate (in the same) whispered out 'n aloud now...

"Truth is Stranger than Fiction!".. A momentary pause. Then..

"Does that make sense?".. he outwardly pondered, in the seconds after.. This, followed by his surrendering .. " ..'f course!.. TOTAL!... So... Whatever!..."

Either way now.. he knew, for sure (in his heart-of-hearts) that (just like Ole Hank), he HAD tried (in his own writings and singing) to lead people to 'what's right'!.. And, 'what's real'! Yes, 'n that he'd, likewise, 'given it his all' too!.. And, done his ABSOLUTE BEST! .. Even publicly 'confessing some of his very own sins and life secrets' to help them more-readily see, that they (too) could change! ..'n make things right!.. And, for the better, if they would only choose to! Yes, Nate had sincerely 'tried to the extreme'!.. No matter WHAT anyone thought about it all!.. That was just the SIMPLE TRUTH, 'n all he could say 'bout it! Yes, now.. it was all.. in the Hands of God .. So, he just gave up his thinkin'-'n-worryin' 'bout it anymore!..

Instead, bringing forth his pad and pen now, he jotted down a few lines....

God Gave Me This Guit'r

God gave me this guit'r

To help me find release

From the sickness, all around me

To give me a little peace

And to teach me things like patience 'n

Persistence, 'n that life

Is not summed up in money, the

True author of all strife

Yes, God gave me this guit'r

With no promise of wealth or fame

Or even that I'd, one day, grow up

T' make myself a name.. No..

He gave it just t' see me through

The blank, stark bleakness of these roads

That lead to Him through wastelands

Of such bitter, heavy loads

He stopped there.. Remembering he was in church. Well, in a way, it was 'sort of a prayer'!

He re-focussed his thoughts (instead) on his sister, Tess.. and how her life had never even been lived. Sixteen short years. Dear Lord, he couldn't even conceive of having died at that early an age. What a long life he had had, in comparison! That was surely something to be grateful for! What a wonderful gift!.. It's no wonder they call it.. 'the present'!

Then.. catching site of his Dad's ring on his small finger, he remembered again how (as a child) he had watched its reflection bounce about his Father's work place. Yes, in that little alcove room. He watched it 'ricochet' again now, in his mind; thinking, in the same, of the unexplainable incident that had occurred, on this more-recent return. At last, giving it up, he considered..

'Why was I so angry with him?' (meaning 'back then')

Having lived and matured enough now to see, he further-considered how his Dad had never really quit his Art… No, really what he had done was just to transfer his creativity and love-for-it into becoming a 'creative' Father! One, that loved his children more than any of his own selfish desires.. Painting his pictures in them instead! Sure, he wasn't a 'perfect man'.. Hardly! .. But, then, who is?

In the furthering introspect (and as a more educated adult now), he likewise realized that his Dad's illness itself, was not something 'brought on' by the things that he (himself, as a boy) had always believed.. Nor, the results of his Father 'leaving anything'.. True, those things might have 'compounded' the suffering! .. But, in greater fact.. it all had been the result of something much-more 'deeper-rooted'! Yes, life experiences and of-the-like.. And, things that his Father simply could not control! And yet, despite all of this, he had never 'ran away' from his responsibilities. Yes, absent, during his occasional bouts.. But, then.. always right 'back at the steering wheel' there-after! No, he was hardly a quitter! .. 'Cause, REAL MEN don't ever run away!.. Or, quit !.. No matter what! And, that.. he had surely and never done!

Twisting the ring on his finger now and looking at it, in the same.. he considered its stone.. 'Red.. The Color of Sacrifice'.. thinking like he'd read that in the Bible somewhere?.. Either way, that had been the one thing he himself had never totally been able to do.. So, really… who was the truer and greater hero? Yes, in a world full of 'false gods' and self-centered people that are admired by the masses, the TRUER and REAL HEROES are 'the selfless'!.. And, they… NEVER receive honor! … At least, not in this God-forsaken world!

Then, there were all the seeming- 'nonsensical' things that he had said to Nate, through-out his years of growing-up. In re-thinking a number of them now, he realized that 'they had made sense'! Yes, perfect sense!.. Only, he'd just never been mature enough to gather their deeper meanings then! This and how.. his 'actual living experiences' had now given him the greater knowledge to see their definite-and-accurate validity! Life should truly be lived in reverse! Maybe in 'West of Eden', it will? 'least, God willin'!

All of a sudden and like out-of-nowhere, it dawned on him!.. And distracted him from his continuing thoughts. Yes, a far-off recall returned (That he hadn't thought of in a long, long time!).. and he remembered now, how his Father had told him (many, many years past) that he had came into this very chapel, when he had first seen their house (just across the avenue)! Yes, when it had been up 'for sale'!.. This, to say a prayer and ask God to help him get it.

Nate, in this moment, remembered all of the many years and the 'too-numerous' disappointments, that his Dad (and everyone else, in the family) had experienced prior, in the search for one. He recalled how sick it made him feel, each time.. Especially, for the sake of his Father. Yes, the 'watching him get his hopes built up, all for nothing'! It was truly sad and painstaking! But then, God did (at last) answer his prayers.. giving him (and them all, as a result!) a small, but 'just right' home! Yes.. where just 'so many' wonderful.. (and yes, a few sad..) memories were made. A house EXACTLY where it had to be, too! A home that everyone had just 'taken for granted' ultimately!.. Especially, his younger siblings, who'd never witnessed all of the former heartbreaks.. And, only knew 'the security of having it'! That, and just so many of the other things

they'd never known about their Father, and who he'd been before! But, then..
Nate, too, had never fully appreciated him! A quiet man.. who took a lot of
verbal abuse and dis-respect, without saying a single word in his own defense. A
patient and forgiving man!.. never once speaking an unkind word about anyone..
Even when it would have been totally 'justified'!.. It truly amazed Nate, for the
totally 'forbearing' Christian man that he had been! And, sure.. there had been
those 'tramautic' and upsetting moments, here and there (During his illnesses)!
.. But, much more than not, he had been a very loving and caring Father!.. Hey,
life's not perfect!.. No more than any of us, who live it!

Getting up, he solemnly walked to the front altar. There was a stand
placed there with numerous, unlit candles upon it. Putting in the dollars that he
considered sufficient for the offering box, he lit two.. "that's for you, Willie
Boy... 'n you, too, Tess.."

Before blowing out the long wick, he reached to the top row and lit one
more candle, in the dead-center..   ".. and that's for you, Dad... Sorry if I mis-
judged you.. I just didn't understand...."

Extinguishing the flame now and returning the stick to its place, he
quickly made the Sign of the Cross. Then, he turned and began out.

Looking back in his near-exit, he confirmed that their lights were still
shining and hadn't gone out.   Seeing that they were still glowing, he was
content.. and in so, left the building.

"When our mind's eyes meet, someday..

You'll look into my once reality..

And see me in there...

Peeking back out at you."....

Mark Brine

.. to the Musical Artists and Composers of the other material that would hopefully be included in this Novel's (eventual..) Movie/Theatrical Soundtrack (If the existing screen-play of this work ever comes to fruitation!); especially and particularly... James Forte!

James & his dear wife, Nancy were the absolute 'salvation' of my stay in New England (2004-2005).. Their friendship & encouragement helped me survive the bitter 'Winter from Hell' .. and the desolate times I encountered, upon returning there. And might I say, as well.. the simple 'finding' of James' music was a true joy and total epiphany for me!.. For one I will note, that I sincerely have never heard a more beautiful classical 'masterpiece' than "Angel Voices/ Wendy's Flowers"!.. It is an absolute 'classic'!

..As, too, are just so many of his created works! They suit this novel's mood perfectly (I believe!).. Not to mention, that they are 'all-the-more fitting', as well, for their 'indicative'-ness to the region! Might I further say.. I only pray that the world will find James' music 'preferably' in his lifetime! If not, at least, 'beyond it'! As.. It is 'pure genius'!

.. to Tracy Knight.. for her earnest and heartfelt work on the above-noted Screenplay. A true 'Angel' of a person!.. and surely, a 'gift from God'!

.. to my unknowing friends at the Newtowne Grill & Tavern in Porter Square (Cambridge, Ma.), where I spent many a cold winter's night jotting down the very basics of this novel.. All the while, sipping on a tall 'Sam'. Yes, cornered into an intimate and warm booth, most times it was reasonably-quiet and peaceful-enough to afford me the opportunity and 'congenial' atmosphere to 'bring back' a lot of my memories from the past. Yes, of those 'old' days! Who says 'you can never go home'?

.. to Christopher ("Christoph"), my Grand-boy.. who helped me create 'new memories' of Stiles Pond.. on our many fishing trips and Boxford- 'eat-outs' there. He was the truer and 'greater reason' I returned to Cambridge (on both of my extended stays)!.. And, this, as well.. because, he once told me that he "was worth it!"… And, I believed him! (Of course!).. I pray he'll always remember that (of himself)!... For it's eternal truth!!

..And, might I add.. if there was ever anyone that I have known, who 'loved hearing a good story' better than he, it is truly 'beyond-me' to name them! May you (my ole pal), one day, pass-on a few, as well! Love you, so deeply!

..and, in the same, to.. Michelle ("My Lil' One").. who (very maturely-for-her-age!) understood why her Grandpa had to focus-in-on and concentrate on her brother, during these times. I'm very proud of her for that, and everything else! Love you, so deeply, too!.. not to forget, your Mommy, my 'Jenipher'!

.. to Everett Dickey.. for the Dog Tags. And, for the many years of his friendship and encouragement! .. And might I likewise add, Ev was the first person (that I know of) to read this novel in its starkest-most 'skeleton' form; all the way through (Several times, as it developed, as well!).. and, in so, always urged me to continue onward! Yes, this and his fore-mentioned 'gift' were profound and catalytic 'inspirations' that truly helped me to follow through! For the latter (after all of the years.. and their 'strange' and very 'timely' reappearance!) made me feel, that.. yes, Willie could, very much and in fact, "hear me"! .. And, had more to do with this novel than even I myself would suspect! This, and the 'too many' other 'odd occurrences' that took place at-and-during my stay in Arlington, Mass. (on Pleasant St.) in the Fall of 2000… where and when I began the research and the writing of this work. Yes, there's just so much that can be said of a completely-vacant, third-story room.. in an old Victorian mansion!.. And, one with an expansive 'overview', afforded by its dormer and gabled-like windows! Yes, I assure you!… There's so much to see beyond!

.. to Paul "Mac" MacDonald.. for his life-long friendship .. and his tremendous support on this project. His words of encouragement were priceless! My 'Third' Brother .. Always!

..to Ken Rohr.. for the inspiration, the time you took.. and your welcoming kindness.

.. to Keeve Brine, my son.. who is forever helpin' out his ol' Dad on his many projects. Your name (Which I created) means.. "The one I've waited for, for so long" .. and now I can truly say, I know why! For, the best and most cherished things in this life are all like that!.. They 'take time'!.. It's just the way the Master created it! And, you are 'my'.... 'living proof' of it!

.. to Christine Downey (my Sis!).. for the return of 'the letters'.. and the many 'shared' recalls! They meant a lot to me (and offered me 'much-deeper incites' than you'll ever know)! And, thanks too.. for your efforts 'above and beyond the call' with this project, in general. They were.. are.. and will always remain.. deeply and greatly appreciated!

.. to Karen, my darlin'.. who deserved a 'better man'! Your endless support and constant belief in me has truly been my earthly 'rock'! And.. You will never know just how 'desperately' I've tried to make 'good' for you, Babe!.. that you might ONLY know 'Pretty Things' in your life!

.. to (last, but hardly not least!) my 'Loving' Mother. Yes, 'Loving' can not be said enough! She has stood by me (life-long) in 'everything' .. All of my craziness!.. and dreams!.. and always sought to help! Without her, I could've never 'went back', for one! My greatest hope would be to, one day, be able to say to her (As Dear Jesus has been said to have told his Mother, in doing what she did not truly understand), "Behold, Mother.. I make all things new!"

.. And, likewise to.. my Father. Yes, my 'artistic', devoted and 'saintly' Father!

My Truer Hero!.. And the 'Real" Hero of this Book!   I especially thank him (as well) for helping me draw its front cover artwork!..   Not to mention, my whole life!....

.. And greater than all ... to God.. who gave me 'life' .. and the greatest parents in the world to support me and teach me how to live it! With absolute sincerity....

Mark Brine